THE GAIA GAMBIT

THE GAIAN CONSORTIUM SERIES: BOOK 3

CHRISTINE POPE

DARK VALENTINE PRESS

THE GAIA GAMBIT

ISBN: 978-0615871714

Copyright © 2013 by Christine Pope

Published by Dark Valentine Press

Cover design by Christian Bentulan

Ebook formatting by Indie Author Services

CHAPTER ONE

"HAVE YOU EVER HAD A HUMAN WOMAN, CAPTAIN?"

Rast sen Drenthan turned toward his commanding officer and tried not to frown. "No, Excellency."

What might have been a smile twisted the edges of Admiral sen Trannick's scarred mouth. "You should. They're delicious."

Rast didn't reply at first, but instead glanced past the admiral's bulky shoulder at the pale yellow sun of the Chlorae system. Three planets, but only one mattered. Chlorae II, site of the richest deposits of millenite yet discovered. Millenite, vital for the subspace propulsion systems of starships the galaxy over, whether Gaian, Stacian, or Eridani.

Too bad the Gaians had been the first to find it.

Odd that sen Trannick would mention human women, considering it was one particular specimen who had been a pebble in his boot for some time now. Captain Lira Jannholm, commander of the *Valiant.*

Officially, the cruiser was listed as being assigned to the Gaian Exploration Commission, and not the Defense Fleet, but Rast knew better. The cruiser had settled in almost as soon as the initial GEC team reported its findings to the government back on Gaia. The *Valiant's* stated mission was to provide support personnel to the scientific team, but all the parties involved knew it was really there to make sure that no interlopers attempted to interfere with the Gaians' claim.

"Perhaps on my next leave," Rast told the older man, his tone deliberately casual. It wouldn't do to offend the admiral, but Rast wondered exactly what his commanding officer had intended by asking such a personal question.

"Perhaps sooner," sen Trannick replied, and this time there was no mistaking the smile that lifted his distorted lips. Those scars had been earned during the siege of Arlinais, when he had stayed to pilot his own ship through the maelstrom and take out the Gaian flagship, thus banishing the troublesome humans from that sector once and for all.

Rast did not answer, but a prickle of unease began to work its way from under the heavy *trinials* of knotted hair that fell down his back. As suited a captain, the dreadlocks were banded in copper and gold, and suddenly felt heavier than he could ever recall.

"This Captain Jannholm," the Admiral went on. "What do you know of her?"

Probably far less than you, Rast thought, but he only said carefully, "She is young for her rank, but tenacious. She knows we are bound by the treaty, and so maintains her patrols but refrains from engaging our forces. Her orders are strict, I imagine."

"They are."

"I beg your indulgence, Admiral, but I'm not sure what you expect from me in this situation. Any attack on the *Valiant* would surely lead to retaliation, both by the Gaian Defense Fleet and the Council's security forces."

The admiral's grin widened. "Not an attack, sen Drenthan—a wager."

Stacians were notorious the galaxy over for their love of a wager, and the admiral was a particularly ferocious gambler. Rast had never quite understood his people's predilection for finding a reason to gamble on everything from the number of chicks in a *cheris'* clutch to the number of days in a woman's pregnancy, but he knew better than to reveal such an un-Stacian attitude. No, he had limited himself to the sorts of harmless wagers that kept him in the game but could cause no real trouble. He had the feeling, however, that what the admiral was about to propose was far from harmless.

"Are we wagering on what it would take to get the good captain to abandon her defense of the millenite?"

"Oh, I know better than to bet on that. She is, as you say, tenacious. But I also know you're an ambitious one —and no harm in that. You would do very well in command of a system fleet, and not stuck out here in the hinterlands playing *treltha* and *minsk* with the Gaians." The smile returned, even as sen Trannick continued, "Offer to withdraw if Captain Jannholm will spend one night with you."

Had the admiral gone mad? It might have been easier if he had, but Rast saw no signs of madness, only a canny gleam in the other man's copper-colored eyes that seemed to indicate he knew exactly what his subordinate thought of such an outlandish wager.

"Excellency, whatever we might think of the Gaians, Lira Jannholm is the captain of a starship, not some harlot in an Iradian brothel. Surely—"

"Are you saying you will not do it?"

The edge in the admiral's voice was obvious, and Rast quickly backpedaled. "No, Excellency, of course not. But— "

"Best not to keep Captain Jannholm waiting, sen Drenthan."

As there was clearly no more to be said, Rast bowed from the waist and then exited the admiral's chamber, cursing his luck in being given this post in the first place, cursing his commanding officer's ruling vice, and cursing Captain Jannholm most of all—for if she had been some grizzled veteran, the admiral would never have cooked up this unlikely scheme.

"Message coming in for you, Captain," said Lieutenant Ramirez from the communications console. His brows drew together. "It's—it's from the captain of the Stacian ship."

Lira Jannholm swiveled in her chair so she could see the comm officer more clearly. "Come again, Lieutenant?"

"Captain sen Drenthan." Ramirez's shoulders lifted slightly. "He's requesting a private channel."

Stranger and stranger. The Stacians didn't normally approach their Gaian adversaries with polite requests for private communications. No, generally, they were more inclined to take what potshots they could, if they thought the Eridanis and the Zhore and the other senior members of the Council weren't paying attention. After all, those small attacks never caused any real damage, although they did tend to make the Gaians more on edge than ever...which was the whole point of the exercise. Still, Lira knew she couldn't ignore such a request.

"Patch it through to my ready room," she said, and rose from the conn.

The *Valiant* was certainly not the grandest member of the fleet, and so her ready room was a small chamber barely three meters square. But at least in there she could have a modicum of privacy.

She pushed the button on the comm console, and the image of a Stacian officer flickered into existence in the space above the desktop. As she had never actually met a Stacian in person, she didn't have much experience trying to differentiate between them. This Captain sen Drenthan seemed a typical enough representative of the species—golden-skinned, eyes dark copper, the masses of his coarse dark hair twisted into ropes that fell down his back. Humanoid, yes, but taller and bulkier than most Gaians, with bony ridges along his cheekbones and brow.

The Stacian's expression might have been considered pleasant on his own world, but she found herself wanting to step backward from that penetrating glare.

"Captain sen Drenthan," she said coolly, as if having an enemy commander contact her privately was something that happened every day. "You wished to speak with me? I feel I must remind you that under Section 56, Paragraph 112, of the Eridani Accord, contact between opposing forces is supposed to be limited to cases of extreme emergency, or—"

"I am well aware of the strictures of the treaty, Captain Jannholm." He paused, and the gleaming copper eyes cast downward for a second or two, as if he were weighing what he intended to say next. "However, the treaty was written to foster peace, and what I wish to say to you may help to achieve that end. I would see you in person, here on my ship."

"You would…" For possibly the first time in her life, Lira found herself at a loss for words. Certainly she had never thought the Stacian commander would invite her over as calmly as if he were extending an invitation for afternoon tea. She gathered herself and said, "I'm afraid that is quite impossible."

"I am willing to offer up ten of my crewmen in exchange—as a gesture of goodwill. But once I have spoken with you, you will understand why I wished to do so in person."

Her tone flat, she responded, "Abandoning my post in such a way is completely out of the question." It crossed her mind to request that he come to visit her here on her own ship, but a second glance at those forbidding brows and that stern jaw told her such a demand would at best be ignored.

"I would not call it abandoning your post. Tell me, have you never once left the *Valiant* to assist the scientists down on Chlorae II?"

He had her there. She had gone planet-side from time to time, since part of her assignment here was to make sure that the scientists had complete access to all the resources they needed. What they all knew was that the *Valiant* served mainly as a placeholder, a babysitter until the GEC's heavy transports could arrive with the equipment, personnel, and materiel necessary to establish a full-fledged mining colony on the planet.

"That is not the same thing, Captain," she told him.

"Perhaps not. But you will still be serving the interests of peace."

"I had no idea the Stacians were so interested in peace," she returned. Although she had been halfway hoping that he would show some reaction, his expression did not change. At least, she didn't think it did.

"There is probably much about us you do not know, Captain Jannholm."

Well, that was true enough. She watched him for a few seconds, the barbarian splendor of his hair and uniform strangely at odds with the sterile interior of her ready room. Possibly she was making a huge mistake, but she hadn't achieved her current position without taking a few calculated risks.

"Make sure your second-in-command and chief

weapons officer are among those you exchange," she said.

He bowed from the waist. "As you wish it, so it will be."

———

Captain Jannholm was smaller in person than he had thought she would be. Something about her stance, the straightness of her shoulders, had bespoken a taller woman, but she barely came up to his shoulder, slight even for a Gaian.

Not that she seemed to notice her lack of height. She stepped into his chamber with her head high, the stars of her rank gleaming on the high collar of her dark-gray uniform. He signaled to the two security officers who had escorted her in, and they bowed, then exited the room.

For a few seconds, neither of them said anything. She seemed content to merely survey her surroundings, from the hangings on the wall to the rugs of woven *chikka* fur on the floor. Rast had heard that the Gaians mocked the Stacian ways, saying their practice of taking luxurious furnishings with them into space proved they were barbarians. For himself, he had never understood the reason for making one's surroundings as spartan and spare as possible. Save perhaps, that the Gaians were notoriously money-pinching in their ways, and perhaps having such uncomfortably sparse ships was one way of saving a few units.

Then Captain Jannholm fixed him with a direct stare, and asked simply, "What is it you wanted to say to me?"

Now, with her standing before him, broaching such a subject seemed more impossible than ever. She was not, as he had told the admiral, some whore from the brothels of the outer territories. Everything about her seemed correct, from the coil of dark hair on the back of her head to the gleaming toes of her polished boots.

And although he had always thought Gaians plain, with their too-smooth skin and distressing lack of personal ornamentation, he looked on this Lira Jannholm and found her oddly lovely. Perhaps it was something in the curve of her mouth, or the color of her eyes, a clear blue-green that evoked images of deep water, so rare on his home world, and so unlike the copper and gold and bronze hues shared by his fellow Stacians.

But reticence was not a trait the Stacians commonly shared, and he saw no point in indulging in it now. "For some days we have been at an impasse, Captain."

"Is that what you call it?"

"No doubt you have been cursing my name and wishing me to leave."

Something flickered near her mouth, a hint of the beginnings of a smile before her expression smoothed itself once again. "I didn't know your name to curse it, Captain sen Drenthan. But I will admit that my life would be easier if your government would just recognize the fact that the Consortium had first claim to this world, and allow you to withdraw."

Unwittingly, she had given him the opening he needed. "But that is exactly what I have come here to propose."

Her brows lifted. "The Stacian government would never permit such a thing."

Cool thing she was, cool as the color of her eyes. Of course, she had no way of knowing he'd already been granted such permission by proxy, through Admiral sen Trannick offering the wager in the first place. "The Stacian navy does not operate under the same constraints as the Gaian fleet. Individual captains may choose to make such decisions based on their individual situations."

"And what precisely is the situation?"

He admired how she stood her ground, facing him straight on, even though he towered over her by several handspans and could easily have overpowered her if desired. Quelling a smile of his own, he said, "I will withdraw from the system...if you will spend one night with me."

For a few long seconds she didn't move, didn't blink. Then, slowly, "Is this a joke?"

"A joke?"

The even pallor of her skin didn't change, although Rast knew humans had a tendency to flush red when faced with uncomfortable situations. She said, her tone even enough, "I suppose I should be glad you said this to me in private, but really—why precisely did you ask to meet with me?"

This wasn't going quite as he'd planned. He'd expected disbelief, anger, embarrassment. He certainly hadn't thought his proposition would be viewed as some sort of jest.

"This is why I asked you to meet me in private. Or would you rather I had asked you such a question in front of your bridge crew?"

"I would rather you didn't ask such a question at all. Has the Stacian fleet stooped so low as to consider such matters even worthy of discussion?"

He might have asked himself that same thing. But trying to explain the intricacies of the wager to this alien woman, of the millennia in which the rituals had evolved, would help very little. To be sure, he didn't always understand them himself. However, he knew that to back out was inconceivable. He could only pursue his suit to the best of his ability.

"Are Gaians so rigid that they are incapable of exploring alternate means of diplomacy, of peace?"

Finally a few spots of color flared in her face, high up along her cheekbones. "I would gladly meet you at any arbitration table if your offer of withdrawal is sincere. But to expect an officer of the fleet—"

"I expect nothing. I can only ask. The choice is yours whether or not you consider the withdrawal of Stacian forces from this system worth your...sacrifice."

He chose the word deliberately, to throw in her face the distaste she must be feeling. Gaians and Stacians had always been adversaries. Truthfully, besides those women who sold themselves to every comer, whether purple-skinned Eridani or hairless Menari, he knew of no Gaian woman who had ever paired with a Stacian man. And of course it was unthinkable that a Stacian female would ever lower herself to bed a Gaian male.

"I will return to my ship now," Captain Jannholm said. "I trust you will allow me safe conduct for that."

"Of course," he replied. Only a very naïve man would have expected her to give an answer immediately. "Shall we say, twenty-five standard hours for you to render your decision?"

Her eyes narrowed, but she only said, "You will hear from me before that."

Her tone seemed to indicate she had a good deal to say on the subject, but held her tongue to avoid argument. In a way it was amusing to see her veiled outrage, the manner in which she lifted her chin and marched out as soon as he activated the controls for the door so she could exit.

He thought he had a very good idea of what her answer would be.

After returning to her ship, Lira immediately headed for her ready room. What she really wished was to disappear into her quarters, but she had only begun her rotation four hours ago; such a deviation from schedule would have been noted at once. The curious stares of her bridge crew as she greeted them curtly before retreating into her ready room had been bad enough.

Another devout wish was for a good stiff belt of

brandy, but such things were rare in the Chlorae system and even rarer on board her ship. She settled for pouring herself a glass of water and staring into the viewscreen on the far wall, the one that showed the form of the Stacian cruiser where it perched in an orbit to match the *Valiant*'s own course precisely.

Of all the—

Over the years, she'd heard a good deal about the Stacians, their warlike tendencies, their fearlessness, their unpredictability. Theirs was a harsh desert world, one where the original lush biosphere that had led to the evolution of sentient life had been decimated tens of thousands of years earlier by a meteor strike. They had lost their oceans and their forests, been driven into the planet's network of caves, emerging only to hunt the fierce predators that had survived the global cataclysm. They had taken the technology that had been the gift of the Eridanis —a race who prided themselves on sharing their knowledge freely—and crafted themselves into a space-faring power. But of all the things Lira had heard of the Stacians, she'd never heard that they particularly coveted Gaian women. So why Captain sen Drenthan would make such a proposition to her, she couldn't begin to fathom.

A swallow of water, then another. The outrage began to ebb, as she had known it would. She couldn't afford to let her emotions get the better of her. Much as she would have liked to tell that arrogant Stacian exactly what he could do with his proposal, she wasn't in a position to give free rein to her emotions. She had to analyze the situation and decide what to do next.

The responsibility for making such a decision must rest solely on her; Gaian regulations regarding fraternization were strict. What sen Drenthan had proposed was something she must keep strictly to herself.

The reinforcements from Gaia were on their way, that much she knew, but the stalemate here could last for some weeks before she might hope for any relief. The lumbering transport ships that carried supplies and colonists traveled far more slowly than the sleek cruisers of the GDF. And once those ships arrived, it was her responsibility to make sure they made planet-fall safely, without any interference from the Stacians. It would be far simpler if the Stacians would just withdraw and relinquish their claim to the millenite, a claim that was specious at best. Yes, they had first visited this system, but only to take the crudest readings for their databases. It wasn't until the Gaians actually landed on the second planet that the Chlorae system's true worth was realized.

If she did the unthinkable—if she went to him—would he keep his word? She did not know this Captain sen Dranthan, but she knew the Stacians took their bond seriously, which was why the other sentient races had such a difficult time pinning them down to treaties and accords. Once a formal agreement was in place, the Stacians would honor it. That was part of the reason why the Eridani Accord was viewed as such a success.

But to coldly give herself to him, to let him...

The thought trailed off, and she drank some more water in an effort to banish those unwanted images. He was so very large, and so savage-looking, with those fierce ridges along his brow line and the mass of twisted hair down his back. Never mind that in other ways he was as humanoid as she, with ten fingers and toes, two arms, two legs. Scientists had been arguing for generations whether the galaxy was rife with instances of confluent evolution, or whether some long-ago race had seeded its kind throughout the stars. In the day to day, it didn't matter so much. Gaians had been intermingling with Eridanis since within a decade of first contact, and the other humanoid races had followed suit, save the Stacians and the mysterious Zhore. Then again, no one had ever seen a Zhore outside their enveloping hooded cloaks, so their humanoid nature was still a matter of conjecture.

But Captain sen Drenthan was not a Zhore, but a member of a race that had been skirmishing with the Gaians for the last hundred years. She found it hard to believe that he had suddenly been so overcome with lust for her after glimpsing her on the comm screen that he was willing to relinquish his people's claim to the Chlorae system. What, then, was his motivation?

Perhaps he had already been given the order to withdraw, for whatever reason, and had come up with this preposterous proposition as a final means of humiliating her. Why she should be made the object of such torture, Lira had no idea, but since she and the Stacian captain had been dancing around one another for the greater part of two standard months, she could see why his patience might be wearing thin. She knew hers was.

Then again, if he was being sincere...

He had sounded serious enough, with no hint of mockery in his tone, but whether that meant anything, she couldn't be sure. She supposed she should just be glad that his command of Galactic Standard was as good as hers, since she'd heard that some Stacians refused to learn the language at all.

The comm beeped, and she ran her finger over the screen to allow the incoming message to display itself there. The smart ions that composed the screen material read her fingerprint and decrypted the words.

Gaian Exploratory Commission to Captain Lira Jannholm:

Schedule for accession of Chlorae II mining colony accelerated. Expect arrival of first colonists in two standard days. Increase security in advance of their arrival. Acknowledge.

Mouth dry despite the half glass of water she had just drunk, Lira pressed her thumb against the screen in the location designated for acknowledging receipt of official communiques. Not for the first time, she wished very much that the GEC, despite its notoriously parsimonious ways, had sent more ships than just her *Valiant* to protect its interests on Chlorae II.

Her gaze seemed drawn inexorably across the ready room to the viewscreen that still held the image of sen Drenthan's ship. It floated against the blackness, its hammerhead shape reminiscent of a predator that had once swum in old Gaia's oceans.

Well, Captain, it seems you might have gotten your wish.

Lips thinning, she turned back to the comm unit.

"Lieutenant Ramirez? Send a message to the Stacian captain."

"Message, ma'am?"

"Tell him to expect me at twenty-two hundred." And she switched off the comm before Ramirez had a chance to reply.

For a few seconds she sat there in silence, staring ahead but seeing nothing. Then she shut her eyes.

You've done it now, Lira.

CHAPTER TWO

RAST WASN'T SURE WHICH HAD SURPRISED HIM MORE—
that Lira Jannholm had said yes, or the alacrity with
which she had given her consent. Something must have
happened to force her hand, but exactly what that
something had been, he couldn't hazard a guess.

Curtly, he informed his second-in-command that
he would be receiving the Gaian captain for a diplomatic visit, and that she would be staying for some
hours. Commander sen Larnack was too well-trained to
display more than a millisecond of surprise, but even
that brief dilation of his pupils was enough to show
what he thought of such a pronouncement. The crew
had already been discussing Captain Jannholm's earlier
visit, truncated as it had been; Rast could only imagine
what they would think after she arrived late in the
ship's rotation and didn't leave again for some hours.
Stacians, disciplined as they could be, also had an

unfortunate tendency toward gossip when their superiors weren't around.

In this case, he guessed they would have plenty to gossip about.

For himself, he experienced a distressing nervousness as the hours wore on. That was not like him—he was not some youth to be intimidated by an attractive woman. Then again, he had never been with a human female before. Human and Stacian anatomy matched up, more or less, but it was not a field of investigation to which he'd devoted much study besides the cursory survey of the humanoid races he'd been given during his fleet training. He was no diplomat, but a soldier.

A chime sounded from the communications console embedded in his desk. He opened the channel. "Sen Drenthan."

"Captain, the Gaian commander is here."

"Send her in."

He stood then and waited for her in the center of the chamber. The door opened, and she moved past the guards who accompanied her. They bowed to their captain before exiting, leaving him alone with Lira Jannholm.

She certainly did not have the appearance of a woman come to an assignation. The same high-collared uniform covered her to her chin, and her hair was still bound in a tight coil at the back of her head.

At first he thought he might mention something of her swift decision, but one glance at the compressed lines of her mouth told him that was probably not a very good idea. Instead, he turned away from her, going toward a small table placed up against the far wall. On the table stood a bottle of lavender Eridani wine and two glasses.

"A drink?" he inquired.

"Do you think getting me drunk will make this any easier?"

He shrugged, and went ahead and poured two glasses, then extended one to her. "I don't know —do you?"

For a second she hesitated, her mouth still grim. He thought he saw her shake her head slightly before she took the glass from him. "I suppose we'll just have to find out." And she took two very healthy swallows of the potent wine.

As he'd spent a good deal of his late adolescence and early adulthood tossing back large amounts of the fungus-based rotgut brewed in the caves of Stacia, the Eridani wine did not pose much of a challenge to his own head. Still, he only allowed himself a measured sip from his own glass. No use getting done up at this stage of the game.

Then again, perhaps there was some value to taking the edge off. With the two of them circling one another like two *trelths* marking their territory, it would be a long time—if ever—before they got down to business. So he lifted the glass again and matched her two gulps of wine with three of his own.

Surprisingly, a wicked glint came and went in her sea-colored eyes. "I hope this isn't going to turn into a drinking game. You have an unfair weight advantage."

"True enough," he replied, staring down at her

slender form. She seemed light enough to pick up with one hand. He would have to test that hypothesis later.

She seemed to catch the weight of hidden meaning in his eyes, and glanced away.

Damn. He had known this was going to be uncomfortable, but he hadn't realized quite how agonizing the reality would prove to be. He was no seducer of women. His previous liaisons had been with equally willing partners. But this Gaian woman seemed to be anything but willing. The data he had on her said she was just past thirty standard, so she couldn't possibly be some inexperienced virgin. No, her reticence had to be because of his race.

"You've never met a Stacian before," he said, hoping he might put her at ease by showing that he was willing to continue the conversation.

"No," she admitted. "I've seen vids, of course, but..." A brief laugh. "You look much taller in person."

"Do I?" He stepped closer to her.

To his surprise, she did not try to move away, although he thought he saw her fingers tighten around the glass of wine she held. "Yes," she replied. "Then again, I'm probably a little biased, considering most of the galaxy is taller than I am."

"Oh, I don't know about most," he said. "The Eridanis are quite similar to you Gaians when it comes to height, and I've met several Eridani women who are no taller than you."

"Have you?" Her expression appeared almost curious. "I wasn't aware the Stacian navy had that many direct dealings with the Eridanis."

Of course it didn't; the Eridanis tended to work with what scientists his home world possessed, and beyond that, those of his people occupied in the diplomatic corps, or the Federation's colonial government. However, the Eridanis occasionally assisted in the design of the ships that now populated the Stacian navy, and it was in that capacity where he'd met quite a few Eridani engineers and scientists. However, since he wasn't certain how much the Gaians knew of Stacian/Eridani interactions, he thought it better not to reply directly.

Instead, he lifted his shoulders—a gesture apparently common to all the humanoid races—and said, "Oh, they come and go as consultants, as required. That is all." He didn't bother to add that he had found none of those Eridani women particularly lovely. Certainly not like this Lira Jannholm, this delicate creature who somehow still gave the impression that she had been wrought of fire-hardened steel. Yes, she was slight, but he thought no less of her for that. She had the graceful, compact strength of the low-flying *darakh*, with its ability to elude the attacks of Stacia's most bloodthirsty predators.

He told her, "It is no hardship, the difference in our heights," and then lowered his mouth to hers.

She tasted of the wine, sweet and dark and somehow forbidden, her lips fuller than those of a Stacian female. He felt her tense as their lips touched, but she did not draw away. Her mouth opened slightly, and their tongues met.

A spike of heat touched his loins, and he hardened

almost at once. Understandable; it had been some months since his last liaison. But he thought somehow he would have reacted the same way even if he had been with another woman only hours earlier.

The table was close enough that he could set down his glass without moving away from her. He did so, then reached up to the mass of hair at the back of her head. It should not be confined so, but allowed to fall loose. Hard little pins held it in place, and he plucked them out one by one, letting them drop to the rug beneath their feet. Finally her hair slipped free, falling in shining coils over her shoulders. No Stacian woman had hair that glistened so. He wanted to run his fingers through it, feel it slide across his skin like the finest Iradian silk.

"You shouldn't—" she began, but he silenced her with another kiss, even as her hair slid against his cheek and neck.

After all, they had far better things to do than talk.

Up until the moment he kissed her, the whole situation had possessed an air of unreality. After all, what sane woman would have walked calmly into the cabin of an enemy captain, his promises of safe conduct notwithstanding?

But then he was all too real, the hard lips against hers, the spicy scent that seemed to permeate his skin and clothing, something reminiscent of sandalwood and yet subtly alien, while at the same time more enticing than anything else she had ever smelled. And his hands touching her hair, gently and with some sort of strange awe, as if he had never felt anything like it before. Perhaps he hadn't.

She had to stand on her tiptoes to reach his mouth comfortably, and he must have noticed, because then his arms were around her, lifting her, taking her out of the office or audience chamber or whatever it was, and carrying her to a smaller room dominated by a tall bed made of some substance she couldn't quite identify in the dim light but which looked almost like polished stone.

This was madness, though, that she should let him reach beneath the placket on the front of her uniform jumpsuit and draw the zipper there downward, just before he pulled the garment away from her. If this had been a Gaian ship, the air that met her bare skin would have been chill, overly air conditioned, but the Stacian ship was warm and smelled faintly of the same spices that seemed to permeate Rast sen Drenthan's hair and skin. He pushed her down on the bed, his hands stroking her bare flesh. If she closed her eyes, she could imagine those hands belonged to a human man, as they felt much the same, although the fingers that now reached up to caress her breasts were just a little too long, a little too strong.

But it would be the coward's way to shut her eyes against this reality, that it was a Stacian who touched her so, who traced his way down the sensitive skin of her stomach until his breath came hot against the flesh between her legs, who pushed his tongue into her and tasted her.

She cried out then, fingers working into the coarse ropy masses of his hair, pulling him closer to her. She had had other lovers, of course, but none who seemed to know exactly where to touch her, who made love to her with his mouth, not as a means to an end, but just because he seemed to derive almost as much satisfaction from pleasuring her as she did herself.

The orgasm hit hard, and she bucked against him, still holding the metal-studded lengths of his hair, gripping him as waves of ecstasy pulsed out through every vein, along every nerve ending. Her own breathing sounded hoarse as she gasped through the last lingering ripples of pleasure. Only then did he stop, and pull himself up to lie next to her. For the first time she realized he still wore his own uniform, which scratched against her naked form.

Either Stacians didn't know about or believe in zippers; her fingers had to work their way down a set of carved bone buttons to free him from the heavy jacket. The same ridges that traced their way along his brow and cheekbones showed along his collarbones as well, and a tattoo in dark red flared in a sunburst pattern across the warm bronze skin of his chest. Otherwise, his body did not look that different from those of the other men she had known, although he was more heavily muscled. And when she tugged down his uniform pants, it was obvious that all parts of him were equally oversized.

No time to worry about that, though. Her fingers closed around his shaft, although her thumb and fore-finger couldn't touch. He moaned, and she bent down to take him into her mouth, her other hand going lower to move through the coarse, crisp hair and caress all of him. Again, no real surprises there, save his size; the differences between Gaian and Stacian were clearly minor.

From the rhythms of his body, and the intensity of his breathing, she guessed he was close to climax, but she didn't want him to spend himself too quickly. She shifted her position, thinking it was time to take him into her—but he surprised her by sitting up, then reaching an arm around her waist so that he lifted her bodily from the bed. Her back touched the cloth-covered wall, and he lowered her onto him, pushing inside her.

She cried out, clinging to him. If she hadn't been so wet, so ready, he might have hurt her, but as it was she could only wrap her legs around him, holding on through every thrust, each one pushing a little deeper, somehow bringing them that much closer. Again those pulses of pleasure began to surge through her, and she rocked her hips against his, reveling in the sensation of him filling her.

It could have been five minutes, or half an hour. Impossible to say for sure, although his arms never seemed to falter as he held her up. All she did know was that, just as the third or fourth—or was it the fifth? —orgasm flooded through her, finally he gasped, and the hands against the back of her waist tightened. Then he held her in place for just a few more seconds before carefully lowering her to the floor.

Her knees wanted to buckle, but somehow she managed to stagger back to the bed and sink down on it. The coverlet was of some soft, velvety material, while under it were sheets that felt very much like any other sheet she had ever touched. The cool fabric slid across her naked body, and she found some comfort in its familiarity. At the moment, she didn't want to think about what she'd just done...or how good it had felt.

"That looks comfortable," said Rast sen Drenthan, and he lifted the bedclothes so he could slip in next to her.

"Mmm," she responded, not trusting herself to say anything more than that.

His body was warm, seeming to radiate banked heat. It was the sort of body to snuggle up against on a cold winter night. Only it wasn't winter, and he wasn't a lover or husband. No, he was one of her people's sworn enemies, an alien she had just given herself to in order to secure some security and peace for Chlorae II.

How her own body had betrayed her by succumbing to his touch, she would have to leave for another day. *Just an automatic reflex*, she told herself, *like flinching when you stick yourself with a pin.*

"So you'll leave the system now?" she asked, not looking at him, but instead staring up at the ceiling. Even that seemed to have been covered with some sort of cloth. The Stacians had little patience for a starship's metal interior, apparently.

He made a sound that might have been a chuckle

before shifting so he could more or less look down at her. "That wasn't the bargain," he said.

Cold doubt replaced the afterglow of sex. "But you said—"

"I said I would withdraw after you had spent a night with me. It has barely been an hour."

He hadn't meant that literally, had he? But Lira realized, as he pulled her toward him once again, and she felt him hard against her thigh, that he had indeed meant a night.

A very long night.

———

She slept for a while, there at the very end. Rast found himself wanting to let her alone, to allow her to lie there with the glorious silk of her hair spread out on the pillow, but he knew he should rouse her. By then it was very late, in the second watch of the night, or oh-five hundred, as the Gaians would say it. Of course there would be crew on duty both on her ship and his, but not as many as during the part of the shift that correlated with the daylight hours on their home worlds. Better that she should slip out now.

Her skin was soft under his hand, and he let his fingers linger there for a moment on her shoulder before he shook her gently.

"Lira."

Soldier that she was, her eyes snapped open instantly, and she sat up. "What is it?"

"Time for you to return to your ship."

She glanced away from him, gaze straying to the scattered clothing on the floor of the cabin, then nodded. Still not looking at him, she slid out from underneath the covers and went to retrieve her discarded uniform and underthings, pulling them on with a grim air that seemed to bespeak a distasteful task now over and done. Only after she had pulled the zipper of her severe garment almost up to her chin did she speak again. "And you will withdraw?"

Hands knotted before him, he bowed to her, the formal gesture of acknowledgment. "As soon as you are safely returned to your ship."

She nodded. "Then it appears we're done here."

"Yes," he replied, trying to ignore the pang of sadness that moved through him at the thought of her leaving so abruptly, never to be seen again. "Yes, we are done here."

What the few crew members who were up and about at that hour thought of the sight of their captain, moving through the corridors with kiss-swollen lips and hastily braided hair that would have fooled no one, Lira really didn't want to know. No teenager sneaking back into her house after a midnight assignation could have looked any guiltier, she thought. But there wasn't much she could do about that. Matter transmission still was beyond the scope of the scientists and engineers, so she couldn't just transport herself directly into her cabin to avoid the curious stares of those she passed on the way back to her quarters. No, she had to pretend her appearance was perfectly normal, and be glad she had gotten back before the daytime rotation began.

At least she had slept a little; her days at the academy had trained her to get by with only a few hours of sleep, although the scant ninety minutes or so she'd gotten in the Stacian's bed were not quite enough to get her through the day. Some caffeine would mend part of the weariness, and a splash of cold water on her face would help with the other, and after that she'd just have to cope as best she could. With the Stacian ship leaving, things should be quiet enough, and maybe it wouldn't matter too much that she wasn't at the top of her game.

She'd just finished pinning her hair back up when the comm console in her cabin beeped at her. "What is it, Lieutenant Ono?"

"Captain, the Stacian ship—it's leaving! Just accelerated out of orbit and is moving away. Looks like they're setting up for a subspace jump."

So Rast was being true to his word. She brought up the exterior view on her screen, watched as the hammer-headed ship glided away from the *Valiant*. A brief shimmer as the ship's main drive kicked on, and then they were gone.

For some reason, she found it difficult to swallow the mouthful of coffee she'd just drunk. Exhaustion, obviously. She was simply too tired to be glad about the

Stacians' departure. Give it a few hours to sink in, and she would be fine.

Better to believe that Rast sen Drenthan had worn her out than to admit, on any level, that she was almost sorry to see him go. Frowning, she swallowed the rest of her coffee and all but slammed the mug down on her desktop. A few hours on the bridge should clear her head of the Stacian's lingering influence.

The bridge crew was noticeably quiet as she strode over to her chair and took her place, but at least they were disciplined enough to attend to their duties without any whispered exchanges or significant looks.

Of course the scientists called up from the outpost, as their instruments had told them the circling enemy had suddenly disappeared from Chlorae II's skies.

"Any explanation?" asked Noor Singh, the chief geologist in charge of the expedition.

Thank God the scientists at least didn't know anything of her nocturnal visit to the Stacian ship. "None," she replied. "My guess is that they were called back for some reason. We were given no notification— not that I would have expected any."

"Odd. But it makes our lives easier. Not much longer now, correct?"

"Correct. Command's last communique indicated that the first group of colonists and support staff should be here within forty standard hours, give or take an hour or so."

"Excellent. Thank you for the update, Captain."

Dr. Singh signed off, and Lira settled back in her seat. So far, so good. No one had asked any awkward questions, and within less than two days she could hand over the planet's security to the newly arrived personnel. In fact, she should probably be getting new orders any time now.

"Captain?"

She turned toward Lieutenant Ramirez, who had replaced Lieutenant Ono at the comm station. "Yes?"

"Incoming transmission from Command. They wish to speak to you in private."

Talk about timing. That must be Admiral Horner from Regional HQ, contacting her about her next assignment. Usually she received those orders directly on the bridge so the crew could know right away where they were headed, but no matter.

"Patch it through, Lieutenant," she told Ramirez, as she eased herself out of her chair. Unfamiliar muscles protested the movement, and she repressed a grimace. Rast had given her quite the workout last night.

Better not to think about that now, though. She went into her ready room and pressed her finger against the screen there to allow the transmission to display.

Admiral Horner's unsmiling face filled the screen. His expression didn't surprise her all that much; he wasn't known for his cheery disposition. But somehow the look on his face was even grimmer than usual.

"Admiral," she said.

"Captain." His dark eyes seemed to narrow just the smallest fraction. "The *Valiant* is ordered back to base. Immediately."

"Sir?" Almost involuntarily, Lira glanced across the

chamber to the viewscreen that showed the space around the ship. The only reason she could think of for such a precipitous recall was that the reinforcements had shown up far ahead of schedule, but all was still black and empty, the *Valiant* clearly the only vessel anywhere near the planet.

"What was unclear about my orders, Captain Jannholm?"

She said quickly, "Nothing, sir. But we'll be leaving the Chlorae system undefended—"

"That is not your concern, Captain. Your only concern is getting here ASAP. Understood?"

"Yes, sir. Of course, sir."

"HQ out."

The screen went dark, and she found herself sitting there and staring blankly at the space that the admiral's face had occupied until a few seconds ago. What the hell was that all about? Could HQ really be considering leaving the scientists and the millenite on the planet completely without defenses? It was insane.

Since questioning orders was the quickest way Lira could think of to get bumped back to ensign, or even sent to the brig, she knew she would do as she was told. The strategic geniuses at HQ must have some very good reason for ordering her away. She'd let them handle the fallout.

All she could do was hope her own crew would keep their questions to themselves as well. This time, she simply didn't have any answers.

CHAPTER THREE

REGIONAL HQ LOOKED MUCH AS IT ALWAYS DID—FILLED with busy, hurrying people, mostly Gaian, although the odd purple-skinned Eridani could be spotted from time to time amongst the crowds. With the *Valiant* safely docked in one of the giant space station's arms, she allowed most of the crew, save a skeleton staff, two hours of shore leave. That seemed reasonable enough; she doubted Admiral Horner would send them back out on another assignment immediately. In general, HQ liked its ships' crews to have at least twenty-four standard hours between missions, and they had just had a hard two-day run to get here as quickly as possible.

The admiral's offices were located on one of the station's upper decks. She took a lift there. No one spared a glance at her, and no reason why they should. She was just one of thousands in the dark-gray uniform of the Gaian Defense Force, just another member of the fleet pursuing her own business...or at least the admiral's business.

The same redheaded adjutant who had overseen the admiral's affairs ever since Lira was posted to this sector gave her a curt nod as she entered the reception area. "He's waiting for you, Captain."

That in itself was a little odd. Admirals generally didn't wait on captains, but rather the reverse. Then again, she'd contacted Admiral Horner's office as soon as the *Valiant* had docked, and possibly her arrival had coincided with a rare opening in the admiral's schedule. She should be glad he was ready to see her right away and that she didn't have to cool her heels in the reception area the way she had several times in the past.

The space station orbited a gas giant in the New Perth system; the planet's ruddy-hued shape dominated the large windows that made up the far wall of Admiral Horner's office. Lira had always found the view a little intimidating, although she could never say quite why. After all, she'd grown up on the Gaian base on Ganymede, orbiting Jupiter. She was used to such sights. But something about the angle of the planet as it was framed in those windows always made it seem as if it was about to crash in on her.

The admiral stood in front of the window, his back to her. She paused just inside the door. "Sir."

He did not turn, but instead replied, "Captain Jannholm."

His voice had never contained much warmth, but today it sounded positively glacial. Some of that cold seemed to transfer itself to her, and a little shiver worked its way down her back. She began to wonder exactly why he had summoned her here.

"Reporting for my new orders, Admiral," she said. At least her voice didn't shake.

Finally he did shift so he faced her, but she almost wished he hadn't. At least then she wouldn't have to see the expression of cold contempt on his lean features.

"Your new orders, Captain, are that you are removed from the *Valiant*'s command. You are stripped of your rank, and discharged from the Gaian Defense Force."

The words made no sense. They were only a jumble of syllables, meaningless as an alien tongue. She stared at the admiral, thinking there had to be some mistake, knowing there was no possible reason he could be saying such things to her.

Her mouth was dry. It seemed impossible to unglue her tongue from the roof of her mouth so she could speak, but she knew she must respond.

"Sir, I don't understand. What could I possibly have done to deserve—"

His voice cut across hers. Years of training forced her into immediate silence.

"What did you do to deserve such treatment? Consorting with the enemy, that's for one. That is enough, and you know it. Bad enough if you were a civilian, but as a ship's captain? Unforgivable."

He might as well have thrown a bucket of cold water over her. Dread choked her throat. How could the admiral have known? Did he have a spy secreted somewhere amongst her crew, or had some ambitious subordinate seen in her visit with Rast sen Drenthan the means of removing her so they could move that much farther up the chain of command?

She had no way of discovering how the information had been leaked. It didn't matter now. The only thing that mattered was damage control. "Admiral, I can explain. The Stacian captain approached me, offered to withdraw—"

"And you fell for such a simple ruse?"

"It was no ruse," she returned. "He did leave. We all saw him leave. It's recorded in the ship's logs."

The admiral's brows drew together. "Oh, yes, he left —only to be replaced by a squad of five Stacian *Trenth*-class cruisers no more than eight standard hours later. The arriving colonists didn't have a chance."

"They didn't have a chance," she repeated, her words barely above a whisper. No, they wouldn't, not with five heavily armed cruisers waiting for them. Something in her pushed her to continue her own defense. "If the *Valiant* hadn't been called away—"

"It would have made no difference, and you know it. The *Valiant* would have been completely outmatched, and your crew lost along with the colonists and the scientific team."

The team. So they were gone as well, the men and women she'd come to know over the past few months, Dr. Singh and Dr. D'Ambrosio and all the others. Her hands curled into fists. What a lie Rast sen Drenthan had spun. She had no idea Stacians could be such good liars.

More arguments rose to her lips, but she knew she needn't bother to voice them. The admiral was right—her one ship could not have held out against five of the Stacian fleet's largest and best-equipped cruisers. He probably hadn't thought of it this way, and wouldn't care to be told of the fact, but Admiral Horner's abrupt summons to regional HQ had saved her life and the life of her crew.

How far out from the disputed system had those cruisers been hiding? Long-range scans had shown no sign of any other enemy craft in the space around Chlorae II. Then again, the signal must have been given as soon as Captain sen Drenthan had left. Those cruisers could have been out of scanning range and still able to get to the Chlorae system in less than a standard day. Sensor equipment could do a lot, but it still had a difficult time finding a moving target that was parsecs away, especially if that target kept popping in and out of subspace. That was a common tactic to avoid enemy scans.

Very likely it had all been a joke, some perverse trick by the Stacian captain to show his dominance before calling in the reinforcements that would bring Chlorae II and its valuable ore under Stacian control. Oh, there would be repercussions, of course. The sector council would condemn the act, and the Eridanis would pronounce on the importance of following the strictures of the treaty, but of course the Stacians could just claim that they had first rights to the millenite, since they were the ones to initially chart the system. It was all very muddy, but this war would only be staged in the courts and around the bargaining tables that had taken the place—for the most part—of bloody battlefields.

It had all been for nothing. She had compromised her honor, and risked the lives of her crew, for a lie. Slowly she reached up and unclipped the stars from the collar of her uniform, then laid them on the shining stainless steel surface of Admiral Horner's desk. She did not bother to speak. What, at this juncture, could she possibly say? His cold-eyed stare told her without words how much he condemned her...and how lucky she was that she would only suffer the disgrace of a dishonorable discharge, and not a full court-martial and life imprisonment in the GDF brig on Europa.

Still silent, she turned and left the admiral's office. She knew she would never return.

Rast entered Admiral sen Trannick's chambers and wondered what the reward for his success might be—reassignment to his home world's system defense fleet, or perhaps even a promotion to commodore and his own regional command. One could never be sure, when carrying out a wager so successfully, but the admiral had been known to be generous when someone pleased him.

Unlike the Gaians, the Stacian commanders maintained their offices shipboard, and not on a space station or moon base. Also unlike the Gaians, those of high rank generally had quarters that would be considered sybaritic by most impartial observers. Admiral sen Trannick's chambers were no exception; tapestries of Iradian silk covered the walls, and a rug with intricate but muted patterns cushioned the floor. Carved stone jars holding the ubiquitous *merh* that scented Stacian clothing and hair ointments were placed around the room to cover up the synthetic odors that always seemed to emanate from the great starships' ventilation systems.

The admiral rose from his desk as Rast entered, the older man's scarred face cracked in a great smile. "Ah, sen Drenthan. Quite the success!"

That it had been. If only he had made the bargain for two nights instead of one. All during the journey here he'd ached to touch Lira Jannholm again, to bury himself in her. What would it have been like to lie down with her and know that she still would be there in the morning, instead of fleeing at her earliest opportunity?

"Thank you, Excellency," Rast said. "Truly, I was a little surprised Captain Jannholm even agreed, but you must have known more of her character than I guessed."

"Oh, that." The admiral shrugged. "An amusing ploy, but not the real story."

"Oh?" Rast didn't much like the sound of that. After all, his commanding officer had seemed fairly invested in suborning Lira Jannholm, in getting Rast a taste of a human female.

About that, the admiral had been right. Lira did taste delicious.

Rast asked, his voice somewhat sharper than he had intended, "And what is the real story?"

The familiar rapacious glint returned to Admiral sen Trannick's eyes. "Someone reported her actions to her commanding officer. They recalled her immediately to base...and so I sent in a squad of *Trenth*-class cruisers to attack the outpost on Chlorae II. The arriving colonists had a nasty surprise waiting for them, I'm afraid."

Over the years Rast had learned to think before he spoke, and so luckily he did not say what first sprang to mind—that the admiral's actions were a clear contravention of the Eridani treaty, and would lead to bitter and protracted reprisals from the Gaian government. He also did not much like the thought of Stacian ships gunning down unprotected civilians and scientists. It was one thing to face your equals in battle, but lying in wait to shoot miners and their families out of the sky was quite another.

Beyond that, though, he thought of Lira. If she had been recalled, then she must have faced some sort of punishment. The Gaians had no more tolerance for traitors than his own people did. Was she now sitting in a brig, awaiting court-martial? Had they executed her? His knowledge of Gaian methods of punishment was fuzzy at best. Had their roles been reversed, he would have been asked to make the cuts of sacrifice on his wrists and offer his life as compensation for the shame he had brought on the fleet, on

Stacia itself. But he did not think that was the Gaian way.

He cleared his throat. "And what of Captain Jannholm?"

A shrewd copper-hued glance from beneath the admiral's heavy brows. "Made an impression, did she?"

Since he knew showing any concern for Lira's fate would not meet with a favorable reception, Rast made the one reply he thought was safe. "We made a bargain, Excellency, and she comported herself honorably. It would be unfortunate if the Gaian command didn't understand that she was trying to act in their best interests."

"Well, apparently they didn't see it that way. Our Intelligence operatives have reported that she was removed from command and discharged from the fleet."

Odd that he should feel so relieved by the news of her disgrace...but that's all it was. Disgrace, and only in the eyes of those too blind to see what she had really done. He knew she possessed more of a sense of honor than most in the Gaian fleet. She might be disgraced, and stripped of her rank, but at least she was alive. Alive, and apparently free to pursue her own fate, whatever that might be.

"And where is she now?"

The admiral almost smiled. "No one knows. She left her sector HQ and disappeared. But what does it matter? She's gone, and Chlorae II is ours. And you, Captain sen Drenthan, are now the commanding officer in charge of the defense force at Syrinara."

It was a promotion, and an enviable one. Syrinara was the fifth planet from the sun in the Stacian system, and the first one colonized and terraformed after the Stacians adopted the technology the Eridanis had given them, using it to escape their home world's harsh conditions. On Syrinara, which had a milder climate and the refreshing novelty of actual oceans, much of the food that supplied Stacia and its fleet was grown. Besides being assigned to Stacia itself, Rast could not think of a more desirable promotion, one that put him in line to move even further up the chain of command.

"You honor me, Excellency," Rast said at once. He knew a swift acknowledgment of the honor he had been given was the best way to please the admiral.

"I thought you'd be happy. So come, share a drink with me and seal the deal. And, Captain—"

"Yes, Excellency?"

"Forget her. She has served her purpose."

"Of course," Rast replied automatically, although he knew it was not quite so simple as that. No, it would be some time before he could completely erase the thought—and feel, and taste—of Lira Jannholm from his mind.

And at the moment, he wasn't sure what troubled him more...that he could still taste her on his tongue, or the niggling sense at the back of his mind that the admiral was playing a far larger game than Rast could begin to imagine.

Jupiter's red eye glared down from the heavens as Lira debarked from the shuttle and made her way through the domes of the Ganymede base.

What was that old saying?

Home is the place that where you go, they have to take you in.

Of course, no one ever said that the people at home had to be exactly enthusiastic about welcoming you back into the fold...

No one had offered to come and meet her, and she hadn't asked. She didn't have much to bring with her anyway—just two suitcases of sleek composite, one of which was only half full. Ships' captains didn't have that much in the way of personal belongings, or at least GDF captains didn't. She'd left her uniforms behind, and her civilian clothing and other personal items made for a meager enough collection. Well, it made traveling that much easier, although being crammed in the economy-class stateroom she had shared with another woman traveling alone brought home more than anything else the realization that she was not a ship's captain anymore.

She was no one.

Everything around her looked more or less the same, and yet subtly different from the last time she had seen it, some five years ago. She supposed it was she who had changed, and not the base on Ganymede.

The base was a mixture of above-ground domes and miles of subterranean facilities. Because her parents held high-level positions—her mother a botanist overseeing one of the greenhouse facilities that grew food for the colony, her father on the committee that handled the day-to-day management of the base—they lived in a complex in Dome 3, near the moon's equator. No one had bothered terraforming Ganymede; it was too far outside the habitable band to make such an endeavor economically feasible, so the atmosphere was a thin trace of various oxygen compounds too toxic to support human life.

Through the domes the stars still shone, bright pinpricks she could remember gazing at every day of her childhood. They were the spurs that led her outward into the greater galaxy. No staying here on Ganymede or even the Gaian system as a whole—she'd wanted up and out, and as soon as possible. Not much to feel homesick for here, as she'd always had the vague impression that her parents had had children more because it had been expected of them than because they'd actually wanted them. True, they were proud of her acceptance to the university on Eridani at barely sixteen, her expedited track at the naval academy, her early appointment to captain, since those were the sorts of accomplishments that they could trot out at cocktail parties.

She had a feeling they weren't quite as proud now.

Not that she'd gone into any great detail about what had happened, but word had a way of getting around, even with the light-years that separated Gaia's far-flung colonies and bases. All Lira could hope was that people only knew she'd done something so dreadful she'd been drummed out of the GDF. Tough as she wanted to believe she was, she really didn't want to explain what she'd been thinking when she shared a bed with a Stacian. She could only imagine the revulsion on the faces of her parents or her old acquaintances and classmates if the whole sordid story ever came out. Beyond her tawdry liaison with Rast sen Drenthan, though, the deaths of the colonists weighed heavily on her, their stilled voices a reproachful murmur at the back of her mind. Yes, she'd only been trying to ensure their safety, but that hardly mattered now.

Dome 3 consisted mainly of residential units, occasionally broken up by an eating establishment, shop, or pub. Not too many of those, of course. It wouldn't do to have the populace tempted by too much drink. Just enough to give the semblance of someplace to rest and unwind, although the alcohol served on Ganymede was carefully lowered in potency so it couldn't cause too much trouble. She still remembered the first time she'd had a glass of undiluted wine at the university on Eridani—she'd barely been able to walk afterward.

Her parents had a spacious end unit that occupied two levels. As Lira approached the entrance, her steps gradually slowed. Something in her very much wanted to turn and run, to take her meager savings and go someplace where no one had ever heard of Lira Jannholm, disgraced starship captain. But she wouldn't be that kind of coward. No, she'd face whatever might come next with her head held high. Perhaps she had made a dreadful mistake in going to Rast sen Drenthan, but it had been a mistake born of a desire to ensure the safety of Chlorae II, not for any personal gain. Her intentions had been good.

And we all know what's paved with those good intentions, she thought, then shook her head.

Better to get this over with. She paused at the door, set down one suitcase, then reached out with her free hand to push the buzzer.

He should have been completely satisfied. His new ship, the *Tarlentha*, was newly commissioned, sleek and elegant and with captain's quarters that would have pleased a man with far more extravagant tastes than he. The promotion brought with it an extra measure of respect; it was clear the admiral favored Captain sen Drenthan, and his new crew were far more obsequious than his former shipmates, who had tended to be a rowdy bunch. This group ran a tight ship, but Rast had the feeling he would miss the easier companionship on board the *Brensa* before too much time passed.

And yet...

Something about the situation didn't feel right, didn't smell right. He'd pondered the situation, in those few rare moments when his time was not occupied by some demand, some new situation to learn from and absorb. For one thing, the political currents he encountered here on Syrinara were far different from those he had dealt with while patrolling the farther reaches of the Stacian Federation. Some days, he thought he was expending more energy on keeping track of whom to curry favor with and who could be safely ignored than on actually running his ship.

Even so, he had stolen minutes here and there when he could be alone in his quarters, when he could sit and think about how he had gotten here, and the woman who'd been the casualty of his new success. Learning where she had gone proved to be more difficult than he'd thought; after all, he couldn't make outright inquiries through regular channels. But a man he'd had dealings with years before when securing a few black market items for his parents' comfort said he might be able to track her down, given enough time, and Rast had to be content with that for now. At least he knew for a fact that she wasn't dead.

Given all that, he should have allowed himself to push the matter aside until he had more concrete information as to Lira's whereabouts. That proved impossible, however. He kept ticking the timing over in his mind, and something about it didn't seem to add up. Unless Admiral sen Trannick had those five cruisers poised in exactly the right position, they could never have reached the Chlorae system in enough time to intercept and destroy the incoming colonists before they even had a chance to land on the planet's surface. No, it was almost as if he had known the *Valiant* would be withdrawn.

And how was that possible? He would have had to receive some sort of intelligence from within Admiral Horner's office that Captain Jannholm was about to be discharged from service. Rast was willing to believe many things, but somehow he couldn't believe that two such sworn enemies would have colluded to make sure the Gaian colony on Chlorae II was destroyed before it had even begun. Such treachery would make Lira Jannholm's perceived disloyalty pale into nothingness. No, there had to be another explanation.

It could have been luck—if one believed in such things. Once upon a time he might have said he didn't, but he'd seen enough over the years to think there had to be some underlying force at work, one that sometimes seemed to have a capricious capacity to play havoc with the plans of sentient beings, or to bring unexpected favor at a roll of the bones. Admiral sen Trannick had had enough inspired guesses and turns of fortune during his career that one could call him lucky.

Better that—better to think that it was the work of the old gods some still believed in—than to think Stacian and Gaian were working together toward some goal whose motivation he couldn't begin to guess. Because if that were true, it meant everything he had been told, everything he believed, was a lie.

"And how long do you intend on staying?" Her mother's tone, brittle in its casualness, told Lira everything she needed to know about her welcome here. Not that she had expected much different.

She wanted to make an airy comment about staying

here on Ganymede indefinitely, of enrolling in some sort of coursework at the moon's one rather mediocre college, but she didn't feel quite brave enough for that. For a second or two she didn't answer, but only concentrated on chewing the mouthful of eggplant strata she had just taken. At least the food was good; some of the best hydroponics setups in Gaian space were located right here on the Jovian base.

"Not long," she replied. "I just need to explore some options. In fact, I've already had a few offers from independent shippers and charter companies."

This was a bare-faced lie. While one might have thought the skills she'd obtained in the navy would be in some demand, no one had come forward to claim them. Blacklists weren't just for the military. At this point, Lira was fairly certain no one respectable would touch her with a ten-meter cattle prod.

The tight lines around her mother's mouth seemed to relax slightly. "That sounds promising."

"Oh, it is."

They lapsed into a tense little silence. Although Lira had expected her father to be here, he was conspicuously absent—a last-minute emergency had called him away, according to her mother. That was possible, but Lira thought it rather more likely that he wasn't quite ready to face his disgraced daughter, and so manufactured a crisis that would keep him safely away for some hours. And luckily her younger sister and brother were long gone, her sister with the GEC, and her brother a climatologist working on the ongoing Gaian rehabilitation project. At least the human race's home world wasn't quite the polluted mess it had been several centuries earlier, but there was still some ways to go before it began to approach even a semblance of its former beauty.

Her siblings seemed the safest subject to broach, and so she inquired about Janna first, then Liam. Lira guessed her mother knew exactly what red herrings these lines of conversation were, but of course she gave no hint. Marta Jannholm had never been one for confidences, and Lira knew she wasn't about to start now.

The conversation lurched this way and that until the food had been consumed. A gleaming mech came to clear away the empty plates. The machine was a new addition; her parents must have been doing better than she thought.

Glad somebody is, flitted through her mind, and she chided herself for the self-pitying thought. No one had held a gun to her head and demanded that she sleep with Captain sen Drenthan. No, she'd brought that disaster on herself. The Stacian would have to live with his treachery, though. That might be cold comfort, but better than nothing. Although Admiral Horner and everyone around her might think differently, she knew, at bottom, that she had tried to do the right thing.

Still, as she murmured to her mother that she was tired and only wanted to go to bed, she knew this refuge—such as it was—could only be a temporary one. She didn't know where home was, but she realized now it wasn't here.

CHAPTER FOUR

RAST SET DOWN HIS HANDHELD AND RUBBED HIS forehead. This was one of those days when it felt as if the *trinials* hanging down his back weighed twice as much as they normally did, and the news his source had just delivered hadn't done anything to improve matters.

Ganymede. Might as well be right in the heart of old Gaia for all the good the information did him. Perhaps somewhere in the back of his mind he'd had some wild notion that he could go to Lira, speak with her, tell her the five cruisers that had attacked Chlorae II and its people had nothing to do with him. But while a Stacian and a Gaian might meet face to face in the wilder hinterlands of the galaxy, such a thing was completely impossible in the heart of the Gaian system.

For a second or two he entertained the notion of having his source pay to hire a Gaian to approach Lira on Ganymede, but that was just as foolish. For one thing, he knew the more people he brought into his confidence, the greater the chance that one of them could betray him to his superiors. A tumble sanctioned by the admiral was one thing. Openly pursuing the woman he'd been told to forget was quite another.

It was time to let her go. She was safely back home, and it comforted him somewhat to know she had gone back to her family. Even in their brief acquaintance she had seemed so fiercely independent that he found the move unexpected and yet oddly heartening. On Stacia, family was everything—it had to be, to ensure that one's bloodlines survived even in face of that world's less than ideal environment. Indeed, some of Admiral sen Trannick's patronage probably stemmed from Rast's mother being the admiral's distant cousin by way of their great-grandsire's numerous offspring.

Unwelcome as the idea might be, perhaps Admiral sen Trannick was right. Perhaps it was time to forget Lira Jannholm, late of the GDF *Valiant*.

For what felt like the hundredth time that night, Lira rolled over, attempting to find a more comfortable spot in the bed. It seemed too soft after the hard, narrow sleeping accommodations in her quarters on the *Valiant*, the adjustable foam too accommodating. And it didn't help that every time she closed her eyes, she seemed to catch a ghost-trace of the spicy scent that surrounded Rast sen Drenthan. Her mind playing tricks on her, of course; there wasn't a Stacian within parsecs of Ganymede, and even if there were, the recyclers and scrubbers and myriad other components of Dome 3's ventilation system would have made sure that every trace of alien aroma had been thoroughly erased.

This had happened once or twice during her journey here: thinking that she had sensed him somehow, shutting her eyes at night and imagining the heat of his body next to hers. Ridiculous, really. No human male had ever made such an impression on her, so why the hell was she letting this Stacian infest her memories?

She wished there were a way to flush her brain cells the way one might wipe a computer after its memory had been hopelessly compromised. Then she wouldn't keep replaying those images in her mind, of his hands touching her, his tongue between her legs, the heat of his flesh inside her. Somehow her body didn't seem to understand what her brain knew—that he had tricked her, betrayed her. That he wasn't worthy of another thought, let alone this obsession that seemed to have taken hold on some deep, atavistic level she hadn't even known existed before now.

Her body ached with need. Without even realizing at first what she was doing, she reached lower, touched the damp heat between her legs. Stroked, and stroked, bringing at last the release she needed, even as she acknowledged that this was a counterfeit, a pale substitute for the thing she really wanted. And once it was over, she turned her head into the pillow and wept, crying as silently as she had climaxed, hating Rast sen Drenthan, and hating herself for what she'd allowed him to do to her.

There had been a formal reception on Syrinara, hosted by the planetary consul, to honor the new commander of the defense force. Strong wine had flowed—Syrinara had begun experimenting with hybridized Eridani grapes—and Rast found himself not quite as steady of head as he might have preferred. The woman who sat next to him at dinner laughed and flirted and made it quite clear that she'd be more than pleased to have him accompany her to her apartments afterward. So he'd gone, thinking in his half-drunken state that it would be a good chance to banish the ghost of Lira Jannholm forever. Surely a night spent in the arms of a Stacian woman should be enough to convince him of where his true interests lay.

But although he'd managed to rise to the occasion, he found his level of enthusiasm not quite what it should be. Oh, he performed well enough, but all he could think of was how different Lira had felt in his embrace, how different she had tasted. How the silk of her hair had trailed across his chest and set him throbbing all over again.

This woman—Rast couldn't even recall her name— fell asleep soon afterward, and he eased himself out of bed and went to the windows, which functioned more as doors, opening onto a balcony that overlooked a moonlit garden. So unlike their home world, this first colony of Stacia. No, Syrinara had the stamp of Eridani all over it, from the architecture to the manner in which the gardens that surrounded the house had been planted. One might say the Eridanis were generous with their knowledge, but others complained they wanted to make everything over in their image.

In that endeavor they had met their match in the Gaians, who had also developed a cruder form of the subspace drive that allowed starships to travel the galaxy and which also permitted the wide-flung colonies that had sprung up in the centuries following those first thrusts toward the stars. The Gaians possessed their own advanced technologies, while the Stacians, he had to admit, had lagged far behind. This was not a popular viewpoint, and most Stacian histories emphasized his people's resourcefulness in surviving after the meteor forever changed their planet's climate. However, one couldn't argue with the reality that living in caves and hunting by night did not exactly produce the correct conditions for developing computers and spaceships and mechanoids.

At any rate, Stacia did not want to lag behind, and so eagerly took the Eridani technology as it was given, unlike the Gaians, who tinkered with it as it pleased them. These days, most new starships were being built with the Gaian-engineered Gupta drives, which achieved speeds even the Eridanis hadn't been able to manage. The irony that those drives also powered the

Stacian cruisers which had headed off the Chlorae II colonists was not lost on Rast sen Drenthan.

"Why so wakeful?" came a throaty voice from behind him.

He turned to see the woman he had just bedded sitting upright, watching him. She had not bothered to cover her bare torso, and the smooth golden skin of her breasts was turned copper by the ruddy hue of Syrinara's oversized moon.

Normally such a sight would have made him harden immediately, but now he only gazed at her with dispassion, wondering what sound he had made that had woken her. More of Lira Jannholm's influence, he supposed, somehow making every other female seem to be a pale imitation of her.

"The moonlight," he lied. "It's very bright."

"True," she said, nodding. "Your first time on Syrinara?"

"Yes." He paused, then added, "I believe I told you that at dinner."

A hesitation of her own, and he had the sudden impression that this hadn't been a chance encounter, that she had been placed carefully to catch his eye and engage him in conversation. Too bad she hadn't done a very good job of taking notes.

"So you did." She smiled, as if at her own foolishness. "I suppose I had a little too much wine."

Rast didn't believe that for a second. Oh, he had drunk a good deal, but not so much that he hadn't noticed she took only one glass for every two of his, and the last one she had left at the table more than half full. Abruptly, he asked, "Who sent you?"

The smile faltered a little, but she managed to tilt her head and give him a puzzled look. "What do you mean?"

"Who made sure you were seated next to me at dinner tonight? Admiral sen Trannick?"

At that question, her smile disappeared altogether. She pursed her lips and looked away from him. "I don't know what you're talking about."

"Of course you do. You're very attractive, but you're not a very good liar."

"I don't see what the harm is. I would have gone with you even if—" And she broke off, her flush made more pronounced by the reddish moonlight.

"Even if he hadn't asked?" Rast finished for her. "And what was the incentive? Did he pay you?"

"I'm not a whore!" she flashed. "There are many women who would have gladly taken my place, but the admiral's wife is my mother's sister-daughter. I had the first right."

"Right to what?" he asked, although he thought he already knew the answer.

"To Rast sen Drenthan, new defender of Syrinara."

"And that is all?"

"'All'?" she repeated, her tone innocent—but, as he had already noted, Rast didn't think much of her skills at prevarication.

"No direction to school me in the attractions of Stacian women? No admonishment to do whatever was necessary to make me forget a certain Gaian female?"

She started a little at that, then stared down at the bedclothes. They, too, were Eridani, he noted absently, fine of weave, intricate in pattern, bits of metallic thread throwing out errant sparkles under the light of Syrinara's moon.

"Ah," he said then. Her silence told him all he needed to know.

Without further comment he went to the chair to retrieve his discarded uniform and began to pull it on.

"That's all?" she demanded, pushing the covers aside and going to stand a few paces away from him. He noted that she had planted herself directly between him and the door. "You would throw this aside for some *slaindar*?"

The word, directly translated, meant "white meat." A slur his people used for the Gaians, even though, strictly speaking, not all Gaians could be described as white. But for the Stacians, the word also meant insipid, useless. He knew the woman standing before him had used it on purpose to wound, to provoke him into some sort of response.

He would not allow himself to become angry. Lira Jannholm's honor was so clear to him that defending it to this female would be a waste of breath. Besides, if he did not acknowledge the remark, then she would have less ammunition to take to the admiral, less proof that Rast truly was still interested in Lira Jannholm.

After fastening the last button of his jacket, he said, "Step aside."

She didn't move. In a way, she was magnificent, the fall of her *trinials* glittering with copper and silver and the dull red sheen of unfaceted carnelian, her breasts rising and falling in angry breaths. A month ago, he would have reached out and taken her again, this time on the floor, against the rug of woven Iradian silk.

Now, though, he only repeated, "Step aside." A touch of steel entered his tone. "Now."

Finally she faltered, and moved a few inches to her left. "The admiral will not be pleased."

"No, I suppose he won't. But that is my problem, not yours."

She looked as if she wanted to say something else, but the expression on his face must have been enough to stop her. In silence she stood as he passed her by and went out the door.

Cool night air surrounded him. He stopped under the spreading branches of an unfamiliar, alien tree, and lifted his head to watch Syrinara's blood-tinged moon for a moment or two.

It was very possible that he had just made a huge mistake. On the other hand, all he felt at the moment was an overwhelming sensation of relief. It would have been too easy to fall into the admiral's trap. Already Rast was past the age when he should have married and begun his own family. Pressure had begun to increase on him from all sides—parents, sisters, brothers. With the admiral flinging an eligible female of good family at him, he might have succumbed...if it weren't for Lira Jannholm.

Odd, though, that only a few weeks ago sen Trannick had been so eager for Rast to bed Captain

Jannholm, and now seemed equally eager to make sure the two were kept as far apart as possible.

Or perhaps not so odd at all...

The base on Ganymede was too regulated, too clean and proper to have the equivalent of the spaceport dive bar Lira had seen on tens of other worlds, but the Big Dipper would have to do. Located in Dome 2, next to the shuttle pad that ferried people back and forth from the mining outposts on Io and Europa, it had its share of what Marta Jannholm referred to as "colorful characters"—meaning they made their living by getting their hands dirty. In a figurative sense, of course, as outsystem miners used automated equipment to do most of their work. And even if they did use their hands from time to time, those hands would of course be protected by the gloves of an EVA suit.

The miners often traveled from world to world, following the next big strike. In that way, they weren't much different from the prospectors of old, although the equipment modern-day miners used would have probably made the "forty-niners" Lira had read about in her history texts fall over in their well-worn shoes.

Anyway, since she had to find something to do with herself, and since the legitimate avenues seemed to be closed—a few carefully worded messages to former classmates at the academy had been enough to convince her of that—she decided her next course of action would have to be pursuing some less-than-legitimate avenues. And that meant hanging out at the Big Dipper and looking studiously at loose ends.

It didn't take too long. After five minutes or so of nursing a reduced-alcohol ale while seated at the end of the bar, she saw a burly character with a week's worth of stubble on his jaw rise from his own table and amble toward her. He nodded at the barkeep, then remarked, as if to the air in general, "I hear there's a transport in need of a pilot."

"That so," she responded, staring down into the wan suds at the edges of her cup as if they were the most important thing in the world.

"Yeah."

The stranger was silent as the bartender handed over another pint and then wandered off to the other end of the bar, where a hard-faced man sat a little too close to a pretty redhead who had to be at least two standard decades his junior. They were both drinking watered-down white wine and not looking very happy about it.

"Last pilot got his arm broke in a fight the other night. Owners want that transport gone ASAP. You interested?"

Of course she was, but Lira knew better than to display too much interest. "What's the cargo?"

The stranger let out a rusty chuckle. "Do you care?"

"I care if it's going to land me in the MaxSec on Titan."

"No worries. Spare drive parts, farm equipment. Harmless."

On the surface, sure. She guessed that "harmless" cargo was hiding some contraband the owner had bribed the proper authorities to make sure was never discovered, but that was just the way these people did business. Once upon a time, she might have cared. Now, all she cared about was getting off Ganymede, away from the no-longer-family that had given her very little refuge after all.

She didn't even bother to ask the destination. What did it matter, as long as it was away from here?

In the end, Rast had given in to his curiosity. It was dangerous, and foolish, but he had to know more of her situation, get a message to her somehow. His source assured him that all would be kept confidential, that the message would be directed through so many different channels no one could possibly guess at its origin.

But then the response came back with one simple word.

Gone.

Left Ganymede some five standard days earlier, apparently piloting a rundown freighter with the ludicrously grandiose name of *Star of Madrid*, whatever a Madrid was.

Destination: Iradia.

He'd frowned at that piece of intelligence. Iradia seemed the last place he could imagine Lira Jannholm.

It was a desert world, much like his own, but blessed with oases scattered across its surface. Those oases had given rise to the moon moth, a huge specimen whose caterpillars produced the fiber woven into some of the galaxy's finest fabrics. In the oases, life was more or less orderly, but the planet's expanses of desert provided safe harbor for a good number of the sector's worst crime lords. If you didn't have business with the silk bosses, it was best to avoid the place. And yet Lira had gone there, flying an old ship that should have, as far as he could judge based on its build date, been scuttled years ago.

The manifest had listed various piece of equipment required for the farming of the sandleaf trees that provided sustenance for the moths. He guessed there was a good deal more on that ship not listed on the manifest, and wondered if Lira had realized the same thing. Probably—she was far from stupid. But what had led her to abandon the safe haven of Ganymede for the dubious honor of flying contraband to Iradia?

That way lay a headache, and Rast's scowl deepened. He'd spent the last week making sure everything he did and said was by the book, so as not to attract any more negative attention from Admiral sen Trannick. The admiral had been less than pleased by Rast's dismissal of the young woman who was his wife's relation, but he hadn't said anything openly. No, his disapproval had been displayed in the coolness of his tone, the way he had saved his heartiest laughs for those under his command who hadn't dared to thwart his wishes.

Rast almost wondered if the admiral might find some way to rescind his gift of Syrinara's defense post, but so far things had moved along unchanged. And that was why Rast had done everything in his power to avoid provoking any more of his superior officer's wrath. By maintaining things as they were, perhaps that small bump in the road could be forgotten, put aside.

The last thing he should do was make any further attempt to locate Lira Jannholm. Bad enough that he had gone as far as he had already. If she had, for whatever reason, decided to put aside all her training and throw in her lot with less-than-savory merchants, there wasn't much he could do about it. She was a grown woman, capable of making her own decisions.

And yet...

He had been to Iradia, just once, newly commissioned on his first posting, eager to see the galaxy, to explore the stars that had glittered so brightly in the clear skies of his home world. As a first impression of those faraway planets, Iradia hadn't been all that inspiring. His ship's crew had been admonished to stay within the safe confines of Aldis Nova, the site of the main spaceport and the planet's largest oasis, spanning a good two hundred kilometers across. But of course he and several other of the junior crew members had laughed at the warnings and ventured outside the safe zone. After all, they were from a harsh desert world as well. They'd been confident they could handle anything Iradia or its denizens threw at them.

Eighteen standard hours later, the group had

limped back into Aldis Nova, missing two of its members. The bosses that controlled the desert just outside the oasis hadn't taken kindly to a contingent of Stacian interlopers entering their territory, and made it clear through an ambush in a canyon some ten kilometers beyond the safe zone. Despite all his training, it was Rast's first firefight—and his last. Not much need for that sort of thing on board a starship, and he found he liked it that way. It wasn't cowardice to know he'd be a happy man if he never had to see a compatriot bleed out in his arms again.

Those bitter recollections did not do anything to improve his mood. And if he'd found Iradia so hostile, how would it treat Lira Jannholm, she of the upper-crust Ganymede background and the spotless record?

Well, spotless until she had met him, anyway.

That seemed to decide things. He wouldn't call it a rescue—he had a feeling Lira wouldn't appreciate being thought of as someone who needed protecting—but he knew he couldn't abandon her to Iradia's tender mercies.

It was time to take a leave of absence.

Lira stared at the captain of the *Star of Madrid* in consternation. "You're leaving me here?"

He seemed unmoved by her distress. "I told you the job was only temporary. You been paid. You can get your own passage off-world."

So she could...at a cost that would eat up more than half what she'd just been paid for bringing that garbage scow of a freighter safely here to Iradia. And hadn't that been a picnic, what with blown coolant coils, a balky nav-computer, and a ship's engineer with roving hands.

When they'd landed, she'd been overwhelmingly relieved that she could get off the ship for a few hours, walk around in Aldis Nova, and breathe air that didn't stink of stale coolant and bodies that weren't quite as fastidious about keeping clean as she was. However, she hadn't thought she'd be barred from returning once she'd had her fill of fresh air.

"People come in and out of Iradia all the time," Captain Marquez said, with a shrug of his fat shoulders. "You shouldn't have too much trouble getting another gig."

That might be true. Too bad she wasn't all that keen on picking up another piloting job, considering how well this one had turned out. Not that she had much of a choice at this point.

"Sure," she said, and bent down to pick up her satchel, which contained pretty much everything she owned. A few odds and ends had been left behind in her old room on Ganymede, but she somehow doubted she'd be going back there anytime soon to retrieve them.

A hot breeze ruffled her hair, loosening a few strands from the tight coil she wore at the back of her neck. The wind was coming from the west. It seemed as good a direction as any.

She turned away from Marquez and strode off into

the swirling crowds of Aldis Nova. She wouldn't let herself think about what might happen next.

To say that Admiral sen Trannick was angry would probably be an understatement. Rast had somehow doubted that his request for a leave of indeterminate length would pass by unnoticed...but he'd rather hoped it would.

"Leave?" the admiral demanded, and tossed the handheld containing the leave-of-absence forms on his desk. "After getting a post most men in your situation would have killed for?"

"Sir, I know it's somewhat irregular, but it is necessary. I am fully prepared to relinquish my command on a permanent basis if that's what is required."

As he spoke the words, Rast was a little astonished at himself. Hadn't he spent the last decade working toward such a post? And now, to throw it away to pursue an alien woman who no doubt hated him for what he had brought her to?

On first examination, it was insane. But Rast prided himself on his instincts, which so far had never steered him wrong. Somehow he knew he was meant to be with Lira Jannholm...just as he also knew the command of Syrinara's defense force was not his intended destiny. Something about it felt wrong, wrong as the admiral's own actions and reactions had been of late.

What drove that wrongness, he didn't yet know. He only knew that he had to leave, and as soon as possible.

"'Personal family business,'" sen Trannick read, after retrieving the handheld from the desktop. "What could be so urgent that it would take you away from your command?"

"As stated, your Excellency, it is a private family matter that I am not at liberty to discuss."

A bald lie, of course, but Rast had known that would be the best tactic to avoid as much unpleasantness as possible. Family was sacred, and the privacy of a family's concerns even more so. As much as he might want to probe, the admiral would most likely forbear from asking any further questions.

Rast's guesses proved correct, as Admiral sen Trannick frowned down at the handheld for a few seconds longer before saying, "Then go. I will not ask your business...but know if you don't return within one standard month, don't bother to return at all."

"Of course, your Excellency." Rast bowed from the waist, the proper response. As any further conversation seemed superfluous, he took his leave and exited the admiral's office. A ship was leaving for Eridani in a few standard hours; that gave Rast just enough time to put matters in order before it departed. From Eridani he could get another flight to Iradia.

One standard month. A lot could happen in that time.

Somehow, though, Rast doubted he would ever return to reclaim his position in Syrinara's defense force.

CHAPTER FIVE

LIRA STARED AT THE GLASS OF IRADIAN BRANDY SITTING on the bar in front of her. Only one glass, and a small one at that. She knew she could never allow herself more than a single glass. Any more, and she might find she'd start drinking and never stop.

A few weeks ago, if someone had told her she'd end up like this—drinking in a disreputable little tavern in Aldis Nova and working for one of Iradia's most notorious crime bosses— she would have recommended that they seek out a good psychiatrist. But life did have a way of playing little tricks on you.

After Captain Marquez dumped her so unceremoniously, she wandered the city for a while, knowing she would have to find lodging at some point, and wondering how much of a chunk it would take from her meager funds. There was a Gaian consulate here, and she supposed she could always go there to send a transmission to Ganymede and ask her parents if they would transfer some money to her. That, however, seemed even more distasteful than having to beg for a slot on a third-rate transport.

So she'd wandered some more, and drifted into a seedy little cafe, and ordered the least expensive item on the menu—a bowl of some sort of grain-based milky dish. It was while she was nursing her meal along that someone dropped into the seat opposite her and remarked,

"Heard you were a pilot."

She'd glanced up to see a well-dressed man a few years older than she watching her carefully. From his pale lavender skin she guessed he was at least part Eridani. "Who told you that?"

"I hear things."

Turned out he did. When he first hired her, he gave no hint of who his—and her—new boss actually was. She didn't discover that until she showed up at the location he'd described to her, found herself being patted down by two enormous men, and then saw the man himself waiting by the door of a sleek Sirocco-class ship, a Gaian-engineered rich man's toy designed for both in-atmosphere and subspace travel. This one was so new that it even had a carefully scaled-down version of the Gupta drive that powered the GDF's starships. She'd heard of the new Siroccos but had never seen one. Maybe a desire to pilot that beautiful machine had fueled her decision to sign on with her new boss.

Gared Tomas. The name hadn't meant much to her at first, of course, but she figured it out soon enough. He had holdings all over the planet, as well as under the base on Iradia's smaller moon, and he needed someone to take him wherever he needed to go.

"Someone he can trust," Istafa Morain, the lavender-skinned man, told her.

How he'd determined that trustworthy person was her, Lira didn't quite know. But after a few days in Gared Tomas's service, she realized he made it his business to learn everything he could about the people he considered hiring. Probably his agents had hacked into her file with the GDF to steal her personal history and slipped back out again with no one the wiser.

Tomas could have been anywhere between forty and sixty. Hard to say, with the shaved head and the smooth warm brown skin. His eyes were a startling green against that mocha complexion. Some women might have found him attractive. Lira didn't, but mostly because she knew better than to have any type of feelings for a superior besides respect.

Tomas didn't have the same scruples, and made no secret of the fact that he would have liked her to be something more than just a pilot. By that time she'd worked for him for the better part of a standard week, and knew a little more of his temperament and moods.

"You can have a pilot, or a mistress," she told him. "But not both...at least not both in the same woman."

Maybe that had been taking her life in her hands, speaking so boldly. But she found she didn't much care. Hadn't she already hit bottom, working for the sort of man who treated people's lives like trash and who she would've vigorously hunted down if she'd still been part of the GDF?

To her surprise, he'd only grinned and nodded. "Fair enough," he said. "I know I can always trust you, Lira, to speak the truth."

And she hadn't known whether to be relieved that he'd spared her, or disappointed that he hadn't ended her sad existence then and there.

So now here she sat, staring into the brandy's amber depths and wondering how long she'd hesitate this time before taking that first sip, and whether she'd be able to stop when she reached the bottom of the glass.

"Captain Jannholm."

The voice shouldn't have been familiar. After all, she'd only heard it a handful of times. But it haunted her sleep, filled her dreams...that burnished baritone with the foreign edge to its pronunciation. He couldn't be here, though. Why *would* he be here, in the ass-end of nowhere?

One part of her wanted her to stay rooted in place, to ignore him, ignore that insidious voice. She'd never run from a fight, though, and she wasn't about to start now.

Slowly, she climbed off the stool and turned to face him. She was going to do this on her own two feet, and not sitting on a barstool like the local lush.

He looked different somehow. Then she realized it was because he wore civilian clothing, the high-collared tunic and slim-fitting pants favored by the Eridanis and popular throughout civilized space. His trousers were tucked into tall boots instead of the typical sandals or low shoes. The hair was still the same, in all its barbarian glory. And the face, whose features she'd thought must have been blurred by faulty memory. But no, the face hadn't changed—those shining copper eyes, the strong nose and defiant chin.

She'd expected a rush of anger, or even hatred—after all, Rast sen Drenthan was a large part of the reason she'd ended up here on Iradia, servant to a man who thought of all life, human or otherwise, as a commodity to be traded or sold, or disposed of when no longer necessary.

What passed through her mind, however, was a single traitorous thought.

God, he's handsome.

Which was just ridiculous, because his looks shouldn't have mattered one way or the other, and since when had she even been capable of seeing a Stacian as handsome?

Self-disgust hardened her tone. "What the hell are you doing here?"

Probably not the reception he had wanted or expected, but that didn't seem to faze him. Without blinking, he replied, "Looking for you."

"Well, you found me." *And I really wish you'd done so* after *I'd had that first swig of brandy...*

"So I have." He moved a few paces closer and paused, looking around at the somewhat dubious surroundings, the sector's dregs sitting at the far end of the bar or huddled in shadowy corners. "Perhaps I should be the one asking what you're doing here."

"An overwhelming urge to get away from it all?" Her tone was brittle, but she refused to tell him the truth, that she had ended up in this miserable backwater because of him.

She turned then, hoping he would take the dismissal for what it was. Of course he didn't, but came even closer, until he was standing next to her at the bar. How could she have forgotten how tall he was, how almost physically overwhelming his presence could be?

To cover her confusion, she reached for the glass of brandy.

"I don't advise drinking alone," he said, and shifted so he addressed the barkeep, who'd been hovering at the other end of the counter and trying to act as if he weren't listening to every word they were saying. No doubt Gared Tomas would have a complete account of their exchange before nightfall. "One for me as well."

She lifted her shoulders, knowing somehow it would be pointless to tell him to go away. Maybe another woman would have been flattered that he had tracked her down so far from his own sector. Right then she just felt tired, and uncertain whether she had the energy to give him the brush-off…and, even if she could muster the strength to send him packing, whether he would be accommodating enough to comply.

What she did know was that they couldn't have any kind of meaningful conversation here. The bartender was one of Tomas's creatures, and, for all she knew, so was the young woman who wiped down the tables and served as a back-up barkeep when necessary. Asking Rast sen Drenthan to leave with her seemed like the sort of encouragement she really didn't want to give him, but she didn't have much choice.

"No need for that," she announced. "We should get going anyway." And she lifted the brandy and took it neat and fast, the way she'd learned during too many rowdy shore-leave episodes from her academy days.

Rast's copper eyes widened a bit, but then he seemed to catch her sidelong glance toward the bartender, and he nodded. "That restaurant you were telling me about..."

"The very one," she agreed, relieved that he'd picked up on the hint. "I'll show you the way."

She began to reach for her pocket to pull out some *irrads*, the local currency, to pay for her brandy, but Rast forestalled her by dropping a few copper coins on the counter. "Best get going. I'm very hungry."

Holding her tongue appeared to be the best response. In silence, she led him out of the bar and on down the street. A block away was a small courtyard that some previous inhabitant had planted with off-world flowers and ornamental shrubs, with a stone fountain in the center. It provided a quiet space to sit and think—or stand and talk, as the case might be. For some reason the Iradians mostly ignored the spot, intent on their own busy commerce, but Lira had found it to be a welcome refuge in a world she found more than a little hostile.

Iradia's orange-tinted shadows had begun to slant toward dusk. They had only an hour or so before night fell, and Gared Tomas would expect her back by then. She'd been given her liberty this afternoon, since he had no appointments until this evening, but she knew better than to be late.

"All right," she said, after they had entered the courtyard and found it to be empty, as she had hoped. "What in the galaxy are you doing here? And what makes you think I'd be remotely happy to see you?"

That did seem to take him aback. He paused, staring down at her, the black brows forming a "V" shape as he frowned. The ridges above those brows didn't move at all, however. Then his shoulders lifted. "I was worried about you."

"You were—" She broke off then, thinking she would explode into hysterical laughter if she said anything else. Worried about her? That was rich. Too bad he hadn't been so worried about what might happen to her when that squad of five Stacian cruisers showed up in the Chlorae system to engage the Gaian forces there. "No, really, why are you here? Making sure the disgraced captain stays safely out of the way? Or did you realize you'd better make sure I kept silent so I would never reveal what happened between us? I can't imagine your commanding officers would be too thrilled by the information. I know mine weren't."

Again he was silent. Thinking of the best lie to hand her, probably.

After a long moment, he said, "Is this really what you think of me? That I meant to deliberately disgrace you? That I was a party to the murder of innocent colonists?"

Surely he couldn't be that obtuse, or believe her to be that stupid. "What else? Oh, maybe it was a calculated risk, a gamble to see whether my superiors would recall me from my post so the way would be clear for a

Stacian incursion, but it all worked out very neatly for you, didn't it?"

"Precisely," he cut in. He glanced around, as if to make sure the area was clear of listening ears or spying eyes. Even though they were alone, with only the background noise of passing traffic and the rustling of the cycads planted in the courtyard to keep them company, he lowered his tone. "It was too neat. And it was none of my doing."

"Whose doing was it?"

Again he paused. "I wanted to see you because I feared you would think I somehow plotted your downfall. Lira, I did not. I swear this to you on the bones of my ancestors."

A strong oath for a Stacian. The strongest, perhaps, although Stacian cultural studies were not her area of expertise. She forced a dusty little chuckle. "Then what? Just horrible luck?"

"No." He reached out and took her hands in his, fingers strong and warm around hers. And although her first instinct was to pull back, to step away from any contact with him, something in his eyes stopped her, something pleading and fierce. "I thought about this, Lira. I thought a good deal. We were maneuvered, you and I, although you came off the worst for it. I knew nothing about those five cruisers lying in wait—I swear this to you also. But my admiral certainly did...and possibly yours did as well."

She stared at him. That didn't make any sense. Why would Admiral Horner collude with the Stacians to destroy his own people, to make sure

Chlorae II and its valuable resources fell into enemy hands?

It had to be Iradia's dust that made her mouth and throat suddenly so dry. "That's ridiculous."

"I thought so as well—at first. But think, Lira. My superior officer makes a wager with me that I can't refuse. The fallout from that wager is your removal from command. And the consequence of that removal is Chlorae II left undefended, and easy prey for the Stacian squadron that just happened to be in the vicinity. Too many coincidences, don't you think?"

Only one word seemed to penetrate her brain. "Wager?" she demanded, and abruptly pulled her hands from his. "That's why you asked me to come to you? For a goddamn *bet*?"

His mouth tightened. "Such a thing has far greater weight with us Stacians. We—"

"Fuck the Stacians," she said clearly. "And fuck you, too."

She wheeled away from him, thinking it was a good thing the officials in Aldis Nova didn't allow civilians to carry sidearms. Not that the stricture affected Gared Tomas and his thugs, but she didn't need to go armed. Everyone knew who she worked for.

Before she had gone a single foot, Rast reached out and grasped her by the sleeve of her jacket and pulled her back toward him. Instinctively, she jerked backward, preparing to pivot and slip out of the garment as she'd been taught in her self-defense training, but he seemed to have predicted her movements. He caught her other arm in his free hand, fingers like steel digging into her flesh.

"Anger I can understand," he said. "I respect your anger, Lira Jannholm. But what began as a wager became much more. Do you think I would have traveled halfway across the galaxy for a woman I had only been with once if I thought of her merely as a pawn in a bet? Do you believe I would have relinquished a prestigious post in my own fleet for a trifle? There is something between us, and you know it. Don't bother to deny it."

She forced herself to remain still. With another man, she might have attempted a swift kick to the privates, but Rast had shown himself to be faster than she. No real surprise, as she had only the basic self-defense training everyone in the GDF received, while he had learned to fight in the harshest proving grounds of all, the sands of his home world. Knowing he outmatched her physically didn't prevent her from retorting, "I do deny it. You're crazy if you think there's anything between us, that there ever *could* be anything—"

"I see I must prove you wrong," he told her, and then, so swiftly she didn't have time to react, pulled her against him, smothered her mouth in his.

The taste of him swirled through her senses, that spicy flavor which found its echo in his hair and his skin and his clothing. It would have been easy to surrender to it, to forget her outrage, but weeks of bitterness and disappointment could not be abandoned quite so quickly.

She tore away, breaking the kiss, moving fast enough that his hands lost his purchase on her arms. "Don't ever do that again."

"Kiss you?" he inquired, his tone one of silky innocence. "But it's such a pleasant prelude to even more interesting things."

Her body remembered those things all too well, even if her mind wanted to forget them. As for the rest —well, she couldn't allow herself to believe anything he said. There might be a few things that would drive a man to travel parsecs to find a woman, but she had a difficult time believing love...or lust...was one of them.

She forced herself to focus on his earlier comment. "So it's your belief that the whole thing was a setup so the *Valiant* would be removed from the Chlorae system."

If he was disappointed in her for guiding the conversation away from the personal, he didn't show it. "Yes, that's what I think. And if that's true, then there had to be forces at work on both sides to make sure everything went smoothly."

"That's one way of putting it." Lira glanced around once more, but no one seemed to be at all interested in their little tête-à-tête, or in entering the courtyard at all. "So why?"

"I don't know yet. But I'm going to find out. And I want you to help me."

His tone was calm, reasonable. But he couldn't be serious. He didn't really expect her to drop everything and go off on some wild goose chase, did he?

On the other hand, if there were any chance of

proving that Admiral Horner had acted treasonously, had discharged her with impunity just to get her out of the way, then she'd be an idiot to let such an opportunity pass her by. Such proof would be enough to get her command back. Maybe not of the *Valiant*, but some other ship of the line. And that would be good enough for her.

"If I agree," she replied, speaking slowly so he couldn't possibly mistake her meaning, "it's just business. Got it? If these bastards really did frame me, then I want them caught and punished, but that's my only reason for working with you."

He nodded, although his jaw looked a little tense. "I understand." A small pause, and he added, "I have no idea where this investigation will take us, but I do know that it would be best if we had our own ship. Too easy to trace our movements if we have to book passage on a commercial ship, the way I did coming here."

That made sense, although a shiver of unease worked its way down her spine as she considered his words. The sort of ship he had in mind couldn't exactly be picked up at a corner used transport lot. No, very few people had access to a ship small enough for two people to crew and yet with the subspace drive capabilities necessary to hop from star system to star system.

A note of warning entered her voice. "I hope you have a ship in mind."

"Oh, I do," he said cheerfully. "I want you to steal the *Mistral*."

All things considered, she took his suggestion rather well. For a few seconds she merely stared up at him, blue eyes narrowed slightly. Then she crossed her arms and remarked, "Oh, is that all?"

"Yes, that's all."

Her mouth pursed. He doubted she did so only to distract him, but because he could still feel the pressure of her lips against his, he had to make an actual physical effort to listen to her next words...which were far from flattering.

"You're insane. Do you have any idea exactly who Gared Tomas is, what he's capable of? I've got enough problems without having someone like Tomas out for my blood."

He'd expected such a reaction, and had his arguments ready. "It is true that this Gared Tomas is no one to trifle with...for a Gaian, at any rate. But the *Mistral* is the only Sirocco-class ship on Iradia, correct?"

"Yes," she replied grudgingly.

"So, if his best and fastest ship is stolen, what exactly will he use to pursue us?"

"I'm guessing he could call in a few favors."

"But not before we'd already left the system."

"Probably not."

She didn't like it, of course. He read her reluctance in the frown that tugged at her brow, in the way she crossed her arms as she thought it over. But he didn't need her to love his plan, only recognize that it was a necessary step in achieving her goal of discrediting Admiral Horner.

Rast would never admit it, but he didn't altogether

like the plan, either. However, he also knew they needed a fast ship, and one they could fly on their own without having to rely on easily traceable commercial starships or the chancy assistance of a chartered freighter. They might get someone trustworthy to take them wherever they needed to go...or they might not.

Upon his arrival on Iradia, he'd spent some time learning what he could about Gared Tomas. A nasty customer, but one whose reach didn't extend far from the Iradian system. Rast guessed that once he and Lira were safely away in the *Mistral* and headed toward Gaian space, Tomas probably couldn't do all that much to catch up with them. Of course, they wouldn't dare to show their faces in this sector again, but that was no great loss.

The concept of the theft itself didn't bother Rast overmuch. Gared Tomas traded in misery, human and otherwise, and the *Mistral* had been purchased with the profits from his peddling in drug trafficking, extortion, and a list of other crimes too lengthy to recount in full. Taking the ship from such an individual seemed almost the noble thing to do. The man certainly didn't deserve such a fine vessel.

"How many men are there when you go to perform your preflight checks?" Rast asked.

"Two, usually. Mingus—he's one of Tomas's bodyguards—and most of the time Istafa Morain, Tomas's right-hand man. Sometimes Morain doesn't accompany his boss off-planet, but we can't count on that." She sounded resigned, as if she knew she'd just committed to an insane scheme but didn't quite know how to back out of it.

"And how long before Tomas actually comes on board?"

"About a quarter-hour, give or take."

Plenty of time for them to eliminate the bodyguard and the lackey and be on their way. "This Mingus. He's big?"

Lira turned a look of not-quite scorn on him. "He's Gared Tomas's bodyguard. What do you think?"

"But I should be able to take him." Rast didn't see much difficulty; after all, even an average-sized Stacian was larger than most Gaian males, and he was big for a Stacian.

"If you get the drop on him," she allowed with a shrug. "Yes, he's Gaian, but he's got to be almost seven feet tall. We're not all shrimps like me, you know."

"Oh, I plan to," he replied, and rested a hand on the pulse pistol he wore concealed under his long jacket. With any luck, the bodyguard wouldn't even see Rast before he shot the Gaian in the back. No worries about honor here; Lira had already made it abundantly clear that they weren't dealing with a couple of upstanding citizens. Besides, the men in question were Gaian, not deserving of the considerations he might extend to a member of his own race.

He didn't stop to decipher why he no longer considered Lira Jannholm a member of that group.

CHAPTER SIX

SHE'D DONE A FEW CRAZY THINGS SINCE BEING FORCED from the GDF, but this definitely topped them all. Rast seemed blissfully unconcerned about the repercussions of stealing a spaceship from the planet's most powerful crime lord, but Lira couldn't be quite that zen about the situation. Yes, it was true that part of Gared Tomas's success lay in consolidating his power on Iradia and one of its attendant moons, but that didn't mean he couldn't call in a few favors if necessary.

Worry about that later, she told herself. *You're not even on board yet.*

True, some might call Tomas arrogant for having so few men guarding his ship. On the other hand, most people knew better than to even look at the boss cross-eyed, let alone attempt something as insane as trying to steal the *Mistral*. Also, he made sure the ship was a moving target, berthing it at various locations both in and out of Aldis Nova. Even Lira never knew until the day of a trip exactly where she would be climbing up the gangway into the sleek little ship. Morain knew enough to get the ship to lift off, achieve suborbital altitude, and guide it into that day's hidey-hole, but he lacked the training to manage the life-support systems necessary for extra-orbital flight, or the knowledge of how to set up the ship's computer to safely guide it from the planet to its moon and back again.

So Tomas operated on the concept that the fewer who knew about where he or his ship were at any given time, the better. As she'd sat in the bar earlier that afternoon, he'd sent the code to her handheld to let her know where she was headed. *Sundowner*, which meant the berth on the western outskirts of Aldis Nova, in a mean area given over to warehouses and a few factories where the moon-moth silk was dyed and prepared for shipment off-world. Its location meant that most of the stink from the dye factories would be blown westward, away from town, given the region's prevailing winds.

She wrinkled her nose now as she approached the ship's docking pad, an abandoned warehouse with the roof conveniently blown off in some long-ago skirmish between crime lords. There wasn't much wind today, and the acrid scent from the factories seemed to have settled on the area like a stinking cloak, burning at the back of her throat.

Rast had said nothing about what he planned, only that she should go in and approach the ship just as she always did. "Best to give them no reason to suspect you," he'd told her. "Besides, you've worked with these men. I don't want any hesitation because you know them and may lose your nerve over some imagined connection."

She'd wanted to argue, but deep down she knew he might be right. Both Mingus and Istafa Morain were hideous excuses for human beings, no doubt about that, and usually she would have said she'd have no problem putting a pulse bolt between their eyes. However, she'd also seen fellow crew members freeze in combat for no apparent reason, and she knew she couldn't risk such a thing now. Not when they only had this one chance.

So she walked calmly toward the entrance to the warehouse, hands out where the currently hidden Mingus and Morain could see them. No doubt they were scanning her, too, and for that reason she went unarmed just as she always had. Aldis Nova was a rough town, the roughest she'd ever seen, but she probably could have walked naked down its streets and not encountered any difficulty. That was the surety of Gared Tomas's protection.

"Hold," came Morain's voice, and she paused just outside the doorway.

Then the door slid open, and Mingus came out, looming over her as he always did, watching her with a leering expression that seemed to tell her exactly what he would like to do to her, if she weren't Tomas's pilot. And as always she stared ahead, not allowing him to see how he disturbed her.

Morain followed, elegant and spare. She found herself wondering how a man like him had ended up here on Iradia in the first place. Not that it mattered how he got here.

What mattered was that he was going to die here.

"All clear," said Mingus, and Istafa Morain nodded.

"Go on," the lavender-skinned man told Lira. "She's all yours."

"Got it," she replied, about the only response she would allow herself in that moment. *All right, Rast... now or never.*

The thought had barely crossed her mind before an orange-red pulse bolt flashed from somewhere above them, striking Mingus directly in the chest. He crumpled to his feet as Lira let out what she hoped was a convincing little yelp and darted forward past Morain, into the interior of the warehouse where the *Mistral* waited. The half-Eridani already had his own gun out, but he ignored Lira, obviously thinking she was only trying to get to the safety of the ship and away from their unseen attackers.

An exchange of pulse shots echoed behind her, but she didn't dare look back, only pounded forward to the ship, which awaited its passengers with the door open and the narrow little gangplank extended to the shabby floor of the warehouse. Everything depended on getting the *Mistral* ready for immediate takeoff, as there was no guarantee Morain wouldn't call for reinforcements before Rast took him out.

The ship was approximately thirty meters long, with the entrance located in the center of the passenger compartment. Lira hurried past the heavily padded seats and their matching low tables, and on into the cockpit. Even though she was its sole pilot, the *Mistral* had been designed to accommodate a copilot as well. She ignored that seat and slid into the one that had become her home for the past few weeks. First to reach under the copilot's seat, locating the device Tomas didn't think she knew about, and yank the wire that connected it to the ship's propulsion system. Then it was on to flipping switches, tapping the commands into the nav-computer that would send them out of the Iradian system altogether, into a neutral location a few parsecs outside the uninhabited Corael system where they could stop to catch their breaths and figure out what they were going to do next.

If, of course, Rast managed to kill Istafa Morain. The man was cagey, no matter what sen Drenthan might feel about the relative battle prowess of Gaians, or half-Gaians, in Morain's case. And if the Stacian had somehow met his match...well, she'd just have to do some damn quick reprogramming before anyone noticed the nav-computer wasn't set for a quick jaunt to one of Iradia's moons.

Heavy footsteps sounded behind her, and she forced herself not to look back, to keep working away as if she fully expected Morain to come in and tell her everything was fine and that Tomas would be along in a few minutes.

Rast fell into the seat next to her, dropped a satchel made of some unfamiliar hide on the floor, and flashed her a ferocious grin. "Ready? Because I believe a quick getaway is our best option right now."

She had to ignore the relief that flooded through

her, concentrate instead on getting the last of the coordinates programmed in. "Just about. So Morain didn't give you any trouble?"

"The half-breed?" He gave a snort of contempt. "Hardly. You'd think someone like Gared Tomas would choose a better shot for his right-hand man. But I'm guessing our little firefight drew some attention...and the dead bodies will draw rather more."

"Around here?" she scoffed, then amended, "Well, if it were anyone except a couple of Tomas's goons, no one would bat an eye, but..."

"That's what worries me."

"No need to worry." The nav-computer let out a chime, informing her that its calculations were complete. "We're out of here."

And she pulled back on the ignition lever, feeling the atmospheric propulsion system kick in, the ship vibrating ever so slightly beneath them. She pushed it further, and they shot straight up, through the shattered roof of the warehouse, lifting away from Aldis Nova, its dusty streets and shabby buildings spreading out beneath them, all painted orange and red with the colors of sunset. Farther still, and the city shrank to nothing, swallowed up by miles of ochre desert, until the desert itself became the color of the planet's flat disc, and black space surrounded them on every side.

Still without speaking, she urged the *Mistral* forward, hurrying them away from the gravity well of the planet and its accompanying moons, sending them into open space where she could safely engage the subspace drive. Only after the odd flickering colors of subspace had surrounded them, and she knew they were safe from pursuit, did she turn to Rast.

"Well, you've got your ship," she said. "What next?"

———

He enjoyed watching her fly, watching her slender fingers work the controls, her fine profile to him as she stared out the viewscreen and into the onrushing heavens. "Where are we headed?"

"Next system over, but I figured we had to go somewhere before I could plot our final destination. Tomas would never suspect us of stopping so close to Iradia, and anyway, it's pretty dead space around there. We can hang for a while and decide on our next course of action."

"And Tomas doesn't have any way of tracking us?" Rast found this a little difficult to believe; if he'd owned a fine ship like this, he would have made sure it had some sort of tracking device secreted away on it.

"He did," she admitted. "You're sitting on it."

"I'm what?" he demanded, halfway lifting himself off the seat before he realized the harness would keep him from getting very far. In exasperation, he began to undo the buckles.

"Relax." Her voice held some of the first amusement he'd yet heard from her. "He had a tracker installed there, but I located it early on. It's deactivated. But I also need to hack into the computer and change the

Mistral's I.D. signature and registry. Otherwise, they'll still be able to find us eventually."

Now free of the harness, Rast shifted in his seat so he could see her better. A small smile was playing about her full lips. "You can do that? Fine upstanding GDF captain that you are?"

"*Former* captain," she reminded him, with only a faint edge to her voice. "No, it's not something they exactly taught us at the academy, but a friend of mine showed me a few tricks back in the day."

"A friend," Rast said. He wasn't sure he liked the sound of that. Generally, those sorts of friends turned out to be a bit more than friends.

"All right, a former boyfriend. From my brief rebellious stage."

Rast crossed his arms, waiting to hear the rest. At least, he assumed there was a rest.

"In fact, he might be the best person to help us now," Lira continued. She didn't give any indication of noticing that her words had sparked a reaction in Rast, but perhaps she didn't much care. "Jackson Wyler. I met him my first year at the academy, but he didn't last long. Not much of one for rules, Jackson."

"Indeed."

"Indeed," she repeated, and this time she had a distinct glint in her blue eyes. "He decided that hacking computers was much more fun than taking orders, so he dropped out. But we kept in touch...that is, he kept in touch with me. He seemed to genuinely enjoy tracking me down wherever I ended up, sending me little notes, that sort of thing. It was more a game for him than anything else."

"Hmm," said Rast. He'd meant it to come out as a more or less noncommittal grunt, but what emerged from his throat sounded a bit too much like a growl.

"At any rate," she continued, "since I have a pretty short list of questionable people who might be able to help us down the road to discovering who's maneuvering behind the scenes, I can't think of anyone better than Jackson to provide some assistance. Unless you've got some hacker contacts you haven't told me about."

Of course Rast didn't. While he knew the Stacian military employed its own versions of what the Gaians referred to as "hackers," his people did not find the same perverse joy in those sorts of activities as some Gaians seemed to. Sneaking around, searching for vulnerabilities in code, devising underhanded ways to suborn computer networks...none of that was anything close to what a Stacian would regard as honorable behavior.

However, he also knew that in their current situation, he and Lira would have to enlist the help of someone with that sort of background, or their investigation would be effectively ended before it had even begun. So he said, with a good deal of reluctance, "And where can we find this Jackson Wyler?"

"He likes to play at being respectable," she replied.

That didn't sound terribly promising. "Yes?"

"So right now he's living on New Chicago."

Rast tried not to groan. New Chicago. Only one of Gaia's oldest and most settled colonies. Short of flying the *Mistral* straight through to Gaia itself, he couldn't think of a worse place for a Stacian to be headed. He would stick out there like that strange aquatic creature known as a whale might if it were dropped in the middle of a Stacian desert. But there was no help for it. To New Chicago they must go.

And the gods help him if the GDF discovered an enemy combatant right in their midst...

Stacians couldn't exactly go green, given the ruddy-gold hues of their complexions, but Lira could tell from Rast's reaction that he was less than thrilled about heading to New Chicago. He'd probably be even less thrilled after she told him he'd have to remain aboard the ship while she went to go see Jackson, but really, they didn't have many options. Maybe someone in MI7 might have been able to come up with a way to effectively disguise Rast sen Drenthan so he'd blend in with a population that was mostly Gaian, but short of cutting off all his hair, covering him in body makeup, and hoping no one would notice the ridges on his brows, Lira couldn't quite think how. And she had a feeling that anyone who made a move to cut off those luxurious falls of dread-locked hair would find their own throat cut in short order.

After a brief stop in the Corael system, just long enough to program in the new route, the *Mistral* continued on to New Chicago, which would take the better part of a standard day. Just as well, because she had work to do.

First a hack into the ship's computer, following the logic path that led her to the subroutine that stored the transponder codes and the registry information. Once inside, she changed the starship's name to *Chinook* and gave her registry as Jordarian. That was far enough off the beaten track that no one was probably going to investigate too closely; on the other hand, Jordares was known for its rich mineral deposits, and so no one would question an expensive ship like the *Mistral*...that is, the *Chinook*...coming from such a home base.

As she worked, she was conscious of Rast's gaze on her, copper eyes keen, blinking just slightly less often than a Gaian would. His physical presence was more than a little distracting, but she couldn't allow herself to get sidetracked.

And maybe at some point she'd have time to really stop and think about what she'd done, about how she'd allowed herself to become a fugitive, trapped in this ship with a man who should have been her enemy... and yet, strangely, was not.

Crazy as it might sound, she thought she trusted Rast sen Drenthan. He'd said very little of how he'd managed to track her down, but she knew he must have walked away from a prestigious post in order to come on an insane mission that might never yield any useful fruit. He'd told her he wanted to know the truth about his superior officer's actions, and she believed him.

However, one reason didn't necessarily preclude

another, more personal motivation. He didn't try to hide the fact that he was watching her. From time to time, their eyes would meet, and a small shiver would go through her. Memories of him had been overwhelming enough. His physical presence, in the tight confines of the Sirocco-class ship, was something else altogether.

Time enough to worry about that later. In a few hours they'd be in New Chicago, and she'd be facing Jackson Wyler, a man she hadn't seen in person for more than ten years. She'd never flattered herself that his occasional notes and vids meant anything except proving his cleverness, his ability to find her wherever she was posted, even if said posting was classified. Even when she had been orbiting Chlorae II, a planet few people even knew existed, those cheery little notes would surface from time to time, inquiring as to her health, inviting her to pop in for a drink if she were ever in the neighborhood.

Well, she was in the neighborhood now...

———

"So you expect me to sit here and cool my heels like some underage *trenth*, some useless appendage?"

Part of Rast's outrage probably stemmed from the realization that he should have guessed she would propose such a thing. A Stacian could not walk down the streets of New Chicago's largest city and not expect to attract some attention. Whereas Lira, though of course lovely enough to draw notice wherever she went, was typically Gaian in appearance, and her slim dark gray pants and short blue jacket were plain enough that they would not have stood out on any of the Gaian Consortium worlds.

She appeared coolly unconcerned by his apparent anger. "Actually, yes, I do. Jackson knows me, not you. He's not going to let some unknown Stacian march into his house—if we could even get you there without drawing down every police officer within a kilometer's radius. Or have you forgotten that the Gaian Consortium and the Stacian Federation are at war?"

"Not technically," he replied, and wished he didn't sound quite so much like a sulky adolescent.

"Technically, no, but for all intents and purposes..."

"I know." He wished he could reach out to her, take her hands in his, but he guessed from her brisk no-nonsense manner that this was not the time for such things. Later, perhaps. He had no idea where their quest would take them, but he hoped the journey might be a lengthy one, so he would have plenty of time to soften that flinty exterior. Hardening his own voice, he said, "And you trust this Jackson Wyler?"

"'Trust'?" she repeated, and lifted her shoulders. "Trust is a strong word. I wouldn't say he's a particularly trustworthy person. On the other hand, I think he'll find it amusing to provide some assistance, especially since the parties involved are high-ranking members of the Stacian and Gaian militaries. Those are the sorts of people Jackson would just love to see brought low. So I think he'll help me...and I don't think he'll tell anyone else."

"But you don't know for sure."

A smile then, brittle as the ice crystals that some-times formed on a ship's viewscreen as it re-entered atmosphere. "If I've learned anything so far, Rast, it's that nothing in this life is for sure."

And with that she walked out of the cockpit, heading for her assignation with this Jackson Wyler.

It felt strange to be walking the streets of a large city again. The Gaian Defense Fleet Academy she'd attended had been on the outskirts of Rilsin, the biggest city on New Chicago's sister planet of Nova Angeles, but after she'd graduated, Lira hadn't spent much time in population centers. Aldis Nova was big enough in its own way, but Michende here on New Chicago could have swallowed the Iradian town in one of its suburbs.

Of course Jackson hadn't responded to the news that she was here with anything more than an expression of simple pleasure and eagerness to see her again. With that he'd transmitted his home's coordinates to her handheld, which auto-matically plotted the best route from the spaceport to her journey's endpoint, providing helpful suggestions for which airbuses to take and offering to subtract the cost of the fares from her credit balance.

She knew better than to do that, of course; such

transactions would immediately alert anyone who was looking for her as to her current whereabouts. No, she always carried some cash with her, mainly because it had turned into a habit during her academy days, and partly because most people on Aldis Nova didn't want to engage in any commerce that didn't involve hard currency.

All around her were people involved in their own affairs, heading to work, heading home from work, taking a break for the midday meal. A place as big as Michende never stopped, its streets filled twenty-two hours a day. At first Lira felt self-conscious as she moved among them, certain that something about her dress or her person proclaimed that she shouldn't be here. Soon enough, though, she realized that none of these intent, hurrying people cared the slightest bit about who she was or why she was here. In that she found something strangely reassuring.

A little more than a standard half-hour after she left the spaceport, she arrived at Jackson's building. It was located in a well-kept, high-end part of town, with skyscrapers of permaglass towering on all sides and carefully tended planters of both native and alien flora growing in the medians of the streets and in boxes along the sidewalks. Typical of Jackson to carry on his dubious business in such a respectable neighborhood.

The door opened as she approached it, and a mech stepped aside, saying, "He awaits you in the penthouse, Ms. Jannholm."

How ostentatious, to have a mech playing doorman. But she only nodded and went on to the lifts, noting that one waited for her. Once she was inside, it shot upward immediately, without her having to voice her destination or press any buttons.

Trying to impress me, Jackson?

Making sure she wore her best poker face, she exited the lift on the fifteenth floor and found herself in an expansive foyer, decked out in expensive Menari travertine and with orchids she thought might have come all the way from Gaia blooming in spare black glass pots set on carefully arranged low columns of more travertine. Directly ahead of her was a door. It opened as she stepped forward, and Jackson Wyler came out to greet her.

"My dear Lira," he said, spreading one hand back toward the apartment from which he'd just emerged. "Come in. So glad to see you!"

"It's nice to see you, too," she said, wondering what exactly his game was. Not that they'd split up under exactly acrimonious circumstances, but still, this sort of effusiveness wasn't the sort of thing she expected from an ex-boyfriend. Yes, that seemed the proper term. They'd been physically intimate, of course, but neither one of them had had much idea what they were doing. Unlike Rast sen Drenthan.

A mental head shake then, even as she almost found herself wishing she'd brought a sidearm, but that was just foolish. You couldn't go two steps on New Chicago carrying a gun without the scanners picking up on it and sending out the alarm to every law enforcement officer in the immediate vicinity. If a frontier world like Iradia let you walk around the streets with a pistol strapped to your belt, fine—after all, what else could you expect from places like that?—but they did things differently on New Chicago.

"Looks like you're doing pretty well for yourself," she commented, after taking a brief glance around the room and noting the expensive low couches of real leather, the floor of some kind of pale wood, the vertigo-inducing views of Michende from the floor-to-ceiling windows.

"I do all right," he allowed, moving toward a table that held a pitcher of some pale green fizzy liquid and a couple of glasses. "Mileni mineral water?"

"Sure." At least he wasn't trying to get her drunk. That was a good sign...wasn't it?

Lira approached him after he'd poured the water and took the proffered glass from his hand. Even though ten years had passed since she'd last seen him in person, he didn't seem all that changed. Maybe a little broader through the shoulders and midsection, the even features more defined. A man now, definitely not a boy. But the piercing green eyes were the same, and the shock of blond air, artfully styled to fall into his face in a calculatedly careless manner.

In her mind's eye she saw Rast, black hair pulled severely back from his face, bound in its barbaric rings of copper and gold. It was a style that did not forgive, but his features needed no softening, no tricks of the stylist to make them more attractive. She wondered then what he would think of Jackson Wyler and decided she really didn't want to know.

"So..." Jackson began, and then paused, studying

her. "Your message was customarily oblique, but I gather you're in need of some assistance?"

"You could say that." She swallowed some of the mineral water, feeling it fizz against her tongue and throat, leaving behind a mild aftertaste of lemon and mint. "I suppose you heard what happened."

The green eyes had an amused glint. "I did. I have to say I was a little surprised."

"Only a little?"

"All right, more than a little." He drank from his own glass of water, then set it down. "A Stacian, Lira? I had no idea your tastes were that...exotic. No wonder you dumped me like a ship dropping its wastewater before it enters orbit."

"As I recall, you were the one who did the dumping. Anyway, it's...complicated."

"I figured it must be. So what's the real story?"

Although she didn't much care to go over the whole sordid thing again, she knew she'd have to give Jackson enough details that he'd know she wasn't holding out on him. His main love was information, so information she'd give him. In cool, terse sentences she outlined what had happened in the Chlorae system, and how she'd been summarily discharged for her actions.

"The thing is," she went on, "Rast and I are almost certain the whole thing was engineered, which means that Admiral sen Trannick and possibly Admiral Horner conspired to make sure that Chlorae II was left undefended. I don't know why, or how, but I figured you would be the best person to get to the bottom of it."

"I'm flattered," Jackson replied, but his eyes

narrowed slightly. "'Rast,' eh? So you two are on a first-name basis now?"

"We're working together, if that's what you mean."

"And what does he get out of all this?"

She blinked. "The truth."

"Ah."

Which could have meant anything at all. After a pause of a second or two, which she guessed he did deliberately to put her somewhat off balance, he went to the computer console at the far end of the room. Like everything else in the place, it was state-of-the-art, with an array of flat screens, heads-up displays, and even holographic projectors. God knows what multi-terabyte monsters those sleek displays and graphite keyboards were hooked up to. At the moment, though, all she cared about was that they would be powerful enough to cut through whatever layers of obfuscation Admiral sen Trannick and Admiral Horner might have put in their way.

"Let's start with the easy part," Jackson said, cracking his fingers. Lira tried not to wince. He'd done that back in the academy, too. It hadn't gotten any more tolerable over the intervening years.

"Easy part?"

"We'll start with Horner. I haven't had as much experience hacking into Stacian systems, but I could probably crack the GDF's algorithms in my sleep. Here we go."

And he began typing away in a brisk staccato, as the screens around him flashed with numbers and symbols, only to fade away into more complex arrangements of numerals, information ebbing and flowing as he drove down into fleet manifests and appointment calendars and financial records, not so much hacking as gently unwinding one bit of data from another, swirling down to a place where he could find the pertinent pieces. Lira watched as he worked, and sipped at her mineral water, and tried not to compare Jackson's pale, soft-looking fingers with Rast sen Drenthan's capable golden-skinned ones.

"Hmm," Jackson said finally, and pushed his chair away from the keyboard. Although he hadn't drunk anything the entire time he'd been working, at this point he did reach out to retrieve his neglected glass of mineral water, which he drained in one gulp.

"So what does 'hmm' mean?"

"It means I can't find anything. Not one frigging thing. The admiral has even paid all his energy bills on time. Not even a demerit from his time at the academy."

"So..."

"So, nothing. The guy's so clean I'm surprised he doesn't squeak when he walks."

"Well, hell," Lira said, trying not to let the disappointment show too clearly in her tone. It would have been so easy if Horner were the dirty one. Well, maybe not easy, precisely, but at least this all would have started to make a little sense.

"Not to worry, dear Lira." Jackson cracked his fingers again. "This just gives me a chance to test my mettle. I'm not sure how long it's going to take, though..."

"That's fine," she replied automatically. This was

what they'd come to New Chicago for, after all. She'd wait as long as necessary.

"Then you might want to amuse yourself with the local broadcasts. I don't do well with an audience when I have to really go at it with a hacksaw."

She found that difficult to believe, considering Jackson's appetite for attention, but only shrugged and wandered back out into the living room, where she found the remote for a vidscreen that covered most of one wall, and turned the receiver on. Quickly she brought the sound down to barely above a whisper, so it wouldn't disturb Jackson at his work.

And although she really didn't care about the local elections in Michende, or the new plan to upgrade the city's airbuses, she made herself focus on the screen and not the rapid-fire typing she heard emanating from the alcove where Jackson was working. Even so, her thoughts wandered, back to the *Mistral/Chinook*, and the man who waited for her there.

She wondered what he was up to.

CHAPTER SEVEN

WHILE HE UNDERSTOOD THE LOGIC OF STAYING BEHIND, Rast didn't like it. He didn't like it at all.

Small as it was, the ship seemed to echo with Lira's absence. He wandered out into the main passenger compartment, lip curled a little at the overstuffed couches and their accompanying tables, the whole setup designed to look like some rich man's living quarters and not the interior of a spaceship. Then he had to shake his head at himself. Wasn't that exactly what Stacians did with their own ships? To be fair, that was only with their personal quarters. The common areas were utilitarian enough, though still probably indulgent by Gaian standards, with their warm-toned floor coverings and wall panels.

Driven by some impulse, he moved through the passenger compartment and on down the small corridor that separated the ship's two sleeping chambers. One was bigger than the other, taking up the rest of that side of the ship, while the other was half its size, the other half occupied by the bathroom—which actually had a real shower stall and not just a chemical scrub unit.

The smaller bedroom looked as if it had never been used, and contained only a narrow cot and an equally narrow table with a mean little chair that was bolted to the floor. The main bedroom, though...

Rast's eyes narrowed as he looked on what had obviously been Gared Tomas's own sleeping quarters. Here was luxury to rival a Stacian captain's cabin, with a large bed covered in quilts and sheets of Iradian moon-moth silk, a fur rug on the floor, hangings of more silk on the walls. A cozy table and two chairs somehow fit into one corner. Just the sort of place for Tomas to indulge his legendary tastes, even while traveling on business.

And were you to his taste, Lira? Rast wondered, then tried to tell himself that was ridiculous. After all, she would have to be truly desperate to slide into bed with a man such as Gared Tomas...

How desperate was she when she slept with you?

Good question. That was different, though. She had been trying to ensure the safety of the scientists on Chlorae II, whereas with Tomas it would have been a simple matter of self-preservation. Although, come to think of it, that was a far stronger drive than altruism...

No. He wouldn't let himself think of that. Best to get out of here, so he could avoid any further mental images of her wrapped in the crime lord's arms, and nightmarish visions of him pounding into her, taking her here on the silk-covered bed.

Rast drove a fist into the doorframe and swore, then turned and headed back to the cockpit. He needed to stop being such a fool. For one thing, he had absolutely zero evidence that Lira's relationship with Gared Tomas had been anything but professional. This jealousy was stupid. Yes, Rast had spent a night with her that made him want nothing else save her flesh, her taste, but that gave him no claim on her. She had made no promises, spoken no words of love. She had done what she thought she had to do, and left.

And now...well, now she was all business again. He flattered himself to think that perhaps he had seen something in her eyes from time to time, just a hint of attraction, or interest. But that could all very well be fancies born of his need for her. Until he had far more concrete encouragement, he would have to hold himself back. Somehow he knew that an ardent pursuit would only drive her away, perhaps forever. And that would make this whole crazy venture a supreme waste of time.

Speaking of which...

He glanced down at the chronometer on the instrument panel and realized she'd been gone for almost two hours. True, she'd said she had no idea how long any of this would take, but waiting was not a Stacian's strong point. His people were more action-oriented.

And this man she was reaching out to, this Jackson Wyler. How reliable was he? An ex-lover, and possibly one who might wish to rekindle that relationship, or at the very least ask for certain favors in return for his assistance.

No, Rast told himself. *You are letting this woman drive you to distraction. Soon you will think every humanoid male between twenty and fifty standard is a potential mate for her, and then you will be fit for nothing. Think like a warrior, not a lovesick* resinth.

Very well, then—a planet rich with a mineral every government in the galaxy needed. A captain removed from duty, leaving that planet unprotected and ripe for the taking. His people had come out on top in this scenario, but why? Chlorae would not have fallen to the Stacians if Captain Lira Jannholm had remained in position above the planet. Rast put very little past Admiral sen Trannick; his hatred of the Gaians was well known. But what was in it for Horner? How much would he have to be paid to allow his government's enemies to take control of a world his own people needed so badly?

Rast didn't know...he could only hope that when Lira returned, she might have the answers to at least some of these questions.

———

"Shit-fuck-damn," Jackson said distinctly, and Lira sat upright on the couch, then pushed the "mute" button on the remote.

"What is it?"

"Come here."

So she stood and went over to where he was working, but the screens all around him showed nothing that looked remotely recognizable to her. Strings of numbers ebbed and flowed, twisting in and around themselves like some sort of brain-bending light sculpture.

"What is it?" she asked, after staring at the displays for a few seconds. "Remember, I'm but a lowly ex-ship's captain. This sort of thing is kind of above my pay grade."

Jackson settled back in his leather-upholstered office chair and let out an exasperated breath. Clearly, whatever he'd been working on had had some sort of effect—his carefully arranged hair was now standing on end in various spots, as if he'd run irritated fingers through it while hacking away at Admiral sen Trannick's records.

Suddenly, he jabbed an index finger at his keyboard, and all the screens went black. "Didn't want to look at that anymore," he said, in cheerful tones that belied the expression of supreme annoyance on his face. "I don't know what your Stacian admiral is up to, but it's obvious that it's something he really doesn't want anyone to discover. Everything to do with his financial records is guarded by a hydra."

"A what?"

"A hydra. A mythical beast with multiple heads. In hacker parlance, though, it means continually shifting code. Every time I try to penetrate it, hack into a section, it generates new code using a different algorithm altogether. I can't pin it down. It's like trying to wrestle a greased Iradian sand-snake."

That didn't sound good at all. No wonder Jackson had resorted to invective, which he rarely used, saying that swearing was a sign of an unoriginal mind. "So what now?"

A frown creased his brow for a moment. "I can't help you."

"You can't?" She felt almost as she had back in Admiral Horner's office, when he'd coolly told her that everything she'd worked for was about to be taken from her. Jackson Wyler, encountering code he couldn't crack? She couldn't conceive of such a thing. "Maybe— that is, if you had more time…"

"Lira, I could sit here and hack at this thing until our children were old enough to drink, and I still don't know if I could get past it."

A faint heat touched her cheeks when he said "our children," but she only shook her head and replied, "I don't believe that. I've never seen you encounter code you couldn't break."

"Well, you're seeing it now." Abruptly he stood and moved past her to the other side of the room, touched a button on the sleek black cabinet there. The countertop split apart, and a tray bearing a couple of glasses and a bottle of what looked like very old brandy rose up from beneath it. He grasped the bottle and poured approximately two fingers' worth of spirits into one of the glasses. "Interested? It's hundred-year-old Armagnac."

"No, thanks." She didn't even know what Armagnac was. At the moment all she could think was that she had failed. She'd brought a stolen ship with a Stacian naval officer on board it into the heart of one of Gaia's oldest colonies, and she had nothing to show for the risks she'd taken. "Really, Jackson, I just think—"

"You think what?" He turned back toward her, bowl-shaped glass in one hand. "You think if I sit back down there and keep working away like a good little elf, I'll just magically figure out how to hack that code? It doesn't work that way."

"I don't believe you," she said firmly. Firm, because the other way lay panic. "I don't believe any code is truly unbreakable. There has to someone who can hack it."

Another large swallow of Armagnac, and he gave her a mirthless grin. "Oh, there's someone."

"Who?"

"I don't know."

Oh, this was classic Jackson Wyler. "You know there's someone, but you don't know who he is."

"She," he corrected. "Don't know her name, don't know anything about her except where she is."

"And where's that?"

The grin widened, taking on truly shark-like qualities. "Gaia."

For some reason Lira had to quell the impulse to burst out laughing. Gaia. Of course. Couldn't be somewhere out in the hinterlands, some barely patrolled outpost at the edge of Consortium territories. No, this mystery woman had to be on Gaia itself, at the heart of the Gaian government, in some of the most heavily guarded space in the galaxy. She took a breath.

"So how do I find her?"

"You don't."

Lira crossed her arms and stared levelly at Jackson. "So why bother to tell me about her if I can't even find her?"

"You don't find her. She finds you. Give me your handheld."

Mystified, she withdrew the device from her pocket and gave it to Jackson. He tapped something into it, then gave it back to her.

"Send out that code from the subspace radio on board your ship. She'll pick it up, and decide whether or not to help you out any further after you've spoken with her."

"That's it?"

He shrugged. "Take it or leave it. She's the only chance you've got, as far as I'm concerned. You might want to mention that your cause is just. She seems to be a sucker for that sort of thing."

Her cause was just. Was it? Or was she manufacturing plots where there were none, simply to avoid the fact that she'd made a spectacular error in judgment and now didn't want to acknowledge her mistake?

Too late to turn back, though, not with a ship stolen from one of the Iradian sector's worst crime lords, not with an AWOL Stacian officer riding in the copilot's seat. And now she had nothing to go on except a code that might or might not summon some mystery woman who might or might not be willing or able to help her.

Put like that, the whole thing sounded worse than ever. Maybe she should just point that stolen Sirocco-class ship out to the farthest frontiers, to some world where no one would be able to find her—after dropping Captain sen Drenthan off somewhere along the way.

Somehow that felt wrong, though. All right, maybe he could stick around a while longer...just in case. If nothing else, he'd proved to be very handy in a fight.

"Well, thanks, Jackson," she said finally. "I'm sorry I dragged you into all this."

"No worries. It brightened up what would otherwise have been a dull day—although I would have preferred not to get my ass kicked by that hydra."

She gave a philosophical shrug. "I suppose it helps us accept our place in the universe if we come up against something we can't beat every once in a while."

"That doesn't sound like you, Lira. As I recall, you never were the accepting sort." He was watching her carefully, as if trying to gauge how disappointed she really was.

"The universe has taught me a few things over the past decade."

"Has it?" After taking another drink—the fumes of which she could smell from where she stood—he set down the glass and moved a little closer to her. "As in, maybe dumping me wasn't such a great idea after all?"

Belatedly she realized that Jackson had never been very good at holding his liquor. Tone light, she replied, "You dumped me, Jackson. Remember? And I quote, 'I'm not going to waste any more time on an uptight by-the-book bitch like you'...end quote."

He blinked. "I said that?"

"You did."

Another blink. "I was an asshole."

She gave a philosophical shrug. "I probably was, too. Anyway, Jackson, I'm grateful for the help you were able to give, but I really should be getting out of here. God knows what trouble Rast has gotten into while I've been gone."

"Rast." Jackson shook his head. "You and a Stacian. That's something I thought I'd never see."

"You're not seeing it now. We're just trying to get to the bottom of this thing. That's all."

"If you say so."

It wasn't worth arguing over any further. "Thanks, Jackson," Lira said, her tone final, and went back to the living room and out the door, trying to ignore his stare on the back of her neck, the speculative look that seemed to say he knew far more about her relationship with the Stacian captain than she did.

She certainly hoped not.

The ship was equipped with state-of-the-art surveillance equipment that scanned through all 360 degrees of the rented landing pad on which it sat. Since he had nothing better to do, Rast seated himself in the copilot's chair and watched the images on the display in front of him cycle through the cameras. Dull enough, since the landing pad was empty, and nothing in those images changed except the angle of the light overhead.

Only then he saw movement, and realized it was Lira returning at last, almost three hours after she had first left. Thank Alenthan. Rast got up, intending to meet her at the door...and then saw the dark shapes of several men emerging from the secondary entrance to the landing pad, the one near the nose of the ship.

That couldn't be good. A shouted warning rose in his throat, but that wouldn't help. She couldn't possibly hear him.

Suddenly the little ship felt far too large. He bolted for the door, flung it open, and rushed down the gangplank, hearing as he did so the sound of pulse bolts firing. And Lira was unarmed.

Swearing, he dropped to the ground and rolled under the ship, pulling out his own pistol as he did so. From that position he could see Lira lying on the rough concrete of the landing pad, her hair spilling free from the its knot at the back of her neck.

No. The denial rose in him, a furious black negation of what he'd just seen. She couldn't be dead. He wouldn't allow it. She had just dropped to the ground to give herself what cover she could.

But she wasn't moving, and he pushed himself forward, rising from beneath the ship to strike at the unknown assailants the way a sand snake might lie coiled under a concealing rock. One pulse bolt took the first man directly in the chest, and he dropped at once. The second shot went a little astray, hitting the other man in the leg. He stumbled but managed to fire back, the bolt whizzing by only a few inches from Rast's head.

Teeth bared, Rast shot again, this time blasting the pistol right out of the man's hand, leaving a blackened stump where it had been. The human dropped to his knees, moaning in pain, as Rast came to tower over him.

"Who are you?" he demanded. "Who sent you?"

But the pain must have been too much, because the man fell over on his side, face going slack with unconsciousness. And that brought back to Rast the realization that Lira, too, lay crumpled on the surface of the landing pad.

With a growl Rast turned and ran to her, dropping to his knees at her side. He turned her over carefully, fearing the worst. A trailing edge of reddened flesh near her temple and some singed hairs told him she had taken a glancing shot, but no worse. And as he held her, she opened her eyes and stared up into his face.

"Did you get them?"

"Of course."

With a groan she shifted more or less out of his grasp and into a sitting position. "Can't believe those sons of bitches got the drop on me. I hate not being able to carry a sidearm." She reached up to rub her temple, scowled as she encountered the burned flesh and singed-off hair. "That's going to take a while to grow out."

Females. Their priorities could be so odd. And besides, if she would just wear her hair down, the spot in question wouldn't even be noticeable.

"Are they dead?"

"One is. The other...I'm not sure."

"Well, let's find out."

Ignoring his outstretched hand, she staggered to her feet and stumbled her way over to where the second assailant still lay in a limp little heap. "Hey," she said, and prodded him with the toe of her boot.

Moaning, he rolled over onto his back and stared up at her with frightened dark eyes. Definitely not dead, then.

"Who sent you?" Lira demanded.

Another moan, and a shake of the head.

She crossed her arms and glanced up at Rast. "Maybe he needs a little more convincing."

"Be glad to oblige." And he reached down and grasped the man by his collar, dragging him upright, holding him so his feet dangled an inch or two above the floor of the landing pad. "You answer when the lady asks you a question."

"T-Tomas!" the man gasped.

Lira's scowl deepened. She nodded slightly, and Rast shook the man like a rag doll.

"I told you—Gared Tomas!"

"And how did he find us?"

Sweat stood out on the man's brow. Rast could smell the stink of him, the fear rising from his pores. Probably not one of Tomas's actual men, but a local hired to carry out his dirty work.

"The ship—"

"What about it?"

"Second tracker—in the cargo hold."

"Well, shit," Lira said, her disgust with herself clearly evident in the downward tilt of her mouth. "And here I thought I was being so clever."

"Anything else?" Rast demanded, giving the man another shake.

"No—not that I know of. Just told us to come here, secure the vessel, and wait for one of Tomas's agents to come get it. That's all."

It probably was. Rast couldn't imagine that Tomas would have asked the men to do anything more complicated than that. Still, one would have thought the crime lord would send more men than these two fools to secure such a valuable ship, let alone take out the two people responsible for killing his right-hand man and best muscle. Rast's eyes narrowed. "Are there more of you?"

"No—no, just Davvin and me, that's all—"

"He's lying," Lira said coolly. "There's no way Tomas would send only these two losers to recapture the ship. I'm sure there are more on the way."

"No—"

"Any reason to keep this one alive?" Rast inquired, as the man squirmed in his grip.

"You mean besides the oath I swore to protect the citizens of the Consortium?"

"You're not an officer of the fleet anymore."

"Thanks for reminding me." She shook her head, then added, "Let's just get out of here...but make sure he won't do anything about it."

"Not a problem." And Rast took his pistol with his free hand and rapped the hired gun across the head with it. At once the man sagged, and Rast dropped him on the ground.

Lira was already heading toward the ship, so Rast lengthened his stride just a little to catch up with her.

"What about the second tracker?"

"I'll deal with it once we're out of here. Now I know where it is, it shouldn't take too long."

He understood the wisdom of getting away as quickly as possible, so he nodded and let her move ahead so she could get to the cockpit ahead of him. Good thing, too, because even as he pushed the button to retract the gangplank, he saw three more men emerging from the landing pad's two separate entrances, guns drawn. Ducking out of the way, he engaged the controls to lock down the exit and repressurize the cabin. From outside, he could hear the muffled thump of pulse bolts hitting the ship's shell. He had no idea how many hits the *Mistral/Chinook* could take before its hull integrity was compromised, but he really didn't want to stick around and find out.

"Get in here and strap down!" Lira commanded, and he hurried forward and more or less fell into the copilot's seat as she engaged the atmospheric thrusters and shot them straight upward at a velocity probably never intended by the ship's designers.

The comm squawked. "*Chinook*, you are exceeding the designated lift-off speed by approximately three hundred kilometers per hour. Throttle back, or you will be cited."

"Send me the bill," she snapped, and sent the ship

hurtling at a 45-degree angle away from Michende and out into space.

Rast smothered a grin, but then sobered abruptly as Lira turned to him and asked,

"You know how to fly one of these things?"

"Not a Sirocco-class precisely, but—"

"Just get us out of the system while I disengage that second tracker. I doubt anyone is going to follow us, but just in case New Chicago's planetary security patrol is bored today and decides to write me a speeding ticket..."

"Got it," he said, and turned to the controls, taking a brief read of the optimal trajectory to get them away from the planet and out into the nothingness that lay between systems. The Westin system, where both New Chicago and its sister planet Nova Angeles were located, was something of an oddity, in that the twin worlds were its only planetary bodies. Here, it didn't take too long to get into deep space.

Lira nodded, said a brief "thanks," and hurried out.

Apparently New Chicago's security patrol had better things to do that day, because he saw no sign of pursuit. The space around the two planets was far from empty, though, as freighters and passenger liners and small ships designed only for intrasystem travel shimmered in the darkness. None of them seemed to take any notice of the sleek craft speeding away from the twin worlds, and within a quarter-hour they were quite alone, hanging at the edge of the Westin system.

Here, Rast throttled the *Chinook* back slightly; it wasn't safe to keep heading blindly out into open space.

It had been a while since he'd programmed a subspace jump, but he couldn't even do that if he didn't know where he was heading.

Just as he'd begun to wonder whether he should go down to the cargo hold and check on Lira's progress, she reappeared, looking rather more cheerful than when she left. A small black object, its composite shell cracked open and its innards clearly smashed, dangled from her right hand.

"Got it," she said, and then turned and tossed it onto one of the couches in the passenger compartment. "Also found about a dozen cases of moon-moth silk down there, plus some items that are sure to get us arrested on any civilized world."

He didn't think he liked the sound of that. "Such as?"

"Crate of *katahn*, couple more cases of pulse rifles. The usual."

Rast's frown deepened. *Katahn* was a hallucinogen derived from a species of flower that grew on Menari... and was illegal across the Consortium and in the Stacian Federation as well, due to its mind-ravaging properties and highly addictive nature. "We should dump it into space."

"Probably," she agreed. "But first things first. We need to get our course plotted."

"So Jackson was able to break the code."

"Not exactly."

He raised an eyebrow and stared at her, waiting for her to let him in on the joke.

She appeared to relent, saying, "Horner's clean, or

at least Jackson couldn't find anything on him. Your admiral, though—his information is so well hidden that even Jackson Wyler couldn't access it. But he did give me a lead on someone who might."

"So where are we going?"

A corner of her mouth quirked. "Gaia."

CHAPTER EIGHT

IF THE SITUATION HADN'T BEEN SO SERIOUS, LIRA MIGHT have laughed at the crestfallen expression that overtook Rast sen Drenthan's craggy features. Talk about out of the frying pan and into the fire...

"I'm not exactly thrilled about it, either," she told him as she plotted the coordinates into the navigation computer. "But at least I know the Gaian system. It's where I was born."

"I know," Rast said, and then looked as if he wished he'd kept his mouth shut.

"You know?" she demanded, pausing to give him a very narrow stare. "What, were you checking up on me or something?"

"I had to know where you went. I had to know that you were safe."

Those words, spoken calmly yet firmly, doused the flare of anger as quickly as it had come. It was hard to be angry with the one person in the galaxy who seemed to give a damn about her, about what happened to her. The dark copper eyes weren't exactly pleading, but something in his expression seemed to indicate that he cared very much whether she was upset with him.

The crazy thing was...she wasn't angry. Maybe she should have been. God knows what he'd dug up about her. Then again, Jackson Wyler was the main skeleton in her closet, so it couldn't have been that bad.

"Thank you," she said quietly. In that moment he seemed far too close to her, separated by only a half-meter or so in the cramped little cockpit. Even from where she sat, she could catch a faint drift of the spicy-sweet scent that clung to his hair and clothing, and an unexpected and unwelcome rush of heat seemed to start somewhere in her stomach and end up between her legs.

Taking a breath, she turned back to the computer, and input the last of the data the ship needed to make the subspace jump. Her plan was for them to come back to realspace out beyond Pluto, in the darkness where comets were born. From there she'd transmit the code Jackson had given her and hope for the best. With any luck, the mystery woman would pick up on it quickly and guide them in to...wherever she was.

Rast was silent, watching her as she worked. It was only after she activated the subspace drive and the *Chinook* propelled itself into the strange non-reality that allowed ships to travel between the stars that he spoke.

"How long?"

"Twenty standard." And how she'd manage, cooped

up in here with him for that amount of time while her body did things her brain had told it precisely not to do, she couldn't quite comprehend. Oh, well, one step at a time.

She got up from her seat, noting as she did so a slight wooziness. That pulse bolt must have done more of a number on her than she thought. All the more reason to tend to the necessities. And if she were concentrating on getting some food together, then maybe she could ignore her other, unwelcome appetites.

"Hungry?" she asked. "Because I know Gared Tomas has a pretty decent pantry on this boat."

Most of the food Lira laid out was unfamiliar to Rast, but surprisingly it all tasted good...although it did seem to collect in a leaden lump in his belly every time he contemplated their destination.

Gaia. She hadn't said anything, but it seemed as if this would be another instance where he would have to cower in the ship while she went out and handled business. He did not look forward to that at all. But the only thing more conspicuous than having one Stacian appear on Gaia's surface would be to have two of them show up at the same time.

If Lira was concerned, she didn't show it. She ate with good enough appetite, which relieved him somewhat; it meant she hadn't suffered any lasting harm from that pulse bolt. And all the while he tried not to linger on her mouth, since that reminded him of other, more intimate places it had been, or on her slender fingers, which had shown him that they were skilled at much more than piloting a starship.

Easier said than done. His body wanted things that his mind knew were quite out of reach at the moment. It was a pleasant fantasy, to think that after they ate they might retire to the ship's luxurious little bedchamber and make pleasant use of some of those twenty hours stretching ahead of them, but he knew that wasn't going to happen any time soon.

If ever.

"And if this woman does agree to help us, what then?" he asked.

A lift of Lira's slender shoulders. "I suppose it depends on what she can dig up. Are you willing to follow this through, even if it incriminates your commanding officer, possibly brings shame on the Stacian military or government?"

Perhaps before he had known her he might have answered differently, but he did not hesitate as he replied, "Of course. I want to know why you and I were maneuvered...whatever that truth might turn out to be."

She didn't say anything, but only nodded. In her sea-colored eyes he thought he saw approval, though. Or perhaps he was merely fooling himself.

The silence stretched between them as they regarded each other. He could actually feel the weight of it, feel the heaviness of her gaze on him, as if there were things she wanted to say but couldn't, or would not allow herself to utter.

Then she gave a little shake of her head, and pushed her empty plate away. "We have some hours until we reach the Gaian system. Do you want to take first watch, or should I?"

And with that he knew the moment was gone; the chance to speak had evaporated. He cleared his throat and said, "I will. It's probably better that you be the one on duty when we reach Gaian space."

"Sounds good." She picked up the dirty plates and put them in the sanitation unit, then disappeared into the corridor, presumably heading toward one of the empty cabins so she could get a few hours of sleep.

Damn. Damn, damn, damn.

A heavy hand on her shoulder. "Lira."

She opened her eyes, saw Rast staring down at her. At once she was awake, swinging her legs over the edge of the narrow cot. She couldn't bring herself to sleep in what had been Gared Tomas's bed. Besides, Rast would have to take that one. There was no way he could possibly fit on this cot.

"Time?" she asked, and stood, then reached to retrieve her jacket from where she'd slung it over the back of the cabin's single chair.

"Oh five hundred. We're about eight hours out from the Gaian system."

"Anything come up while I was alseep?"

A shake of the head. Several of the precious metal rings bound into Rast's hair jingled slightly. "No. It is a good ship."

"The best money can buy." She moved past him, heading to the galley so she could get a cup of water to rinse the sleep taste out of her mouth. And after that, coffee. She knew Tomas stocked some of Gaia's best in his pantry.

Rast hesitated at the door to Tomas's cabin. "Are you sure you don't want me to stay up? I am not tired."

"No, you should sleep." She wasn't about to tell him that it was easier for her when he wasn't around. At least then she didn't have to worry about the distractions his physical presence seemed to create for her unruly body. "Don't worry—I'll wake you before we come out of subspace."

He nodded, and shifted as if to move into the cabin. She added,

"You'll probably want to change the sheets on the bed. There should be some fresh ones in that black lacquer cabinet."

"Thank you," he said, his tone formal, but she could see him frown slightly, as if wondering how she could possibly know where Gared Tomas stored his clean sheets.

Not from any intimate knowledge, I assure you, she thought, but said nothing. If she explained that Tomas had expected her to perform certain housekeeping duties along with piloting the ship, it would only sound as if she were worried about what Rast might think of her and Tomas's relationship, which was absurd.

Wasn't it?

At least she was spared further conversation, since Rast disappeared into the cabin, shutting the door behind him. Relieved, she went into the galley, started up the coffee maker, drank some water and splashed some more on her face for good measure, and then went on into the cockpit.

Nothing had changed, of course; the odd distorted colors of subspace streaked past the viewscreen at velocities the human mind simply couldn't comprehend in any rational fashion. Lights glowed on the instrument panel, all in reassuring shades of green and blue. Rast was right; it was a good ship, far better than Gared Tomas deserved. She thought she could get used to this, racketing around the galaxy in this elegant little vessel...if only her reasons for being on it weren't so dire.

Down the hall the coffee maker beeped, so she went back and poured herself a cup before returning once more to the cockpit. Numbers in a blue to rival Gaia's lost skies counted down their time to the end of the subspace jump. Seven hours, twenty-two minutes. Plenty of time to meditate on her sins.

If only that didn't require thinking of Rast...

Maybe that stray pulse bolt had given her more of shock than she'd thought. Because she shouldn't be spending her time right now thinking about the deep, smooth timbre of his voice, of the elegant architecture of his cheekbones and chin, the strength in those golden-skinned hands and how they had felt as they moved down her body…

No, she shouldn't be thinking about any of that. She should be thinking of their angle of approach to the Gaian system, and whether this unknown woman would be able to help them…if she even existed at all. For a split-second Lira wondered if Jackson had made her up, simply as a way of getting back at her for some imagined slight, but she dismissed that notion as foolish and more than a little paranoid. Jackson Wyler was many things, but vindictive wasn't one of them.

So, they would come out of subspace in the dark at the outer edges of the solar system, then drop below the plane of the ecliptic, coming up at Gaia from underneath. Lira wasn't foolish enough to think they would escape detection that way, but it was a route many passenger and private ships took, avoiding the commercial traffic among the middle worlds and the base on Luna. It was the world's southern hemisphere that flourished now, with the enormous spaceports at Buenos Aires and Capetown handling a good deal of the off-world traffic. No one would think it odd that a ship like the *Chinook* would be coming in along such a trajectory.

And so she planned, and stared out the viewscreen, and…once or twice, though she would never admit it to Rast…dozed off, then came to with a start. After the second time she grimly rose from the captain's seat and went to make another pot of coffee.

It was in there that Rast approached her. He looked in better shape than she, rested, changed into more of the civilian attire of a high-necked tunic and straight pants, this suit in a dark brown that suited his warm-toned coloring. He must have been carrying a change of clothing and other necessities in the satchel he'd brought on board.

She wasn't entirely lacking, since she kept a small bag with some toiletries and clean underthings in the closet of the second, smaller cabin, but she hadn't had much of a chance to use them yet.

"I would have come to wake you," she said, handing him a cup of coffee.

He took it from her, held the cup under his nose so he could inhale the fragrant steam. "No need. I just told myself that I needed to wake up in six standard hours."

Lira blinked. "You can do that?"

"Of course. Can't you?"

"No. I have to sleep with the alarm right next to my head, or I'll never wake up."

"Ah. Yes, as I recall, you do sleep rather soundly."

That remark brought a flush to her cheeks, but she managed to say steadily enough, "We're about to drop out of subspace."

He nodded, and said nothing else as she went back to the cockpit and settled into her seat. Apparently he could tell that he had discomfited her, because he remained silent, sipping his coffee, as she took a last reading of their location, then began the sequence that would allow them to safely reenter realspace.

At once the universe dropped in around them, velvet black with a faint sprinkling of stars. As always, the skies of her home system felt sparse, empty, compared to the glory that blazed in the heavens of planets nearer to the galaxy's core. She pulled out her handheld, brought up the sequence of numbers Jackson had given her, and fed them into the comm system, all the while wondering whether they were just some cruel pie in the sky, nothing more than a meaningless combination of numerals.

Rast finally spoke. "That was the signal?"

"Yes."

"And now what?"

"We wait."

"For how long?"

She could only shrug. Jackson hadn't said how long it would take for this woman, this unknown hacker, to respond. It could be dead of night in her part of the world, and she could be safely asleep in her own bed, which meant they still might have many hours to wait.

"I'm going to start bringing us in," Lira said, as she engaged the sublight engines and sent the ship on the route she'd already plotted, flying below the space that contained the heavy ore freighters and the passenger liners and all the other traffic a highly populated system would accumulate. "It'll get us that much closer, and even at max sublight, it'll still take about an hour, hour and a half. And then I have to hope that we'll get an answer by then."

He nodded, although his mouth looked a little grim. Not surprising; she knew she wouldn't be overly thrilled if their situations had been reversed, and they were instead flying into the heart of Stacian space.

To her surprise, the comm came to life only about

fifteen minutes later. A woman's voice, low-toned, with rounded Gaian accents that somehow sounded a bit off, as if she hadn't spent her whole life on that world. "I suppose Jackson sent you."

"Yes," Lira replied, leaning closer to the comm for some reason, even though she knew perfectly well it would pick up what she said no matter where she was in the cockpit. "He said I should tell you that our cause is just."

"'Our'?" the woman repeated. "Is he there with you? I didn't think anything could shake him loose from that penthouse of his."

"No—it's not Jackson. I was talking about my travel companion."

"Who is...?" The woman's words trailed off before she continued, "I can tell from your voice that you're Gaian—off-world colony, though, probably Ganymede or Luna. Is your companion the same?"

"Um...no." Lira hesitated, then realized she would have to tell the truth sooner or later. "He's, well, actually, he's a Stacian."

A long silence then, one so long Lira feared the woman might have cut off the transmission. Not an entirely unexpected reaction, given the perpetual state of not-war that existed between the two governments.

At last the woman spoke again. "Well, that puts an interesting wrinkle in it. A Gaian and a Stacian traveling together. Guess I'll have to hear more about it... and this 'just cause' of yours. Transmitting course coordinates now. Do not deviate from these in the slightest. Understood?"

"Yes," Lira said quickly, not wanting to risk their chances.

"All right. Here goes. We'll see you in a few hours."

And the comm went silent, even as the nav-computer began to show long streams of numbers that traced their path through the Gaian system and their final destination, whatever that was. Of course, she didn't have to sit here idly and let the ship fly on autopilot. A few extra keystrokes, and she could see exactly where they were being guided.

Their destination popped up on the screen, and she frowned down at it. Really? She'd heard it was a wild area, remote, underpopulated. And that was where the galaxy's best hacker was holed up.

Rast sent her a questioning look, then asked, "So where are we going?"

She sat back in her seat, mystified. "New Zealand."

He'd never heard of the place, of course. Gaian geography was not something he'd studied, thinking he would never need an intimate knowledge of his enemies' home world. "What is New Zealand?"

"An island in the southern hemisphere. One of the places that escaped the Cloud."

"The Cloud?" The capital letters were clear in her voice, but he'd never heard of such a thing before.

"What, they didn't teach you Gaian history?"

"Some. Not in any great detail. It was not considered essential."

No reply at first. She appeared less annoyed than preoccupied, perhaps a little sad. He couldn't think why.

Then she said, "Well, we've got some time to kill. The Cloud hit in 2112. North America had been pushing for years for more sustainable energy—solar, wind, even nuclear, once they had interplanetary flight pretty much settled and figured out they could dump all those spent rods on Mercury's dark side. Anyway, that was fine and good, but it didn't keep people from wanting to consume—computers, vehicles, electronic equipment...everything, really."

"So you didn't have fusion yet."

"No. That came around in 2150—better late than never, but it didn't help the billions who died in the Cloud." Her expression darkened as she continued, "The factories in China just kept increasing output to keep up with demand, and they hadn't put in the same environmental controls that the governments in the United States, Mexico, Canada, and the EU had. The air was so bad you couldn't go outside without a breathing unit. And then it just...coalesced. Like a perfect storm of atmospheric conditions and factory pollution. The air turned toxic, burned right through the filters on their breathing units, was swept for thousands of miles across mainland China, on into Korea and Japan and parts of Vietnam and Thailand. Some went up into Russia, too. Billions died. *Billions.*"

Rast didn't speak. He knew that Gaia had undergone some horrific ecological disasters, but he'd never really considered their ramifications, except for a brief dismissive thought that the Gaians had brought such things upon themselves. Now, though, as he gazed at the haunted expression on Lira's face, he understood what a toll it had taken. Billions. He could barely grasp the enormity of that number. Even now, in a time of unparalleled prosperity for his people, the population on his home world barely numbered one billion.

"Anyway," she continued, "although the damage was concentrated in Asia, it still hit other parts of the world—the west coast of North America, for one thing, and the northern coast of Australia. But New Zealand, it was protected, more or less, though never densely populated. A lot of people fled, wrongly thinking the Cloud would hit them there, too. And they just never came back."

"And so it is this place to which we are headed?" he asked, trying to guide the conversation back to the present, back to something that might erase the bleak expression from her lovely face.

"Yes." She stared out the viewscreen for a few seconds, then added, "I suppose it makes sense. If you want to be on Gaia, but be someplace where you don't have to worry about having a bunch of people in your lap, New Zealand is a pretty smart choice."

"What is it like?"

"New Zealand? I have no idea. I've never been there. Actually, I've only set foot on Gaia twice in my entire life. The first time was for my graduation ceremony— they always have it here. Silly tradition, if you ask me.

And the second time was to visit my brother Liam. He's a climatologist, helping with the rehabilitation of the Asian continent."

"So it's still uninhabitable?"

"Large parts of it. They're working on cleaning up the air, utilizing equipment similar to what we use in our terraforming processes, but it's slow going. And it takes a long time to dispose of billions of dead bodies. Hundreds of years, even."

Her tone was too brittle, too careless. Rast didn't dare to inquire whether she'd visited this brother of hers in the region where he was working, whether she had seen the devastation for herself. And did it really matter? She obviously still felt the pain of those deaths, even if they had occurred almost four hundred years ago.

"Do you think it odd that this woman is trusting us?"

Lira smiled then, but she didn't appear all that amused. "I doubt she is. You'll note that she said 'we'll see you.' That could have just been for show, but I sort of doubt it. I'm sure the welcoming party will be quite interesting."

He should have guessed as much. If their roles had been reversed, he knew he'd be awaiting any visitors with a gun in either hand and some reinforcements, especially if he were the type of person who was trying to make sure his whereabouts weren't discovered by anyone in authority.

"But," Lira continued, studying the readouts on the instrument panel, "I'm guessing if she didn't mean to help us, she wouldn't have given us the coordinates at all. So our best course of action is just to stay cool and see what happens. After all, we're not interested in her story—we just want to get in there, give her the pertinent details, see if she can hack her way into Admiral sen Trannick's files, gather the results, and get the hell out of there. We have no reason to betray her to the Gaian authorities. I think she'll see that."

That made sense, but even so, he could feel himself tensing as they moved inexorably closer to Gaia, to a world where such as he certainly weren't welcome. Lira seemed to note his unease, but she said nothing to dispel it, only continued to guide the *Chinook* ever closer, until at last the blue-green sphere of the planet filled the viewscreen. He started a little when the comm came to life once again, but it was only a bored-sounding official inquiring as to their registration and destination.

Lira answered that they were headed toward Adelaide, which he guessed was a lie, but not one that would arouse a good deal of suspicion. And that turned out to be the case, because the official only said, "We have you recorded, *Chinook*. Enjoy your stay on Gaia, and remember to declare any goods purchased here when you leave the planet."

"Will do." Lira turned slightly and even smiled, possibly noting his mystified expression. "Oh, come on, Rast—I know you Stacians just love to mock us mercenary Gaians. So why should you be surprised at the planetary government making sure it squeezes every unit it can out of us unsuspecting tourists?"

"I suppose I shouldn't," he admitted, watching as they dropped out of the black of space and into wreaths of moisture-laden air, flowing over and around the viewscreen. Although he'd been on Gaian-class worlds before, breathed the heavy richness of their atmospheres, something about this one felt different. Perhaps it was only because he was now in the heart of enemy territory, spawning ground of the hated humans.

Not that he hated all of them. He would not allow himself to stare, but he was intensely aware of Lira's presence, of the way her loose hair slipped over the dark fabric of her jacket as she worked the controls, the delicate perfection of her profile as cool white light bathed the ship once they pierced the cloud cover.

But then he found his gaze drawn away from her, on to a shimmering expanse of blue water as they flew low over the ocean, approaching a green island that seemed to rise up from nowhere, somehow insubstantial as a dream, with the clouds that crowned its mountaintops and the mist that hugged its dark forests. The ship banked, dropping even lower, barely skimming the treetops, negotiating a narrow canyon that opened up into a sheltered valley, with lowering mountains on either side.

In the center of this valley stood a sprawling white structure Rast belatedly realized must be a residence of some sort, although it bore no resemblance to the high-rise buildings he'd seen on New Chicago and many other worlds of the Consortium, or the graceful villas of stucco and stone his own people favored when imitating the Eridani style. Incongruously, he noted the outline of an arrowhead-shaped Eridani Vector-class ship parked behind the house.

And then they were dropping straight down, Lira guiding the *Chinook* so that it landed approximately ten meters away from the other spaceship. A minute or so more, as she finalized the landing sequence and put the ship in standby mode, and then she unbuckled her safety harness and stood, gazing down at him with an unreadable expression on her face.

"Let's go meet our hosts, shall we?"

CHAPTER NINE

RAST DID NOT SEEM PARTICULARLY OVER-EAGER TO follow her, but after a brief hesitation he undid his own seatbelts and stood, trailing a few feet behind her as she cycled the door lock and extended the gangplank. And then the door opened, and a fresh cool breeze, smelling of water and something else, something green and growing, flooded in over them.

At least she didn't have to leave Rast behind this time; the mystery woman already knew that one of the people seeking her help was a Stacian. And really, you couldn't get much more remote than this, unless you set down in the middle of the Gobi Desert somewhere. The mountains created an effective barrier, and all around the valley tall trees reached up to the sky. The house did not appear occupied, although that didn't mean much. Its residents could just be waiting for their off-world visitors to make the first move.

"Stop there," said a harsh male voice.

She couldn't even tell where he had come from, because her quick scan of the surroundings had shown no other signs of life. Maybe from the other ship, then passing under the still-steaming belly of the *Chinook*.

Hands held in the air, she said, "We're unarmed."

He moved in front of her then, a swarthy Gaian man of average height. Something about the way he moved, though, the way he scanned her quickly without having to pat her down for weapons, told her he knew exactly what he was doing...and that he was very, very dangerous.

Next he moved to Rast, and although the Stacian towered over him by almost a foot, Lira wasn't sure whether or not her travel companion would be able to best the stranger in a confrontation. She decided she really didn't want to find out.

"They're clean," the man said, and a door on the back of the house opened, and a woman stepped out.

She seemed to be about Lira's age, with long dark red hair. Striking, with her high cheekbones and full mouth. When she spoke, Lira recognized her voice at once. "Anyone follow you?"

"No. I think the authorities were more interested in making sure we reported any purchases to customs before we left the planet than trying to find out if we were up to something nefarious."

"Typical." Her gaze moved past Lira to Rast, and her mouth tightened. "A Stacian. I wasn't sure if you were joking or not."

"Is that a problem?" Something in the woman's voice belied a tension that seemed to go beyond a simple mistrust of strangers, and Lira began to wonder if they'd done the right thing in coming here.

Another penetrating stare, and then the woman shook her head. "No. We're fine. Why don't you two come inside, and we'll start getting this worked out?"

And she led them into the house, the dark, silent man in the rear, his eyes seeming to bore into the back of Lira's neck. That quiet stare seemed to tell her that he'd happily smoke both her and Rast if either of them caused the slightest amount of trouble.

Although she'd never been in a house like this, she recognized its type from images she'd seen in her history books. What they used to call a clapboard farmhouse, sprawling and two-storied, with real wood floors that creaked underneath. They passed through what looked to be the laundry area, and then through a kitchen that was an odd blend of old and new, with a brick fireplace and gleaming polished metal appliances. From there they emerged into what was clearly the dining room, with a long table of some dark wood, scarred and marked by probably centuries of use, accompanied by a set of equally battered chairs.

"Take a seat," the woman said. "Eryk, some water for our guests. It's a little early for beer," she added with a grin. The dark man nodded, eyes narrowed, and then went back into the kitchen.

Behind her, Rast shifted slightly. Lira guessed he didn't think it was too early for a drink. What he said, though, was, "I don't want to break one of your chairs—"

"You won't. They're solid oak, sturdier than they

look. And if they can stand up to Jerem, they can stand up to anything."

Who Jerem was, Lira had no idea. Maybe they'd find out at some point. At any rate, she pulled out a chair for herself, and after a pause Rast did so as well. The aged wood did creak as he deposited himself on the seat, but it seemed to hold...for the moment, anyway.

The strange woman sat down at the head of the table, waiting until the man—her bodyguard? lover? husband? Lira couldn't guess for sure—returned with a pitcher of water and a set of glasses that looked as old as the house. He sat down as well, at the table's foot. Probably not a bodyguard, then, although Lira thought he performed those duties for her...as well as any others that might be required.

"Thank you," the woman said, and waited until both Rast and Lira had helped themselves to some of the water. "Might as well get formally acquainted. I'm Miala Thorn, and this is my husband, Eryk."

Finally Lira put two and two together. She'd heard of Eryk Thorn, the mercenary. His face and name had been attached to scores of "Wanted" communiqués spanning the galaxy. He'd gone quiet the past eighteen standard months, though. Now she knew why. He'd been living here on Gaia in apparent domestic bliss. Who knew?

Still, how the mercenary had ended up here wasn't her business. She said, "I'm Lira Jannholm. And this is—"

"Captain Rast sen Drenthan," Rast supplied, copper eyes wary.

Again Miala's lips compressed. For all her outward friendliness, it was clear enough to Lira that the other woman had no love lost for Stacians.

Rast was no fool. Lira could see that he noticed, too, although he said nothing else after that first introduction, but only sat stiffly in the too-fragile chair, chin out, masses of hair at odds with the clean-lined civilian clothing he wore.

Into this tense little scene came the unexpected sound of a baby wailing somewhere upstairs. At once Miala broke eye contact with Rast and stood.

"My apologies. She just went down for a nap, but she's teething—"

"Take all the time you need," Rast said, nodding a little, as if he knew all too well the travails of mothers with teething infants.

Lira stared at him, once again startled by the revelation of a heretofore unknown facet of his personality. Vaguely she knew that infants had a period when their teeth came in and were therefore fussy and even more demanding than usual, but her knowledge stopped there. The last infant she'd been around was her youngest sister, and that had been almost twenty-five years ago. Janna might have been a fussy baby, but if she was, Lira had blocked that particular datum from her memory banks.

After another murmured apology, Miala hurried out of the dining room, her boots clattering on the wooden steps as she rushed upstairs. Her departure left

Rast, Lira, and Eryk Thorn clustered uncomfortably around the dining table.

Without preamble, Rast said, "She doesn't like Stacians. Why?"

Thorn turned cool dark eyes on both of them. "Why should she? Gaians and Stacians weren't exactly allies, last time I checked."

"It's more than that. And yet she still agreed to help us."

"If she wants to tell you, she'll tell you. And if she agreed to help you, then you'd do better not to question her motivations too closely."

His tone didn't leave much room for argument. Lira tried to cast about for something else to say, finally settling on, "This is quite a house. How old is it?"

A shrug. "About five hundred years, give or take. It was abandoned during the time of the Cloud. But it suits us."

She supposed it would, stuck out in the middle of nowhere like this. A good place for a wanted man like Eryk Thorn to settle down, and equally suitable for a hacker who wanted to make sure the authorities would have a difficult time finding her. How exactly two such disparate individuals had ended up together, she had no idea, but she had the feeling that Miala's and Thorn's story might rival hers and Rast's for improbability.

Just then Miala came back into the dining room, a yellow-wrapped bundle held up against one shoulder. "Eryk, can you take her for a while? Every time I try to put her down, she gets fussy, and I've got work to do."

Silently Thorn reached out to take the baby from his wife, and Lira was treated to the sight of one of the galaxy's most notorious mercenaries cuddling his infant daughter. She had to repress a grin. As she glanced over at Rast, wanting to share the joke, she saw he didn't look amused at all, but was staring at Eryk Thorn with an odd expression on his face, something she almost would have classified as wistfulness...if she didn't think Rast sen Drenthan was incapable of such an emotion.

"All right," Miala went on, her gaze clearly focused on Lira, and not Rast, "why don't you tell me what I'm looking for, and why the great Jackson Wyler wasn't able to help you?"

As much as she hated to go through the whole thing all over again, Lira forced herself to recount the story, although quickly, skimming over what had passed between herself and Rast, and focusing on the importance of the mines on Chlorae II. "And Jackson said there was no way he could beat this hydra code, and that you were the only person he knew of who could. So here we are."

The other woman was silent for a moment, forehead puckered in an abstracted little frown. "Well, we'll just have to see what I can dig up. Why don't you come with me to my office, and we'll start taking a crack at it? We'll leave the boys here to babysit." And she winked at Eryk Thorn, who gazed up at her stoically, the baby gurgling into his dark shirt.

Lira was fairly certain Rast was less than thrilled about being left out like this, but she didn't dare

protest, and instead got up from her chair to follow
Miala out of the room. As she went, she sent the
Stacian an apologetic little glance over her shoulder.
He might have shrugged, just barely, but it was hard
to tell.

Although she wouldn't allow herself to shake her
head, she couldn't help wondering exactly what it was
this Miala had against Stacians...

———

Left alone with Eryk Thorn, Rast found himself
pinned by the mercenary's flat black stare. At
length Thorn said, "You still active in the
Stacian navy?"

This might have sounded slightly more menacing if
the baby hadn't chosen that precise instant to start
making little cooing noises, burying her face into her
father's chest.

*You're not going to find what you're looking for
there, little one. I think your meal ticket just left
the room.*

Still, Rast managed to keep his tone an impassive
match to Thorn's as he replied, "For now. I have a
feeling a dishonorable discharge is looming if I don't
return to active duty soon."

"Doesn't sound like you care much one way or
another."

"I don't."

Thorn appeared to absorb this, nodding to himself

as he stood and got a bottle for the baby out of the refrigeration unit. A flip of the tab on the bottle's self-heating coil, and then he expertly maneuvered the bottle into the baby's open rosebud lips. At once she began suckling, eyes squeezed tight, dark lashes of astonishing length fanned against her plump little cheeks.

Somehow Rast knew that any comments on the mercenary's domestic abilities would meet with a poor reception. Instead, he inquired, "How long do you think this will take?"

"Hard to say. If it's as tough as Jannholm says it is, days, probably."

Days? He didn't like the sound of that very much. The gods only knew what might be going on out there in the galaxy as they hid here in this secret corner of New Zealand, so far away from anything that seemed important. Then again, they didn't have much choice. If they couldn't find out who Admiral Sen Trannick was working with, and what his true motivations were, they might as well just pack up and go home. Not that Lira had much of a home to go to, apparently.

And neither would he, if this venture stretched out too long. He'd been granted a leave, true, but the chronometer was ticking down even now. Besides, if they had irrefutable evidence the admiral was dirty, discrediting the man wouldn't make Rast much of a hero on his home world. Not that he cared about that. He cared about getting at the truth, no matter the cost.

"Well, then," Rast said, and stood, glad to be out of that rickety little chair. He didn't care what Miala might have said regarding its sturdiness; it felt to him as if it was about to collapse at any moment. "Guess I'd better go check on my ship."

Thorn's expression was unreadable. "You do that."

It felt good to get out again, actually, to feel the cool air on his face. Such delicious-tasting air didn't exist on his home world, dry and dusty place that it was. Perhaps long ago Stacia had been like this, green and cool and welcoming, but no more. Glancing around at the cloud-topped hills to all sides, he thought there were worse places he and Lira could have been forced to stay.

The *Chinook* was fine, of course, silvery hull gleaming almost a pale blue as it reflected the cerulean skies overhead. Still, Rast made his customary inspection of its exterior, walking all the way around, looking for any pits from meteorites or other bits of cosmic dust that might have taken their toll. As he came back around to the gangplank, he heard a boy's voice.

"Is this your ship?"

"It is." It seemed simpler to reply that way, even though technically the ship belonged to Gared Tomas. Possession trumped law, anyway...and who was to say Tomas himself hadn't stolen the Sirocco-class vessel?

The boy came into view then, a tall lad of probably ten standard or so, although Rast was not completely familiar with human growth stages. His dark hair and eyes and olive skin, as well as the firm chin and straight, rather broad nose, marked him as Eryk Thorn's blood. Interesting. So was the boy Thorn's from an earlier liaison, or was Miala his mother as well? The child didn't look much like her.

He paused, staring up at Rast. "You're a Stacian."

"Yes." Since the boy's gaze hadn't wavered, was still fixed on Rast's face, he asked, "Have you ever seen a Stacian before?"

"Oh, yeah," Jerem answered. "I was kidnapped by one."

"You—what?"

The boy actually grinned. "Yeah, he wanted my mother to give him the money, since he thought he had a right to it since it was in his brother's compound or something, only it really wasn't, because my mom had taken it years before. Anyway, he wanted to ransom me for it, except not really, because he planned to kill me anyway once he had the money, but the joke was on him because he didn't know who my father was, and he came along and killed him. So it was okay." Finally a pause for breath, and then, "So anyway, that's how I've already seen a Stacian."

Rast tried to find something in this narrative he could latch onto, failed, and instead inquired, "What's your name?"

"Jerem. Jerem Thorn. For a long time I thought it was Jerem Felaris, but it turns out that wasn't really my name...or hers."

"Hello, Jerem. I'm Rast sen Drenthan...but you can just call me Rast."

Jerem squinted up at him. "I guess it's okay for you to be here, or my father would have already done something about it, wouldn't he?"

Of that Rast had no doubt. "It's fine. Your mother is helping my—Lira Jannholm, my traveling companion."

"Oh. That makes sense. She's good with computers. You're getting something done with a computer?"

"Something like that, yes."

The boy seemed to consider Rast for a moment, staring up at him with wide brown eyes. "You don't seem to mind."

"Mind what?"

"That my dad killed a Stacian."

I have a feeling your father has killed a whole lot of people, kid. Of course Rast made no such remark out loud, but said only, "It sounds as if that particular Stacian was a criminal. So I don't mind. I believe your father probably did the galaxy a favor by taking someone like that out of commission."

Jerem nodded solemnly, seeming to take Rast's words to heart. "That's good." He paused, then added, "You don't seem like him at all—the dead Stacian, I mean. You seem pretty nice."

"Well, thank you, Jerem," Rast replied, trying to keep the amusement he felt from seeping into his tone. He didn't want the boy to think he was being condescending toward him. Children that age were sensitive creatures, whether human or Stacian.

"I've never seen a ship like this," the boy continued, moving toward the *Chinook* and staring up at her sleek outlines with some envy. "What is it?"

"It's a Sirocco-class private transport, very new. Only a handful have been built so far. It's the smallest ship to have a Gupta drive."

"It's got a Gupta drive? Seriously? How fast is it?"

Jerem continued to pepper Rast with questions, asking enough that he could tell the boy had a working knowledge of ships and their various functions. Perhaps Thorn had even begun teaching his son how to pilot the old Vector-class ship that sat only a few meters away from the *Chinook*.

"Are you going to take her up soon?" Jerem's eyes were shining, and Rast had the feeling the kid would probably try to wrangle a ride if that were the case.

"I doubt it. We need to lie low while we're here. No point in attracting attention by flying around in her."

Jerem's face fell. "Oh." But then he perked up again. "So are you guys on the run? Are you, like, intergalactic assassins or something cool like that?"

Somehow Rast managed to keep from grinning. "No, nothing like that. I'm a captain in the Stacian navy, and Ms. Jannholm is—well, until recently she had her own starship in the GDF. We're both honest, upstanding citizens."

"Oh, that's too bad." Even as the words left his mouth, Jerem seemed to realize his mistake. He rushed to add, "I mean, it's probably good that you're not assassins, I suppose, but it would have been cool. Nothing ever happens around here."

You say that like it's a bad thing. "Sometimes it's all right for things not to happen, you know."

"I guess."

Looking at the boy's crestfallen face, Rast could only hope he might be blessed with Jerem's version of boredom for a few days. Some peace and quiet would be nice for once.

"All right," Miala said, after she'd sat down in front of her keyboard and indicated that Lira should take the other unoccupied seat in the cramped space that served as her office, "let's see what we're dealing with here."

And she began typing away, her fingernails making a slight clatter on the touch pad of her keyboard, as the screens around her began to flash with strings of numbers and pieces of code that Lira knew she wouldn't be able to decipher, no matter how long she stared at them. Instead she looked away to inspect the workspace, which looked as if it might have been a spare bedroom at one time. Now it was filled with desks, and all of those desks were occupied by flat screens and head's-up displays, although she didn't have any of Jackson Wyler's pricey 3D generators.

And she was pretty sure Jackson Wyler didn't have miniature holo-portraits of his children stuck next to said displays. Roughly half those portraits showed a dark-haired boy of about ten who had to have been Eryk Thorn's son, even though Lira hadn't actually seen the boy yet.

"Well, this is something," Miala said, and Lira startled a little.

"What's something?"

"Jackson was right. This thing is a beast."

"So you can't do anything with it?"

Miala sent her an amused glance. "I said it was a beast. I didn't say I couldn't break it. The problem with Jackson is that he lets himself get flummoxed too quickly. I may have to round my estimate up by a couple of days, but I'll unwind it eventually."

It was probably too soon to feel so relieved, but Lira did allow herself to let out a small, thankful breath. So the situation wasn't completely hopeless after all.

"The weird thing is," Miala continued, "there's only one person I know of who could even begin to write code like this."

"I would think that would make it easier. That is, if you know who wrote it, then you'd also know where it came from."

"True," Miala admitted, continuing to type away. "I guess I'm just trying to figure out why a Stacian admiral would have an Eridani hacker covering his tracks."

After reiterating that he wouldn't be flying the *Chinook* any time soon—and also pointing out that it was Lira who would be doing the actual flying—Rast followed Jerem into the house, where both Eryk Thorn and the baby had disappeared. Maybe she had settled down enough that she'd be able to sleep for a while.

"Are you going to be eating dinner with us?" Jerem

asked, after pouring himself a glass of water and then belatedly asking Rast if he wanted one, too.

"I don't know. I somewhat doubt it. That's really impinging on your parents' hospitality, especially since they'd never even met us before today."

The boy looked disappointed, and Rast supposed he couldn't really blame him. They were so isolated out here, and he probably went weeks or even months without seeing anybody except his parents...and a six-month-old baby wasn't exactly a very good companion.

Rast heard footsteps on the stairs, and Lira came into the kitchen a minute later, her face a study in worry and confusion. She hesitated a moment when she spied Jerem, but then smiled a little and said, "I don't think we've met yet. I'm Lira Jannholm."

"I know," the boy said. "I mean, who else could you be? Rast was already telling me about you and your ship."

"Oh, he was?"

"I was saying how you were the real pilot, and how I sort of doubted we'd be flying the *Chinook* until it was time to leave."

"Well, of course not," she remarked, as if that should be obvious.

"Jerem was also wondering if we'd be staying to dinner, and I said I thought not. We have plenty of rations in the *Chinook*, don't we?"

"Yes, of course. Tomas made sure the ship was always well-stocked."

"Best freeze-dried rations money can buy, I'll bet,"

said Eryk Thorn as he entered the kitchen, sans baby. "We have plenty. You can take some over to your ship."

"That's very generous," Rast said, noting that the invitation was only to share the food, and not actually to sit down to dinner with the family. Not that he could really blame the man; if he'd been in Thorn's position, he doubted he'd be inviting a couple of strangers, one of them from a hostile alien race, to break bread with his family.

"But Dad—"

"Don't 'but Dad' me. Put together a couple of packets for our visitors."

As the boy did as his father ordered, reluctance obvious in his dragging footsteps, Thorn directed his next words to Lira. "Working, is she?"

"Yes. She said it's tough but that she thinks she can do it. Could be four or five days, though."

If Thorn was disturbed by the thought of the two interlopers parking themselves on his property for the greater part of a standard week, he didn't show it. He only nodded, then said, "I'll take a tray up to her later. When she gets like this, I know better than to ask her to drop everything and come down. Best you eat that before it gets cold."

It was a clear dismissal, and Rast took it as such. He shot Jerem a quick grin, to show he wasn't put off by Eryk Thorn's brusque tone, took the packets of food from the boy, and made the smallest of nods toward the back door. Luckily Lira took the hint, thanking Thorn for the food before she followed Rast out to the ship.

They went inside, and she paused to close the door

behind them and lock it. She waited until he had set the food down on the low table in front of one of the couches before asking in acid tones, "You think that's poisoned?"

Since he knew she was joking...or at least he hoped she was...he replied with a grin, "I think we're safe. I have a feeling Miala Thorn might be a trifle irritated if her husband knocked off a couple of guests that way. Besides, I doubt poison is really his style. He seems to be more of a 'shoot you between the eyes' sort of person. Or maybe the back of the head, if that's more convenient."

She gave an unwilling laugh. "You're probably right. So what did they send over?"

"You'd probably have a better idea of that than I would. I don't know much about Gaian cuisine."

"Neither do I. Everything on Ganymede was grown hydroponically or so processed you really couldn't tell what it started out as." Even so, she opened one of the packets, sniffed, and tilted her head to one side, considering. "I think there might be actual meat in there. Not sure what, though. It smells good."

It did smell good, a savory aroma that sent his stomach juices turning. The second packet held some creamy-looking white stuff that Lira said was mashed potatoes...whatever those were.

"And since Tomas kept everything on this ship well-stocked, we can eat like civilized people. Well, mostly," she added, after casting a critical eye on the table where their food rested. "That table's a little low, even for me. But I suppose you'll make do."

"Oh, I will." He watched as she fetched plates and cutlery from a low cabinet on the far side of the passenger compartment, and cheered up even more when she produced two glasses and a bottle of dark-hued wine on her second trip to the cabinet. "Tomas didn't hide much from you, did he?"

Abruptly, her expression darkened. "Oh, he hid plenty. But since he expected me to be his flight attendant in addition to his pilot, I do know where he kept all his dining necessities." She pushed the tab on the cork so it would self-extricate, then poured a measure of wine into each glass. "Dinner is served, I guess."

It was a little awkward to sit on the couch and lean over the table to eat, but the food itself was delicious, if unfamiliar, and the wine smooth and dark and heavy, a good complement to the rich gravy that covered the meat. Since there was no place else for her to sit down, Lira perched on the edge of the couch next to him, distinctly uncomfortable with their proximity.

Rast could not say the same for himself. She was so close he could feel the warmth of her leg next to his, smell the sweet scent of her hair as she leaned over to pick up her glass of wine.

"Miala says she thinks the hacker is Eridani," she said abruptly, after she took a sip.

He hadn't been expecting that. "How can she tell?" He lifted his shoulders, drank of his own wine. Gared Tomas might have been a bastard, but he knew how to choose his liquor.

"Says she only knows of one person who can write code like that, and apparently he's an Eridani."

That remark sent the wheels in Rast's mind spinning. He refused to believe that the Eridanis might be involved in this mess. They were a peaceful, long-civilized race, known for their generosity in sharing their knowledge, their tech. Stacia would still be a backwater world, its inhabitants scratching out a bare subsistence, if it weren't for the Eridanis. No, the most likely explanation was simply that Admiral sen Trannick had hired the best to obfuscate this records...and that "best" just happened to be Eridani.

"Probably doesn't mean anything," he said after a long pause, which he tried to hide by drinking some more of his wine.

Lira's tone was also noncommittal. "Probably."

They both lapsed into silence then, bites of food punctuated by sips of drink. He had no idea what might be going through her mind. His own was preoccupied by her presence, the warmth of her body, the way her hair gleamed in the cabin's overhead lights. How he wished he could pluck the wine glass from her fingers, press her down into the cushions, taste her again. He knew better, though. The day might come when Lira Jannholm would come to him willingly, but it was not this night.

He could only hope that tomorrow might be better.

CHAPTER TEN

A DAY PASSED, AND THEN ANOTHER. HARD TO BELIEVE that she could share cramped quarters like those on board the *Chinook* with a Stacian, of all people, but Rast turned out to be a more than tolerable shipmate, not using inordinate amounts of water in the bathroom, and picking up after himself without having to be asked. She had no idea whether that was normal behavior for him, or whether he simply wanted to make a good impression so she might soften her attitude toward him.

Not that simple, Rast, she thought on the morning of the third day, as he volunteered to take her soiled clothing into the Thorn homestead, where Miala had offered them the use of their laundry setup. *Maybe it's all domestic tranquility now, but once we get back out there...* She gazed up into the blue skies, which had begun to cloud over. Thorn had said it might rain today.

Rain. There was a novelty. She could count the times she'd felt real rain on her face on the fingers of one hand.

Rast returned from the house and paused a few feet away from where she stood, still staring upward.

"Jerem is going to teach me how to fish," he said. "You want to come along?"

She shook her head. The two of them had been spending a good amount of time together the past few days, Jerem obviously entranced with the novelty of having a friendly Stacian around...and his parents probably relieved that someone new was on board to keep him amused for a while.

"You're good with kids, aren't you?" she asked abruptly.

"I suppose so." He shrugged. "I've been around enough of them."

"You? Around children?"

His pained expression seemed to indicate that she didn't know much about Stacians. "I have fifteen nieces and nephews. There might be more on the way...I've been out of contact the past month or so."

"Fifteen?" She tried to imagine fifteen nieces and nephews, all running around and carrying on the way she supposed small children did. The thought was vaguely horrifying.

"I suppose it's my turn to lecture you about your ignorance of Stacian history and culture." He grinned, apparently overlooking the frown she felt etch itself on her forehead. "Family is everything to us. Life was so hard for so long that the biological imperative still remains. Children, and lots of them."

"That's not ecologically sustainable," she replied.

"Now, perhaps. Why do you think my people are pushing so hard to colonize other worlds? You're right —Stacia can't support its current population. So we're moving outward."

"No wonder the Gaians and Stacians are at each other's throats."

"It is unfortunate, but true."

After digesting that for a few seconds, she asked, "And what about you?"

"What about me?"

"Have you been a good Stacian and been busy reproducing with the rest of them?" As soon as the words left her mouth, she wished she could take them back. True, Rast had been on his best behavior the past few days, but she wasn't stupid. She could recognize sexual tension when she saw it. Or felt it, as the case may be. Like the times she caught him watching her. Or hell, the time she'd been in the shower with the warm water cascading over her, and somehow her thoughts had strayed to Rast and how his body had been this warm...and the next thing she knew, she'd been running her soapy hands over her breasts, wishing they had been his hands.

She'd turned the water to cold right after that and gotten out as soon as she could.

He lifted his shoulders. "No. My mother reminds me of my failure every time I speak with her. True, she and my father are proud of me, proud of the rank I've attained...but that does not count for as much with them as three or four children would."

Somehow she managed to keep her voice steady. "So why the delay?"

The copper eyes didn't waver. "I had never found the right mate."

Lira was saved from making a reply by the arrival of Jerem, who held a long, slender object that she supposed was a fishing pole in each hand. The boy looked a little discomfited by her presence, but then he straightened and asked, "Did you want to come fishing, too?"

"No," she said immediately. Even after a few days here, she wasn't entirely comfortable in Jerem's presence. He had so much energy, and she wasn't sure how she should behave around him. But she didn't want to sound rude, so she added, "Maybe next time. I think you'll have your hands full just teaching Rast. There aren't any fish on his world."

"There aren't?" Jerem asked, eyes lighting up the way they always did whenever the conversation turned to life on other planets.

"No," said Rast, and over the top of the boy's head his eyes met Lira's for just a few seconds, as if acknowledging her diversion. "But we have these creatures that dwell in the pools in the caves, called *dalgesh*, that make good eating..."

And the two of them moved off, leaving her there to watch them as they disappeared into the trees, Rast's smooth baritone a counterpoint to Jerem's treble. For a minute she wished she'd gone along with them. But no, that was silly. She should stay here, in case Miala made a breakthrough and needed to talk to her.

Lira sighed, and was about to go back into the *Chinook* when she saw the other woman walking toward her. "You've got something?"

"Sorry to get your hopes up." Miala paused a few feet away and shook her head. "I just needed a break. Some fresh air to get my brain together."

Whether Lira was able to keep the disappointment out of her voice was anyone's guess. "It's not going well?"

"Define 'going well.' I think I'm starting to see a ray of light, but it's tough. I keep darting in and taking stabs at it, but then I have to dance back out of the way so I don't give myself away. It's exhausting."

"I'm sorry."

"Don't be. This is the best challenge I've had for a long time. I was starting to worry that too much domesticity was dulling my brain cells."

Miala's tone was rueful, but she didn't look all that concerned. Not sure of the best way to ask the question, Lira began, "And it doesn't bother you? That is—"

"You mean, does it bother me, one of the galaxy's best hackers, to be sitting here in the middle of nowhere with a boy whose middle name is Trouble and a teething infant and a retired mercenary?" The smile that lit up Miala's face turned her from strikingly pretty to downright beautiful. "I wouldn't trade it for anything."

"Oh." Even to her, Lira's response sounded flat.

"I don't know why you're surprised. I've had enough excitement to last me a long, long time. Besides, I still get enough clients to keep me occupied. It's fine."

Her words reminded Lira that there had never been any mention of payment for Miala's hacking services... never mind camping out on her property for days on end. "About that—I suppose you can help me access my savings without anyone knowing—"

"Please. I don't need your money. Really. The challenge is payment enough." She reached up underneath her long red ponytail to rub the back of her neck. "Although I'd really like it if I could make a dent in the damn thing. This hydra code is a bitch. I'm going to be really annoyed if I actually find my way through it, only to discover that the only thing this Stacian admiral is hiding is a mistress on Bathsheva or something."

Lira couldn't help but chuckle. "I'm guessing it's a little bit more than that."

"You're probably right." For a minute the hacker stared off in the distance, toward the trees that bordered her property. Then she asked, "Boys off fishing?"

"Yes."

"See, *I* think I should be paying you two for babysitting services." Her smile faded, though, and she gave Lira a sober look. "Mind if I give you a little piece of advice?"

Probably. But Lira shrugged and said, "What about?"

At first Miala was silent. With a lift of her shoulders,

as if inwardly dismissing her own qualms, she said, "You probably guessed that at first I was less than thrilled to have a Stacian here."

"I sort of gathered that."

Another smile. "And I'm guessing Jerem's already filled you in on the gory details as to why, so I won't bother with that, either. And anyway, I was wrong in my reaction to Rast. He's a good man."

Not sure where exactly Miala was going with all this, Lira could only nod uncertainly and wait.

Despite that wan encouragement, the other woman went on, "And I've seen how he looks at you...and how you look at him sometimes, when you think no one is watching. It's probably none of my business, but this dance you're doing around each other...you might want to reconsider whether it's really working for you."

Lira found her voice. "You're right. It is none of your business."

Surprisingly, Miala didn't seem offended. "All right, then—I'll finish my piece and get back to work. I've just got this to say: It's a big, cold galaxy out there, Lira. If you have a chance for a little warmth, then I think you should take it."

And with that Miala turned and strode back toward the house, just as the first big drops of rain began to fall. But Lira didn't bother to move, and only stood there as the downpour soaked her hair, her clothing, bringing it with it the sharp scent of damp earth and wet grass.

Warmth. Perhaps that wasn't such a bad idea.

They'd caught a fine string of some silvery fish that Jerem called "trout" by the time the rain began to fall. Jerem was all for staying on—"they bite better when it rains!"—but Rast judged their catch to be more than sufficient for five people.

"Besides," he added, as they gathered up their tackle, "I don't think your parents would be too happy with me if I kept you out here in the rain."

Jerem's expression was an odd mixture of mutiny and resignation. "Like they'd even notice. Mom's busy on her computers, and there's the baby, and—" He broke off. "Anyway, I don't think it's a big deal."

So Jerem was less than thrilled with having a new sister. Well, that wasn't so out of the ordinary, especially since he'd been the only child for so long. Carefully, Rast said, "Yes, but I did say we would try to bring back something for dinner, and your parents need time to prep the meal. So we wouldn't have been able to stay out here all that much longer anyway."

This comment seemed to meet with a better reception. At least the boy appeared to consider Rast's words, then nodded without speaking and picked up the tackle box in a silence that was uncharacteristic for him. They made their way back through the woods, moving more quickly than on their journey out. Rast wouldn't say the rain was exactly unpleasant—the novel sensation of water cascading from the sky was enough to make it interesting, if nothing else—but he could feel his clothing getting soaked and knew he would have to change once he dropped off the fish at the Thorn homestead.

As expected, Miala was nowhere in sight, but Thorn accepted the string of fish with his normal taciturnity, said, "Get upstairs and change, Jerem," then turned back to the knives he was sharpening.

Rast didn't know much about fish, but he guessed those particular blades were intended for something a little more sinister than gutting a trout. Still, he knew better than to inquire, and only said, as he always did, "Need any help?", to which Thorn only shook his head, as *he* always did.

Ritual satisfied, Rast headed back out to the *Chinook*, thus completing the soaking that had begun on his return trip to the Thorn homestead. Once inside the ship, he paused, gave the sodden masses of hair down his back a couple of squeezes in an attempt to avoid dripping water all the way back to his cabin, then pushed grimly on. While novel, rain definitely had its drawbacks.

He'd only taken a few steps when he saw Lira emerge from the bathroom, a towel wrapped around her midsection. Her own hair was damp as well, although not dripping. She stopped, staring at him, as he gazed back at her, taking in the long slim legs and the graceful curve of her throat, the dark valley between her breasts. Yes, he had seen her naked, but something about her current half-nude state was almost more enticing, and heat spread through him at once, banishing the chill of his rain-soaked clothing. This time, he knew he had no chance of forcing back the arousal that stiffened him, made him want to reach out and push her down to the thin synthetic carpet of the corridor, plunge inside her, share some of her warmth.

Say something, you fool! his mind shouted at him, but he found he could say nothing, but only remain there as if he had somehow been glued to that spot. So much of his energy the past few days had been taken up in trying desperately to conceal his desire for her, to make sure matters remained friendly and neutral between the two of them, that for once he found himself completely at a loss.

Then, unbelievably, she smiled at him and looked over her shoulder at the door to his cabin, then said, "I think your bed is bigger than mine."

───────

She hadn't planned it this way. But the way he had looked at her as she stood there in the *Chinook's* narrow little corridor sent a wave of desire through her so strong that she knew she couldn't fight it anymore. What had Miala said? *A chance for a little warmth*?

This was more like raging supernova heat, but she could live with that.

His damp garments fell one by one to the cabin floor, and her towel followed. Naked, they dropped onto the bed, Rast pulling Lira on top of him, his hands

—almost shockingly cold against her warm flesh—moving over her breasts. A moan bubbled its way up her throat, and she arched her back, pushing against him, needing his touch, needing to feel that spark within her again. To feel alive.

Yes, she realized she'd never felt so alive as she did within his embrace.

He slid one hand down her body, reaching between her legs, stroking her, no doubt feeling how ready she already was. And then, with a strength that still shocked her, he lifted her up, moved her forward, lowering her onto his face so he could taste her again, make love to her with his tongue.

Her moans turned into outright cries, but that was all right—no one could possibly hear her through the *Chinook's* walls, built to withstand both the vacuum of space and the infinite pressures of subspace. Thank God that this pretentious cabin's bed had a headboard she could hang onto, to give her something to prevent her from collapsing altogether as the orgasm flared through her. And, being Rast, he wasn't done there, wouldn't be satisfied until she climaxed again, and again...and then she had no choice but to loose her grip on the headboard, to fall down on the silk sheets next to him, mouths finding one another, body pressed to body as he slipped inside her, filling her with his heat and his need as she clung to him, knowing she was lost, and knowing there wasn't a damn thing she could do about it.

A long time later...or possibly only five standard

minutes...she opened her eyes and announced to the ceiling, "I think I'm going to need another shower."

Rast chuckled. Even that slight movement was enough to send the fever-heat racing across her flesh, but she knew she didn't dare reach out for him again. It had to be close to dinnertime, and they both needed to get cleaned up. It was going to be difficult enough to face Miala and Eryk Thorn as it was. She knew she couldn't possibly walk into that house in her current condition, stinking of sex.

"I don't suppose we'd both fit in there...?"

"You know very well we won't. I don't know how you fit in there on your own, frankly. Do you bend space to do it?" She propped herself up on one elbow, gazing down into his face, taking in the high cheekbones and the gleaming copper eyes with their frame of sooty lashes.

"Mmm...possibly. Should I keep the door open so you can watch?"

"Very funny." She shook her head, then added, "If you really want a tandem shower sometime, then we should try the Eridani Majesty on Callia. The bathrooms there are bigger than my entire cabin was on the *Valiant*."

Strange how she could mention the *Valiant* with hardly an inner pang, as if it had inhabited a part of her life long gone. She supposed it was, even though only a few standard months had passed since her dismissal from the GDF. Being a ship's captain had been her sole desire for so long that she'd subjugated everything else to that ambition—and now she was beginning to realize it had been a hollow one. Stars on her collar hadn't kept her warm at night, but she had a feeling Rast would do an excellent job of it.

"We will," he said firmly. "Once we get all this straightened out, and bring the perpetrators to justice, I think we will have earned a long vacation." His gaze sharpened, and he sat up then, all glorious muscle and gleaming golden skin. "That is, if you wish to take one with me."

She didn't hesitate. "I think that sounds like a wonderful idea. And since Callia's an Eridani colony, no one's going to look twice at a Gaian and a Stacian together." Rast lifted an eyebrow, and she amended, "Okay, they'll look twice. But they won't do anything about it."

"Probably not. So do you want to shower first, or should I?"

"You go ahead. I just need a quick rinse-off, since I already took a real shower."

"Done."

He rose from the bed, and she was rewarded with a good, long look at his well-muscled backside and thighs before he went out the door and into the hall-way. A few seconds later, she heard the water come on.

Maybe it was stupid of her to feel so contented, so relaxed. By coming to him willingly this time, she'd taken a huge leap of faith. True, sex wasn't necessarily any kind of commitment. Billions of casual liaisons were enough testament to that notion. Somehow, though, she knew from the way Rast looked at her that he wasn't interested in a quick lay, a scratching of the biological itch, as it were. No, it seemed pretty obvious to her that he wanted a lot more than that.

That in itself should have been more than a little terrifying. To her knowledge, no Gaian had ever willingly entered a relationship with a Stacian...or vice versa. She guessed that in the Iradian brothels there were Gaian women who would lie with Stacians, if enough coin changed hands, but that sort of transaction bore no resemblance to what she shared with Rast sen Drenthan.

Miala had said, *He's a good man*, and within her Lira knew that to be true. She'd fought against the realization, not wanting to acknowledge that someone who was an enemy of her people could be, in his own way, far more trustworthy and honorable than most of the Gaians she'd met. No way of knowing what the future held for them...but it was a big galaxy. Once they got this puzzle sorted out, maybe they could simply disappear. She had very little holding her back. Family? It was a big deal for Stacians, but her own mother had made it abundantly clear that Lira was a disgrace. And she hadn't seen her brother Liam or her sister Janna for more than five years. If she left for good, she wondered if they would even miss her.

Getting a little ahead of yourself, aren't you? she thought, and grinned. Next thing she knew, she'd have herself married off to Rast and settled down on some colony somewhere, with a couple of kids just to round things out. Never mind that she'd never even considered having children, knowing it wasn't an option for a career captain in the GDF. It would have been up to

Janna to carry on the family name, since Liam certainly didn't have any inclinations in that area.

"You're a million miles away," said Rast as he came back into the room, one towel around his waist, another one in his hand as he blotted the dreadlocked masses of hair falling over his shoulder. "Let me guess—the penthouse of the Eridani Major?"

"Yes, that." She had no intention of confessing what she'd really been thinking about. Children? It was crazy.

Besides, she had no idea whether Stacians and Gaians could even crossbreed.

"I'm looking forward to it." He came over to the bed and bent down and kissed her gently, but on the forehead, a soft touch of lips to flesh far more tender than she could have ever imagined coming from such a fierce-looking being. "But in the meantime, we should probably eat something. I'm hoping those trout I caught will look a little more appetizing once they're cooked."

"I would imagine," she replied, taking care to keep her tone light. Despite everything they had just shared, she still wasn't sure how much of herself she could reveal to him. "Not that I would know firsthand, since it will be my first time tasting trout as well."

"I look forward to sharing a new experience with you," he said, and from the gleam in his eyes she guessed he was thinking about a lot more than fish.

She knew she was.

Somehow she managed to repress the flush of heat that went through her as he gazed down at her, forced herself to climb out from beneath the sheets and move past him so she could take her own shower.

It was more than a little frightening to contemplate the effect he seemed to have on her.

Thorn guessed at once, Rast knew. Not that the Gaian did anything except raise one eyebrow the barest fraction of a centimeter before handing over their packets of food, but somehow that was enough. What he made of the situation, Rast couldn't quite decipher. Not that it was any of Thorn's business whether Rast and Lira were sleeping together, of course. But he supposed a man who was as successful a mercenary and assassin as Thorn had been—before he went into semi-retirement—would have some pretty good instincts about behavior, whether human, Stacian, or otherwise.

Of Miala there was no sign; she must be still toiling away upstairs at her computers. Rast felt a little pang at that image, because he thought a woman with a baby that young should be spending more time with her child. Or maybe she was. He hadn't been in her office. For all he knew, it was next door to the nursery, or perhaps she actually kept the baby in the room with her as she worked.

He said nothing, though, except the usual "thank you" as Thorn gave him the food, a phrase Lira echoed as Jerem handed her several additional packets, probably bread and vegetables. It bothered Rast a little to be taking so much from them—even if he had assisted in catching the fish—with no mention of payment. Possibly Lira had worked something out with Miala, but if such an arrangement had been made, she hadn't mentioned it.

They hurried back out to the ship—"dodging raindrops," Lira had called it—and went inside, then shut the door behind them. He resisted the urge to shake the water from his hair, guessing that it would only spray everywhere, and instead set the food down on the table before going to the bathroom to fetch one of the towels he'd used earlier. While in there he also collected one for Lira, who was looking more than a little damp.

She took it from him without comment when he returned to the main cabin, squeezing the wet out of her long hair, then setting the towel aside so she could attend to their food. The aroma that drifted up from the open food packets was unlike anything he had ever smelled before, but he decided he liked it. His stomach growled, and Lira grinned.

"Fishing's hungry work, I guess." She pushed a plate toward him and sat down.

He took his seat next to her, falling into a pattern that felt as if he had been doing it all his days, instead of for less than a standard week. They ate in silence for a few minutes, a silence that could have been awkward but somehow wasn't. Once again he thought of how much he desired her. No, it was more than that. True, her flesh was delectable, but he enjoyed just as much these quiet times with her, these moments when they could simply be together.

And perhaps it was wishful thinking on his part, but he thought with their lovemaking this evening they had somehow turned a corner, that Lira had finally acknowledged the connection between the two of them. What it meant for their future, he didn't know yet. At least now, however, he thought they might actually *have* a future.

"So did Jerem teach you all the ins and outs of fishing?" Lira asked, pausing to take a drink of water. The ship's wine cooler only held about ten bottles, so they had decided to pace themselves.

"I'm sure he thought so," Rast replied. The boy had a great deal more enthusiasm than skill, and probably had scared off far more fish than they actually caught. "It mostly involves a good deal of patience, which, as we both know, is not one of the boy's best qualities."

"True." She shook her head slightly. "He certainly seems to have glommed on to you."

"He's a good boy. I can see how he'd get bored out here, with only his family and no one else his age to run and play with. I suspect the only reason he doesn't get into more trouble is that his father would not tolerate it."

Not that she'd really thought about it that way, but she guessed Rast was right. He seemed to instinctively know the best way to approach the boy...or maybe it was simply because he had spent so much time around children, given all those numerous nieces and nephews.

She opened her mouth to reply, but was stopped by a smart rapping on the door to the ship. Normally they weren't disturbed out here, which meant—

Rast got up at once, and went to the door and cycled the lock. Eryk Thorn himself stood out there, rain sluicing through his short-cropped hair and running down his neck. "She wants you to come inside. She thinks she's gotten it."

CHAPTER ELEVEN

THERE WAS BARELY ENOUGH ROOM IN MIALA'S CRAMPED office for both Lira and Rast to squeeze in. The hacker sat in front of the bank of screens, fingers tapping away so quickly they were a pale blur against the dark gray keyboard, and she did not look up when they entered.

"Don't you even try it, you little bastard," she muttered, and once again her fingers danced over the keyboard.

Lira cleared her throat. "Um...Thorn said you had something?"

"Yep. I have to keep working at it, though—it's like a wormhole that keeps wanting to collapse while you're in it. Anyway, I got in far enough that I was able to see what your Admiral sen Trannick was so keen on keeping hidden. Looks like he's had huge amounts of cash funneled into a bunch of different accounts, some shell corporations, anything to keep too much of it from showing up in one place. No huge surprise, since that's pretty much SOP for anyone who's trying to hide large amounts of money." She pounded in a few more commands on the keyboard.

Figuring she might as well take advantage of the break in the other woman's speech, Lira said, "That's not all that surprising, though, is it? I mean, we all sort of figured he was getting a payout somehow."

"Oh, I know." This time Miala took the briefest of pauses to sip from a glass of water on the side table within arm's reach before continuing, "It's not the money that's the kicker. It's where it's coming from."

"And where is that?" Rast inquired, speaking for the first time. Since there wasn't much available space in the chamber, he had positioned himself within the doorway, half in and half out of Miala's office.

"Eridani," she replied simply.

At that Lira looked back over her shoulder at Rast, whose own expression showed something of the shock that had rippled through her at Miala's revelation. Eridani? What in the galaxy were the Eridanis up to? They were all about peace and cooperation and mutual beneficial coexistence. She couldn't begin to understand why they would be funding sen Trannick, apparently to destroy the brittle détente that currently existed between the Gaian and the Stacian governments.

"You're sure?" Lira asked at last, after she realized Rast was waiting for her to speak.

"Positive. Oh, yes, it's coming from accounts that have been triple and quadruple masked, but once I got past the hydra it was simple enough to unlock the algorithms that were concealing those accounts. Still haven't gotten it tracked down to a specific individual or organization, but that's only a matter of time. Even so, it's pretty obvious—if you know what you're looking for —where the money is coming from."

"Well, shit," Lira said, and Rast nodded grimly.

"This could...this could be a great blow to galactic peace, were it to be made public," he said. "We absolutely cannot do or say anything until we know for sure."

Although she still faced forward, Miala gave a lift of her shoulders that was clearly intended for them. "You're probably right. So what do you want me to do? Give it up?"

"No," Rast said, and although his tone was quiet enough, something about the edge to his voice made Lira look over at him sharply. "I am not saying that at all. Can you give us what information you have so far?"

"Sure thing. Either of you have a handheld? Give me the code, and I'll send it over."

Lira reached down to pull the device off her belt— and the sky outside their window was splashed with fire, painting the dim little room in angry shades of orange and carmine.

What the *hell*—

From below Eryk Thorn's voice came to them. "Ship! Take defensive positions!"

At once Rast whirled and pounded down the stairs, obviously intending to help the mercenary mount whatever defense was necessary.

Miala bolted up from her seat. "Jerem—Leah—"

"Go to the baby," Lira said at once. "I'll make sure Jerem is all right."

The hacker nodded, white-faced, and bolted out of the room, even as the unmistakable sound of pulse fire came from outside, clearly aimed at the front entrance.

Good thing they don't know the Thorn family hangs out in the kitchen, Lira thought as she raced downstairs, cursing herself for leaving her sidearm back on the *Chinook*. Then again, she hadn't thought she would need it. Not here...not in this haven Eryk Thorn had created for his wife and children.

Not such a haven anymore.

Smoke was already drifting down the hallway, acrid, catching at the back of her throat. She burst into the kitchen, saw Rast holding a deadly-looking pulse rifle, Thorn with a pistol in one hand. Without speaking, he reached into a drawer and tossed her the mate to the gun he held. She caught it.

Guess I didn't have to worry about not bringing my gun with me...

Jerem was tucked away into a corner behind the breakfast table. Surprisingly, he didn't look frightened at all. Instead, he had almost an expectant expression on his face, as if he were simply waiting for his father to go into action so he could watch the show.

"Six of them," Thorn said briefly. She noted a brief flash from the screen of a handheld before he slipped it back into a pocket. Surveillance feed, most likely. "Came in a Jecca-class ship, so I'm guessing they're Bathshevan mercs." A sideways glance from those dark eyes, so hard they looked like chips of obsidian. "I'd say you didn't find all the trackers on your ship, except I did a sweep of it myself and I know there's nothing there."

"You did a—" She broke off, realizing it was stupid to argue with him over such a petty invasion of privacy, especially now, with armed invaders breaking the peace of the Thorn homestead. "So what next?"

An incongruous grin, and for the first time she caught a glimpse of what Miala must see in the man. He did have a very good smile. "Let's see how many of them are left."

"Left?" Rast inquired, with a quick, darting glance down the hallway, where the smoke was getting thicker.

"No worries," Thorn said, and pushed a button on his handheld.

Lira heard an odd gushing noise. Almost at once the smoke began to lessen, and she realized Thorn must have installed some sort of fire retardant mechanism in the house.

"They're going to have a tough time getting to the front door," he added.

His words might have been a signal. From outside came a series of small explosions. The grounds surrounding the house must have been rigged.

"But we walked across that hundreds of times—" she began.

"Yes, 'cause I hadn't armed the defenses. Soon as the alarm went off on my handheld, I activated everything. One of 'em might be able to get through. Maybe."

Sure enough, another series of explosions shook the house. Lira wondered how Miala was doing, stuck upstairs with the baby. Then again, she must know how well-protected the house was, so maybe she was hunkering down to wait it out.

A pulse blast echoed down the corridor. Apparently at least one of the attackers had made it through the mine field, and was now attempting to shoot his way through the back door.

"Wait here," Thorn said, and his gaze flickered past Lira to his son, who sat in the corner, dark eyes shining.

"I've got it," she said, moving closer to the boy.

The mercenary nodded, jerked his chin at Rast, and the two of them headed down the hallway. Even though of course she wanted the intruders stopped, she couldn't help but feel a hint of pity for whoever was out there, firing away at the innocuous-looking door, which she guessed was only ordinary on the outside. She had a feeling they weren't expecting to run into one of the galaxy's most notorious guns-for-hire.

"I wish I could see," said Jerem in plaintive tones, and Lira smiled even as she shook her head.

"I doubt your father wants you in the middle of a firefight. We'd better wait back here while they handle it."

"O-kay," the boy replied, looking dejected. "I never get to do *anything* fun."

Any desire to laugh was quickly smothered by the sound of more pulse bolts coming down the hallway. Despite the knowledge that Eryk Thorn and Rast sen Drenthan could probably handle just about anything thrown at them, Lira still felt her throat grow tight with worry. What if there were more of them out there?

What if a stray bolt somehow hit Rast? She'd just begun to acknowledge what he meant to her. She couldn't lose him now. Not like this.

Her hand shook slightly as she gripped the pistol, knowing she would have to shoot if someone managed to make it past the two men. Killing was still something she hadn't quite come to terms with, especially when she had to do it on such a personal level...and in front of Jerem. It felt different when it was one ship shooting at another. You couldn't see the life drain away from someone when you blasted a hole in the side of their ship, even if the end result might be the same.

Relief coursed through her as Rast and Eryk Thorn returned to the hallway, dragging a limp form between them. The unconscious man—or maybe he was dead—wore the dark jumpsuit and body armor of a Bathshevan mercenary, and when Thorn reached down to pull off the man's helmet, the merc's shaved, tattooed head was the final clinching evidence that these interlopers had come from that rough frontier world.

Without speaking, Thorn squatted down and searched the man with brutal efficiency, spilling out his pockets and the pack he wore on his back. With the same economy of movement he rifled through what he found, which wasn't much. Spare battery packs, small wrapped squares of what were probably field rations, a spare laser scope. Nothing, however, that could help to show who he was or where he came from: no handheld, no identification. Which, Lira guessed, was par for the course. Not much use in being an anonymous mercenary force if you carried your pilot's license with you.

Through all this Rast had stood by silently, allowing Thorn to do his work. Although she somehow knew these men had come for her and Rast, still, this was Eryk Thorn's home they had invaded. It was his right to search the fallen mercenary.

Apparently done, Thorn got back to his feet. Never one to wear the most pleasant of expressions on his face, he now looked grimmer than ever, mouth a flat line, brows pulled together. He looked past Lira to his son, saying, "Jerem, go upstairs and tell your mother to come down here. But you stay up there. Hear me?"

"But Dad—"

"Are you defying me?"

"No, Dad." Looking sulky as only a ten-year-old boy could, Jerem stomped past Lira. As he approached the fire door, it retracted, allowing him to continue out into the corridor. A series of heavy thuds seemed to signal his annoyed progress up the stairs.

Thorn waited a few seconds, then said, "I didn't want to say this in front of him. For whatever reason, he's taken a liking to you two. But this is over. I want you out of here. Now."

Lira opened her mouth to protest, and shut it again. What could she say, really? She and Rast had somehow drawn the mercenaries here, threatening the safety of Eryk Thorn's family. He might not have cared if it had only been him, but when he had a wife and a son and a baby daughter to protect—

Like her, Rast seemed to understand, giving a grim

nod before replying, "We'll have to check on our ship, make sure the mercs didn't damage it somehow, but otherwise we'll be away as soon as we can."

Miala appeared then, baby tucked up against one shoulder. "What's this about being away?"

"I told our guests that it was time for them to go."

Her brows drew together. "Without talking to me first?"

"The safety of my family is non-negotiable."

Obviously flummoxed, Miala glanced away from her husband and over at Rast briefly before allowing her gaze to settle on Lira. "I'm really sorry about this—"

"It's all right," Lira broke in. "He's right. We've endangered your family, and that was never our intention. But if you could give me that data—"

"Absolutely." She shifted the baby to her other shoulder; little Leah let out a small, contented burp, and then seemed to go right back to sleep.

"I'll go look at the ship while you do that," Rast said.

"And I'll come with you," Thorn said unexpectedly. "Just in case any of our friends are hanging back at their ship."

A nod from Rast, seeming to indicate his agreement with this idea, and then both men went out the back door, leaving Lira and Miala alone in the kitchen.

"Well, come on upstairs," Miala said, after an awkward pause.

Since there didn't seem to be anything left to do, Lira followed the other woman up to her office, where Miala pulled up the necessary data and beamed it to Lira's handheld. "No time to encrypt it," Miala said. "So make sure you sleep with this thing under your pillow, okay?"

"Okay."

At that moment Jerem's curly dark head peered around the doorsill. "What's going on?"

Miala didn't look up from her computer. "I'm getting Lira the information she needs so they can go."

"Go?" Jerem demanded. "Why?"

Surprising herself, Lira jumped in, as if to keep Miala from having to explain that Jerem's father had basically kicked their two visitors out of the house. "Your mother found the information we needed, so it's time for us to go."

Jerem, however, seemed to see right through her stratagem, and frowned. "No, you're going because those mercs showed up and my dad is pissed off about it."

Out of the mouths of babes... Lira cast a helpless look at Miala, who said briskly, "Jerem, you should know better than to talk about things you don't know anything about. Go back to your room."

"What, I don't even get to say goodbye to Rast?"

"*Now.*"

His lower lip pushed out mutinously, but he heaved an exaggerated sigh and went away, his footsteps heavy across the wooden floors.

Miala sighed. "Kids. I think it's even tougher when they're just too darn smart for their own good."

Not having much frame of reference, Lira could only lift her shoulders before saying, "I should go downstairs and see what Rast found out about the ship."

"Sure. I'm going to put Leah to bed, since she's finally conked out, and then I'll be down, too."

There wasn't much else to say. Lira hurried down the stairs to find both Thorn and Rast in the kitchen. Although Rast did not look exactly thrilled with life at the moment, she didn't see anything in his expression to indicate that the *Chinook* wasn't ready to head out.

"Everything okay?" she inquired.

He nodded. "Looks like it. The explosions didn't reach that part of the property, and it looks as if the mercs were more interested in getting at us than at the ship, so we're good to go."

Good to go. At that moment it came to her full force that they were about to leave. It was only then that she realized how much she'd come to appreciate this little haven of peace and quiet, this spot that the darker sides of the galaxy hadn't seemed to touch.

Well, not until tonight, anyway.

She began, "I don't know how to thank you—" but Miala waved a hand.

"It's all right. If nothing else, cleaning up the yard will give Thorn and Jerem something to do for the next few days, keep them out of my hair."

Despite herself, Lira couldn't help smiling. "Still…"

Eryk Thorn cut in, "You should get moving. We're isolated here, but not so isolated that the scanners in Christchurch might not have picked up on those explosions. I can head them off, but it's going to be tougher if

I've got a Stacian hanging around my property in a stolen Sirocco-class ship."

"Got it." If Rast was annoyed by Thorn's words, he didn't show it. "We're ready. Aren't we, Lira?"

No protests could delay their leave-taking any longer, so she nodded. "Thanks again. For everything. And we'll find some way to get to word to you once we get to the bottom of this."

"You'd better." Miala gave Lira a mock-fierce glare. "I hate unsolved mysteries."

After that there was nothing left to do. She went to Rast then, glad she could have him walk next to her as they left the house. They picked their way across what was left of the yard and went to the *Chinook*. The door stood open, awaiting their return.

At the bottom of the gangplank, Rast paused and stared down at her. "You okay?"

"I'm fine," she lied. "Let's get out of here."

And as they entered the ship, she wondered if she would ever stand on Gaia's surface again.

Although she piloted the ship with the same effortless grace she'd always shown while working its controls, Rast could tell she was upset. Funny how her small expressions, the slightest furrow of her brow, the way she looked away from him out the viewscreen, the hard line of her jaw, were as clear to him now as if she had

just written the words "I am pissed off" across her forehead with glowing ink.

"You want to talk about it?" he asked.

"Not really. I just want to get us out of this godfor-
saken system."

So he waited as she brought them around the night
side of the planet, past its sole stony moon, and out
toward the farther reaches of the Gaian system where
the gas giants reigned. Her mouth tightened as they
passed the largest planet, and he recalled that it was on
one of that planet's moons where she had grown up,
where she had sought refuge after being discharged
from the GDF.

Apparently that refuge hadn't been a very
effective one.

"And now?" he inquired softly, once they were very
nearly to the open space where it would be safe for
them to make the subspace jump.

"I don't know," she admitted. "Straight on to
Eridani?"

He'd thought of that, but no point in diving straight
into the fire. "Probably not wise. We need to analyze the
data Miala gave us first, then plan from there. If forces in
the Eridani government are somehow behind all this, it
would not do to march in with guns blazing. The Eridani
mind is subtle." He grimaced, thinking of how often the
soft-voiced Eridanis got their way at the negotiating table.
"I will admit that I am not the best-suited for this sort of
confrontation. I was trained for action, not stealth."

A wry smile twisted her full lips. "You and me both,

Rast. I'm not saying I'm the 'shoot first, ask questions later' type, but I'm—I *was*—a ship's captain, not a diplomat or a spy. Right now, I'll plot us a course for the dead space around the Charybdis Shoals. No one should disturb us there while we try to figure out what to do next." She returned her attention to the instruments before her, fingers flying as she programmed in the necessary coordinates.

That made sense. What they needed was some breathing room. And he thought then that one of the things he loved about her was her ability to look at herself dispassionately, with very little self-deception or puffery. She knew who she was, what she was good at.

That thought led to some quite delectable things that she was very good at, and he smiled.

"What's so funny?"

"It's not so much that I'm amused," he told her, reaching down and taking her by the hand, raising her from her seat so he could pull her against him. "I was recalling a pleasant memory."

That line between her brows smoothed itself away, and she stared up at him, one eyebrow raised. A faint sweet scent drifted from her hair, and his loins tightened, heat rushing through him at the memory of those silken locks brushing against his cheeks, his chest.

"Which memory is that?" she inquired, but he could tell from a certain gleam in her eyes that she knew very well what he had been thinking about.

"The one we're about to make," he replied, and wrapped his arms around her, lifting her up, taking her back to the cabin, even as the the autopilot took them into subspace, away from Gaia's sensors. Away from everything.

He worried for a second or two that she might protest, but instead she burrowed herself into his neck, that lovely mouth of hers doing some astonishing things to his throat. A smack of his hand against the control to open the door, and then they were inside. He set her down gently, but only so he could pull off her jacket, then draw her open-collared shirt over her head. The curious garment Gaian women wore to support their breasts was still in the way, but she helped him with that, reaching behind her to undo its clasp, tossing it onto the cabin's sole chair. Then her breasts were bared to him, those wonders of smooth pale flesh, tipped with rosy-dark nipples.

It was too much for him to wait any longer, and he bent to take one into his mouth, to suckle her as she gasped and arched her back into him. She was not so far lost in the moment that she couldn't reach down and undo the belt he wore, which dropped to the metal floor with a thud, holstered pulse pistol and all. Her fingers worked hastily on the closures of his trousers, but even so she was still in control, deftly pulling them down, taking him into her hand, moving up and down his shaft.

His turn to gasp then, and with a growl he pushed her down on the bed, needing to taste her and feel her, to reassure himself that they were alive, that she was his. Her hand slipped away from him, but he ignored that for the moment, driven only by the desire to bury his face between her legs, to touch his tongue to the delicate nub there. She cried out as he licked her, but then he felt her shifting beneath him, moving so she could take him into her mouth as well, her lips closing around him, tongue gliding over the sensitive flesh at his tip.

All the blood in his body seemed to be drawn there, to the pulsing core of his being. He knew she could make him come so easily, but he didn't want that—not yet, anyway. So he turned his focus to pleasuring her, to circling that delectable little knot of flesh with his tongue, using quick, feathery movements, the way he knew she liked it. Her moans reverberated along the length of his shaft, and he felt it then, felt her spasm against him, tasted the flood of her juices, that nectar he desired more than anything.

And as she lay there, breasts rising and falling with her jagged breaths, he took her by her tiny waist, turned her over so he could run his hands over the smooth white flesh of her lovely backside, then pushed into her wetness and womanliness from there, hearing the sharp intake of her breath as he took her, pounded into her, felt her move with his rhythm, all the need and heat and desire in his body swirling down, down, to the sensation of her flesh tight against his, fitting better than any woman ever had and ever would.

He came then, a groan tearing itself from his throat, guttural and harsh. She clenched around him, pulsing, her own orgasm coming a second or two after his, her body still rocking with his, drawing every drop from him, until at last he pulled out and fell onto his side, still gasping, and she nuzzled up against him, her face buried in his flesh, her mouth showering kisses into his chest, his stomach.

In that moment he knew he loved her, loved her with a searing intensity that surprised even him. Women there had been before, but never one like this.

He wouldn't allow himself to reflect on the irony of finding the true mate of his heart among the enemies of his people. Instead, he only held her close, held her as her soft little rain of kisses died away, and she slept in his arms, quiet, trusting, her hair a spill of dark silk across her shoulders, caressing the curve of her breasts.

Dream well, heart of my heart. For I will be here to make sure you come to no harm.

CHAPTER TWELVE

THE CHARYBDIS SHOALS LAY APPROXIMATELY TEN thousand light-years away from the Gaian system, and since navigating the area was tricky—odd gravitational fluxes, clouds of gas, constantly morphing asteroid fields—most starships stayed far, far away. No planets here, nothing of any interest...unless you were looking for a quiet, dark corner to plot your next move.

Rast still slept in the cabin, tangled up in Gared Tomas's ridiculously expensive sheets, but Lira had wakened a few hours after they'd made love and quietly slid out of bed, making her way for the cockpit. No reason the ship's automated functions couldn't handle the drop out of subspace on their own, but because the Shoals could be treacherous, she wanted to make sure she was there at the moment of realspace arrival, just in case.

The *Chinook* didn't even shiver as the swirling colors of non-orthogonal space dropped away, and unfamiliar constellations formed around them. Through the viewscreen Lira saw ribbons of pale gas in shades of violet and blue, but they were strangely beautiful, and did not present any immediate threat. A quick scan of the instruments told her the region's problematic asteroid fields were millions of miles away. The course that had brought them here had deposited the ship in a backwater of the Shoals, a place where they could linger unmolested for some time, if necessary.

So she and Rast were safe...for now, at least. Why, then, did she feel so uneasy?

Well, the sensation could have something to do with having just uncovered what could be a vast, galaxy-wide conspiracy...but somehow Lira knew that wasn't the real problem. No, that was just a little closer to home...sleeping in the cabin down the hall, in point of fact.

Lying to herself was useless. No, she'd always prided herself on looking at things straight, even if she didn't always like what she saw. And what she saw now was a man who should have been her enemy, and somehow had become the exact opposite.

Lover? Yes. He coaxed reactions from her body that she'd never experienced with anyone else. It would be easy enough to say that's all it was—just a physical reaction. Chemistry. But that was a lie. Oh, not that they didn't set off sparks between them hot enough to start a forest fire. There was far more to it than that, though.

Hard to admit it, but she actually liked him, liked his sense of humor and the sound of his voice and his gentle patience with Jerem. And somehow all those qualities made the whole situation that much more difficult, because it was a lot easier to dismiss a relationship based purely on sex than one that involved respect, even admiration. Long ago she'd given up on believing she'd ever meet someone who made her feel this way. She'd convinced herself that it was all right, because all she really cared about was being captain of a ship in the GDF, making a difference. Love and romance, kindred spirits, all that? It was for someone else, not Lira Jannholm. A fling here and there, to burn off the biological back-pressure when necessary, but the notion of love, *real* love, was something she'd dismissed years ago.

What a mess.

She pinched the bridge of her nose between her thumb and forefinger, trying to stave off the headache that threatened to build there. Not enough sleep, especially after the insanity of the firefight at the Thorn homestead and their precipitous flight away from Gaia. What she needed to do was focus, to figure out their next move. She and Rast couldn't float out here forever, although at the moment the illusion of tranquility was more than a little seductive.

Somehow they'd have to try to track down whoever it was on Eridani that had suborned Admiral sen Trannick, find out why he'd been paid off in the first place. She had no idea how, though. As she'd told Rast, she was a pilot and a captain, not a spy or a hacker.

A hacker...

No use trying to get Miala Thorn's help—her exmerc of a husband had made it pretty clear that Lira and Rast would get a few warning shots across their bow if they attempted any further contact. However, she couldn't overlook Jackson Wyler as a resource. Maybe now that they knew the root of the treachery had its source on Eridani, he could do a little more to help them. After all, he traded in information...and the revelation that the Eridanis were apparently behind the plot could be worth a good deal.

Another thing Jackson could help them with was new identities. She'd scrubbed the *Chinook* pretty well, and so far they'd more or less stayed off the grid, but if their search for the truth involved any sort of contact with the Gaian or Eridani governments, she'd have to make sure their records were flawless. Probably they'd need to get retinal realignment and fingerprint transplants, too, just to be safe.

So she opened a subspace channel to New Chicago, to the comm coordinates Jackson had given her, and sent him a ping. She had to hope it wasn't too ungodly an hour in Michende—not that Jackson had ever paid all that much attention to diurnal patterns. He worked when the mood struck him, and if that was at 0400, then so be it. Just another reason he quit the Academy; he had never been able to maintain anything resembling a normal schedule.

Less than a minute went by before her ping was answered by a request to open a secure channel. She did so, entering the code Jackson sent her, and a second or two later his voice came over the comm unit. No video. Maybe he had been asleep.

"Miss me already?" he inquired.

Her mouth tightened. Just for once she'd like it if he took something seriously. "Sorry to disappoint you, Jackson, but actually I could use some more assistance."

"Really? Am I going to have to send you a bill?"

"I doubt it. I have some information I think you might be interested in."

"So my contact on Gaia worked out."

"More or less," Lira said, choosing her words with care, reminding herself that Jackson knew nothing of Miala Thorn's identity, save that she was located on Gaia. "But before we go any further, Rast and I are going to need some new documentation—"

"No problem," Jackson cut in, sounding almost gleeful. "I know a guy on Miris Prime whose work is so beautiful it would make you weep."

"I hope weeping won't be necessary, but thank you." She hesitated, not sure how many requests he'd be willing to handle at once. Still, they couldn't function properly if they had to keep looking over their shoulder at all times, wondering who or what was going to jump them next. "Also, while we were on Gaia, we were attacked by a group of Bathshevan mercenaries—"

"And lived to tell the tale?"

"Yes," she said, her tone curt. No way she could explain that the only reason they'd survived their encounter was because Eryk Thorn had been there to provide defense. "They didn't get the drop on us, luckily. However, it would really help if we knew who had hired them."

"That I can do." He was starting to sound happier than a kid who'd gotten a pony for Christmas. "Bathshevan security is notoriously sloppy. They're great at killing. Computers? Not so much." A pause, and then Jackson went on, "So that must be some information you're sitting on, if you're using it to bargain for all this other stuff."

"It is." Now it was her turn to hesitate. She knew the channel was secure, that Jackson had myriad ways of safeguarding all his transmissions, locking them down so hard he could give lessons to the GDF's security people. Even so, saying such a thing to a person light-years away felt odd, as if somehow, despite all Jackson's protocols and defenses, someone might manage to overhear what she was about to say. Her voice lowered, although she knew that was silly. It wasn't as if anyone was in the next room, eavesdropping on her. She pushed her loose hair back over her shoulder, drew in a breath, and said, "The money behind sen Trannick? We traced it to Eridani."

Dead silence, for one second, two, three... In fact, it stretched on so long that Lira began to wonder if the transmission had been cut off somehow.

Then Jackson said, "You're serious."

"Unfortunately, yes."

Another silence. "Shit."

That about sums it up. "Yes, Jackson, it's big. So big that frankly, I don't know what to do about it." Her head throbbed again, and she reached up to rub her brow, wondering if she was going to have to dig a pain-tab out of the first aid cabinet. "Right now I'm trying to do this one step at a time. If I stop to think about the big picture, I'm just going to freak myself out."

"You don't freak out over anything."

"Then this may be a first."

"Okay," he said, after another one of those pauses. "That's some serious information you handed over. I may have to think up more things to do for you just to even the score."

"That's not necessary. Just your contact on Miris Prime is enough for starters, and we'll worry about the Bathshevans after that."

"Sending it over now." Even across the light-years that separated them, Lira could practically feel the excitement coming off Jackson in waves. "I can't wait to start digging into this. Now that I have an origin point—"

"Sounds great," she said wearily. "If you have something new to pass on, let me know. We're going to head for Miris Prime immediately."

"Coordinates have been beamed over." He let out a small sigh, one that sounded almost concerned...for Jackson. "Be careful, all right?"

"I always am," she told him, and flipped the switch, ending the transmission.

Movement behind her made her turn around, and she saw Rast standing there, looking far grimmer than a man should who'd just had spectacular sex less than five hours ago. For a few seconds she wondered if he was angry at her for speaking to Jackson, but dismissed that notion as foolish. Then she realized that he held her toiletry bag in one hand, and she frowned.

"Do you want to tell me what that's about?" she inquired, with a jerk of her chin toward the bag. Somehow she doubted he was looking to borrow her deodorant.

Rast's mouth thinned. "I think I just discovered how the Bathshevans found us on Gaia."

He'd slept afterward, of course, drowned in a satisfied slumber, content, the woman he loved curled in his arms. But sometime later he'd awakened and discovered she wasn't there. At first he was concerned, although almost at once he reassured himself, realizing that she probably wanted to check on the ship, and so had slipped out without disturbing him. He'd lain there for a while, staring up at the ceiling, feeling the almost imperceptible motion of the ship beneath him, wondering if perhaps he should try to fall asleep again. For some reason that idea did not sound wise, so he'd begun picking over the day in his head, wondering how it was that the Bathshevans had tracked them down on Gaia, when Eryk Thorn himself said that he'd double-checked the *Chinook* for any trackers. The ship was clean.

So it had to have been something else that drew down the mercenaries. Somehow he and Lira had been tracked there, even though the ship had been swept. That meant it had to be something they carried on their persons. He'd pawed through the satchel that held his meager belongings, but found nothing suspicious.

Perhaps it would have been wiser to wait and take his suspicions to Lira, but surely she couldn't be upset by a quick check of her things. There wasn't much to see, anyway—one change of clothes, several changes of underthings, a bag that held small containers of cleansers and lotions, a tube of what he thought was lip color, another tube of some liquid apparently meant to darken her eyelashes, although they always looked dark and lush to him.

The lip color tube had an odd little dent at one end, possibly from being thrown carelessly into a bag or a pocket, but even so he thought it merited a second look. He tugged on the casing, finding it to be wedged on there more tightly than he had initially thought. In the end, though, the little metal tube was no match for a Stacian's strength, and he yanked it off—only to have small chip fall out, a chip that he knew had no business being hidden in a tube of cosmetics.

He picked it up, eyeing it narrowly, but he was no expert in electronics, let alone the minuscule devices employed by the less trustworthy of the galaxy's citizens. Best to show it to Lira, and see what she thought. He took the chip and the tube of lip color and dropped them back into the cosmetics bag, then went forward to the bridge.

She was speaking to someone as he approached. Jackson Wyler, from the sound of it, and although Rast would have been more than happy if she never had contact with her former lover again, he knew that Wyler possessed skills and talents that could help them along their road to discovering why the Eridanis were in bed with Admiral sen Trannick. The transmission ended as he approached, and so he only had the impression that she'd gotten Wyler to help them out once again.

When she turned to look back at him, Rast could see at once how weary she was, how shadows stained the fine skin beneath the clear blue eyes. But her back was straight enough as she turned around in her seat to more or less face him, then inquired as to why he was holding her bag of toiletries.

He told her, and added, "I don't recognize that chip, but maybe you do?"

She took the bag from him and pushed past the ruin of her lipstick without comment. The chip she brought up, held between one slender forefinger and her thumb. "Well, goddamn," she said after staring at it for a moment.

"Do you recognize it?"

"Miniaturized subspace tracker. Pretty sophisticated one, too, from the looks of it." An expression of disgust crossed her delicate features, and before he could say or do anything to stop her, she dropped it to the floor of the bridge and ground it to dust beneath the heel of her boot.

Frowning, Rast inquired, "Was that wise? We might have been able to discover who planted it on you if we'd inspected it more closely."

Her eyebrow lifted. "Are you an expert in that sort of thing?"

"Well, no, but—"

"Neither am I. And that goddamned thing was transmitting our coordinates as we sat here. Thank God I know where we're going next, so we can get out of here before anyone else shows up." She turned away from him and began entering commands into the shipboard computer, obviously lining them up for their next subspace hop.

Knowing it was useless to protest, Rast instead eased himself into the copilot's chair, waited for the moment when the ship shot forward and realspace melted around them, to be replaced by the shifting colors and patterns of subspace. It came within the minute; Lira hadn't been exaggerating when she said she knew where they were going.

"So what is our destination?" he asked.

"Miris Prime. Jackson has a contact there who can give us new identities. I'm not saying we won't still be a little conspicuous, but at least that way there's less chance of being tracked quickly."

Given this information, Rast could only nod. Miris Prime was a Gaian world, a planet that had been heavily industrialized because of its rich deposits of various useful ores. By all accounts it was a grim, gray place, but he had to remind himself that he and Lira were not going there to vacation, but for the all-important purpose of masking their identities.

She settled back in her seat, not exactly relaxed, but freed of some of her piloting responsibilities now that the ship was set on its course. Rast thought perhaps she was now ready for more questions.

"Who do you think put that tracking device in your belongings?"

A sigh, as she pushed her hair back behind her shoulders. Another good thing about her being freed of military service—those glorious silken locks were now allowed to fall loose, instead of being bound up in the tight little knot that the Gaian Defense Force's dress code apparently required.

Quietly, she said, "I can't know for sure, of course, but I suspect it was Gared Tomas."

The answer startled him, but on closer examination, Rast supposed the idea wasn't that far-fetched. "Keeping tabs on you, eh?"

"Most likely. Gared Tomas didn't trust his own mother, let alone some woman one of his lackeys picked up in a bar when he was trolling for a pilot." She gave a self-deprecating laugh and added, "I probably wouldn't have trusted me under those circumstances, either. Now that I think of it, I was being a little too trusting. I never considered that Tomas might put a tracker on me—after all, when I was on Iradia, I was easy enough to keep an eye on, and of course I spent a good deal of time directly in his company, flying him between his various bases."

Rast wasn't aware of any particular shift in his expression, but she must have seen something, because she shot him a sideways glance and said,

"And no, there was nothing personal between us."

"Did I say there was?"

"No, but you were thinking it." Something approaching a smile touched her mouth, and she stood, going to him and wrapping her arms around his waist, pushing herself close against him.

It was one of the first voluntary gestures of affection he'd seen from her, and his arms tightened around her, even as he noted the enticing musky scent of their love-making, along with a whiff of something that smelled like smoke, probably from the mercenaries' attack on the Thorn homestead. She felt right there, nestled in his embrace, even though she was such a tiny thing, really, her head not even reaching his chin. For all that, though, he could feel the steel-sharp strength of her, the force of will that had made her a captain at such a young age.

With her cheek still pressed against him, she said quietly, "He wanted me, but I said no, that I was his pilot and only that. There wasn't anything between us."

So those unpleasant visions of her sharing that cabin with Gared Tomas were only that—visions, foolish fancies, far from the truth. "I won't lie and say I'm not relieved."

A muffled laugh. "I'll have to watch out for that jealous streak of yours. No, Rast, there hasn't been anyone for quite a while. I was always focused on my career. What was the point in trying to make a connection with someone? The GDF frowns on its captains—especially the female ones—marrying and having families. That wasn't for me."

"And now?" he asked.

"Now?" She pulled away slightly and looked up at him, one eyebrow quirked. "I don't even know what tomorrow is going to bring, so I'm not going to start thinking about the long term for a while yet."

It would have been too much to expect her to say she would run off with him, start their own version of the Thorns' domestic bliss. Not that he even knew whether Stacians and Gaians could interbreed. Such a notion verged on blasphemy for one of his race, since they had been focused on preserving the purity of their bloodlines for millennia. It was the only way to ensure the future of the Stacian people, as their world made short work of those who were weak or genetically inferior. And now, for him to be considering mixing his blood with that of a Gaian woman? He did not want to think how his family members might react to such a proposition.

"At the moment, it's probably wise to not think too far ahead," he said, laying aside for the moment visions of having this woman by his side for the rest of his life. "But will you come back to bed now?"

She hesitated, and again he noted the weariness etched in her face.

"Only to sleep," he promised, although his body flickered with heat at the thought of taking her again. But he could tell she'd had enough for now. "As you said, we don't know what tomorrow will bring. How long until we reach Miris Prime?"

"Ten standard."

"Well, then," he said, and drew her away from the bridge, back to the cabin that had become theirs over the last few days. "Come and sleep, and leave tomorrow's worries for tomorrow."

CHAPTER THIRTEEN

SHE HADN'T THOUGHT IT WOULD FEEL SO GOOD TO SLEEP curled up against Rast's warm, solid body, to have his calm, regular breaths soothe her into a slumber so deep that she didn't dream, didn't do anything except lie there, as her weary muscles healed themselves and her mind sought its own healing. And when she woke, some seven standard hours later, it seemed the most natural thing in the world to turn to him, to run her fingers along the heavy muscles of his chest and arms, to reach down and take him into her hand, finding him hard and ready. They made love slowly, silently, and afterward took turns using the shower, scrubbing off the last traces of their encounter with the mercenaries and the doubt and worry that had come along with it, and making jokes about one day soon being able to climb into the shower together.

Some of her good humor evaporated when they

came out of subspace and into the Miris system. Like Gaia itself, the system was located far out on one of the galaxy's spiral arms, and the stars here were even more widely scattered than they were in the Gaian system. Miris itself was equally unprepossessing from orbit— dull gray in appearance due to the bands of perpetual cloud cover that wrapped themselves around the planet.

As with most approaches to Gaian Consortium worlds, she was contacted only a few seconds after beginning her approach to the coordinates Jackson had given her.

"Unidentified craft, identify yourself and provide your reason for coming to Miris Prime."

The voice was male, neither friendly nor hostile. She thought she detected a faint note of apathy in his tone. Good. Bored people tended to be sloppy.

"Miris Control, this is the *Chinook*. Sending registry information now." And thank God she'd cleaned up that data days earlier. A dedicated planetary security operative might be able to spot some inconsistencies in what she was transmitting down to Miris Prime, but she somehow doubted the man she spoke with now was anything close to that determined, or talented.

"Thank you, *Chinook*. You're cleared to land in either of the 'ports in Sector Three. Have a nice day."

The connection was closed, and Lira smiled and shook her head, rerouting to Sector Three—which, luckily, was close to where they'd been headed anyway.

"Tight security out here," Rast remarked, lowering himself into the copilot's seat for their final descent.

"I think the weather must get to people on this world. You'd think they'd be a little more alert, since the ore mined here is worth a great deal." She shrugged. "Then again, it's a little more difficult to steal several shiploads of duranium ore than it is to walk away with precious gems or priceless art."

"Is that what thieves are after these days?"

"So I've heard. Things that are difficult to synthesize are of course the most highly prized. Not that I know with any great certainty—after all, the captain of a starship generally isn't occupied with chasing after intergalactic jewel thieves."

"Ah," Rast said, which could have meant anything. Something in his gleaming copper eyes told her he was somehow amused by the idea of intergalactic jewel thieves. Maybe he was considering that as the next step in their careers, once they wrapped up this whole Eridani mess. She wouldn't quite put it past him.

They were now descending through Miris Prime's murky atmosphere, gray clouds swirling past the viewscreen. Somehow it felt instantly colder, although of course the temperature in the cabin was calibrated to be exactly the same twenty-two degrees Celsius no matter what the conditions outside might be. As they dropped even lower, rain began to spatter against the *Chinook*, hissing as it hit the still super-heated alloy.

"More rain," Rast said in resigned tones.

"What, I thought you Stacians prayed for the rain to

come again." She didn't bother to keep the grin off her face as she smiled at his obvious distress.

"So we do, but I think that's because those of us who don't go off-world don't realize how...inconvenient...it can be."

Judging by the information the ship's external sensors were relaying to her, that rain wasn't planning on stopping anytime soon, either. "Well, I guess we'll just have to hope that this contact—whoever he is—isn't too far from the 'port. And that Miris Prime has decent public transport."

Once they'd landed in the docking area designated for their use and had emerged from the *Chinook*, Lira realized she was going to be disappointed on both counts. The rain pounded down, heavier than anything she'd ever seen before, and although they both had coats they could wear to keep the worst of it off, neither of them had any headgear. Of course a ship based on Iradia wouldn't have anything so prosaic as an umbrella among its store of useful items, either, so she and Rast had to stumble through the downpour to a kiosk that looked as if it might supply information on public transportation. That did prove to be its function, but it appeared they were out of luck again, as the branch of the subterranean train that serviced this part of Sector Three was closed for repairs.

"What now?" Rast looked positively miserable, rain sluicing over his golden skin and soaking through the matted masses of hair down his back. Lira wondered how long it would take for all that hair to get dry again and decided she probably didn't want to know.

Then again, maybe the weather was a blessing in disguise. In his civilian garb, with the long black coat covering him to his chin, and in the muddy, muted light, Rast didn't look quite so overwhelmingly Stacian. It might take a second or even a third glance for someone to recognize him for what he was. Even so, Lira knew the less time they spent out in the open, the better.

She pulled out her handheld and squinted at the coordinates Jackson had sent her. They had a walk of approximately a kilometer ahead of them, something normally she would have just shrugged at. But now, in this weather—

"We walk," she said.

"I was afraid you were going to say that." But he only turned up the collar of his coat and followed her as she led him down the slick perma-crete sidewalk in the direction the handheld indicated.

At least the streets were more or less deserted. Lira had no idea whether this was because of the weather, or because Miris Prime was the sort of place whose inhabitants preferred to spend their time indoors. One would have thought that the shutdown of the public transportation system would send people out on foot, but long ago she'd given up trying to understand the idiosyncrasies of the various worlds she visited.

An aircar whooshed to a stop next to them. "Need a ride?" The unfamiliar voice had a slightly tinny quality; it must be coming from an external speaker on the 'car somewhere.

She paused, and could feel Rast bristling to attention next to her, his hand drifting down to where he carried his sidearm.

A laugh emerged from the speaker. "Jackson sent me. So get in, or do you want to walk a kilometer in this weather?"

Tilting her head up at Rast, she sent him a questioning look. He hesitated, then glanced from her to the 'car and back again. An odd movement of his hands, palms rolling skyward, which seemed to be the Stacian equivalent of a shrug.

Well, she could either allow herself to trust a little, or she could walk to their destination in the rain. Sooner or later she'd have to trust the stranger Jackson had sent them to see; it might as well be now.

Chin up, she approached the 'car, Rast only a pace behind her. The rear door slid open, and she got in, Rast following with some difficulty, as the vehicle was clearly designed to accommodate human frames, not Stacian.

As she settled herself into a seat and allowed the automated safety belt to lock itself on her, she stared forward to get a better look at the driver. From what she could tell, he was also Gaian, dark-haired, of Asian extraction. That surprised her a little; so many people from that part of the world had died during the Cloud that they now comprised a much smaller percentage of Gaia's population than they once had, and overall they preferred to stay on their home world, striving to rebuild their peoples and their cultures as best they could.

"Jackson didn't give me your name," she said coolly,

as if getting into cars driven by complete strangers was something she did on a regular basis.

"Hunter Chao. Nice to meet you, Captain Jannholm. Or are you not using the 'Captain' anymore?"

So Jackson had related something of her circumstances. She was not overly happy with that knowledge, but she supposed he'd needed to give this Hunter Chao some information to work with. Next to her, Rast stiffened, obviously expecting to be addressed next.

But Chao said nothing else, only piloted the sleek late-model car through the sodden streets to a blocky-looking building of four stories made of some grayish perma-crete material. He pulled into the building's underground parking area, which was a little more than half full, and pushed a button to open the 'car doors once they'd come to a stop.

Lira got out, and Rast did the same, clutching the doorframe and more or less levering himself out, a fearsome scowl on his face during the entire procedure. Somehow managing to smother a grin, she turned to Chao, who motioned for them to follow him.

They went to an elevator and got in, and he pressed the button for the fourth floor.

Their mysterious host still didn't seem overly inclined to conversation, so Lira followed suit and remained silent as the elevator rose to the building's top floor. Rast looked dubious at best, but at least he refrained from comment as they got out and followed Chao down a hallway as gray and unremarkable as the building itself, and through a door into his—apartment? Office?

It appeared to be a mixture of both, a huge space that took up what must have been one whole side of the structure. On the far wall was a compact kitchen area reminiscent of the one on board the *Chinook*, while not too far away there was a screened-off section that she guessed was the sleeping area. In the main part of the loft were tables and desks littered with a variety of computer equipment, scanning devices, small 3D printers—everything someone would need to duplicate the sophisticated I.D.s utilized by the Gaian government.

"Take a seat," Chao said carelessly, going to one of the computers and typing in some rapid-fire codes. Then he paused and looked up at Lira and Rast where they waited a few feet inside the door. "Oh, hey, on second thought, get rid of those coats first. I don't want you getting water anywhere near here."

Luckily, there was a set of metal hooks on either side of the door whose sole purpose seemed to be keeping sodden outerwear from getting near Chao's precious equipment. Lira took off her coat, and Rast did so as well, although she noticed he was slower about removing his, intent gaze roving the interior of the loft before he began to undo the buttons and then finally hung the garment from one of the hooks. Underneath, they were more or less dry, as their coat fabric had been treated to be water-repellent.

She went ahead and sat down on one of the chairs their host had indicated, but although Rast approached, he remained standing, as if prepared to go into battle at a second's notice, should the situation warrant it.

Chao flicked a glance up at the Stacian and then shrugged, obviously not overwhelmed by Rast's stature, even though he had to be a good thirty centimeters taller than Chao.

"Okay," he said, after apparently satisfying himself with what he saw on the one computer screen in front of him. "Jackson says I'm supposed to give you the full workup. New identities from top to bottom, including new retinal scans."

Rast flinched a little at that, and Chao grinned.

"Don't worry—those big copper peepers of yours will look exactly the same."

"I am not worried about my personal appearance," Rast said stiffly, and again Lira had to fight back a smile.

Maybe you're not, but I am. I've gotten used to those amber eyes of yours. She inquired, "And fingerprints, and full I.D. replacement?"

"Of course. My job is to make sure your new armor is impenetrable." He typed in another quick burst of data. "You, Lira, are no problem. But the big guy?" A quick lopsided grin. "He's going to be a little tougher. You can't exactly hide a Stacian."

Again Rast stiffened. It was clear that he didn't appreciate being referred to as "the big guy," let alone discussed as if he weren't even in the room.

"Jackson trusts you, so I trust you," Lira said simply.

"I am *very* good at what I do." Chao appeared to finish whatever he was working on, and swiveled his chair so he faced both Rast and Lira. "Rast, you're now from Syrinara, a minor bureaucrat in the colony's agro department. That makes it plausible for you to be off-world, since part of what you do is investigate new crops that could be grown on the colony. Okay?"

"Okay," Rast replied, although Lira saw his lips thin a little. He probably didn't much like being demoted to a bureaucrat, and a minor one at that, but really, what their new identities did wasn't the point, only that they didn't raise too many warning flags.

Chao's gaze shifted to Lira, and she wondered what on earth he was going to come up with for her. "You'll be working for MonAg, trying to sell Rast here on your company's products."

At first whiff, she didn't like that much at all. MonAg was one of the galaxy-spanning corporations that had a stranglehold on the Gaian Consortium's policies. If it didn't earn a profit, it didn't get done, and even the GDF had to fight for funding every year as the lobbyists came up with new arguments about its lack of profitability.

A peacekeeping force wasn't about being profitable, but Lira knew that was an argument she'd never win. At least as a captain she hadn't been forced to deal with those sorts of confrontations. Admiral Horner had been in a choice few, that much she did know. Say what you wanted about the man, but he was willing to go to the mat for the people under his command.

On the upside, it would make sense for a MonAg rep to be seen with a Syrinara-based Stacian whose job was agro development. Clever of Jackson to come up with alternate identities that were extremely plausible...and which she and Rast would both dislike, for very different reasons.

"All right," Lira said, after a pause she hoped Chao wouldn't notice but was fairly sure he had. "That'll help explain the *Chinook*, I suppose. A MonAg executive might actually have access to a ship like that, whereas most mere mortals don't have that kind of opportunity."

"Our thoughts exactly. The data is being crunched as we speak. But we might as well move on to the, ah, physical enhancements. Who wants to go first?"

"I will," Lira said at once. Not that she was all that eager to have her retinas sliced and diced, but at least that way Rast could see that it wasn't quite as horrible a procedure as he was probably imagining.

"I will," he said, almost at the same time. His gaze met hers, as if to say, *I refuse to let you step in first just because I am hesitant.*

"Geez, kids, should I flip a coin?" asked Chao, clearly amused by their posturing.

Rast's voice was low, almost a growl. "No need. *I* will go first."

Oh, of all the—Lira threw up her hands. "Fine, go first. It's not as if you're saving me from certain death or something, Rast. I'm going to undergo the same procedure immediately afterward."

A quick flicker of those amber eyes toward her. She wasn't totally adept at reading his expressions, not yet, but she could tell he was not going to entertain any further argument on the subject. Continuing to bicker in front of Hunter Chao would be counterproductive at best, so she just lifted her shoulders and settled back in her seat, arms crossed.

"Now that we've got that settled," Chao said, "care to step into my operating theater?"

Rast made a sound in the back of his throat that might or might not have been a growl. Even the insouciant Hunter Chao looked a little discomfited.

"Um, that chair over there," he told Rast, and pointed.

The Stacian got up from where he'd been sitting and settled himself into the indicated chair, which didn't look terribly dissimilar from the kind used by dental professionals the galaxy over. It squeaked under Rast's bulk but appeared that it would more or less survive the abuse.

Chao stood as well, and went over to an autoclave cabinet, the kind that kept all its contents in rigidly controlled sterile conditions. Before opening it, he dipped his hands in self-skinning latex solution, then reached in to pull out the retinal reassignment instrument, which to Lira's eyes looked more than a little like some of the medieval torture devices she'd once seen in a history book.

Stacians couldn't actually turn pale, but she thought she saw Rast's fingers tighten around the aluminum frame of the chair. It buckled slightly, but not in an area that would affect its usability. All she could do was hope that Chao hadn't noticed.

"Really, this won't hurt a bit," he said, as he bent over Rast's tense form, moving the shining metal device closer and closer to the Stacian's left eyeball.

Even Lira felt herself blinking in sympathy, although she could tell Rast was doing everything he could to keep his eye open as wide as possible. A whir, and a flash of light, and then...

"Next one!" Chao called out, and quick as lightning lowered the device over Rast's right eye.

A second brilliant burst of light, and Rast was blinking up at the ceiling, his forehead furrowed.

"Everything looking all right?" Chao inquired. "No blurriness, no dark spots?"

"No," Rast said slowly, opening and closing his eyes several times in rapid succession, as if to make sure the side effects Chao had mentioned weren't going to appear after a few moments.

"Great. Then it's your partner's turn."

The chair creaked again as Rast got up from it. As Lira passed him, he reached out and put a reassuring hand on her elbow, a quick gentle touch that she wasn't even sure Chao saw. Just as well. She certainly wasn't in the mood to be explaining her relationship with Rast to anyone.

She sat down and leaned back into the headrest. Chao approached her, a little more confidently than he had Rast.

"Ready?"

"Sure." She forced her eyes to stay wide open, although the impulse to blink seemed stronger now that she was trying so very hard not to. Judging by the delicate wire contraptions Chao had set down on a little table nearby, he had the means to keep her eyelids propped up by force if necessary, but she certainly didn't intend to go down that road.

Then he was bending over her, and a flash filled her field of vision. Dancing bright and dark spots followed immediately afterward, and then her vision cleared. She didn't have much of a chance to do react, however, because Chao was leaning down once more, this time over her right eye. Again the world was obscured by a flash of brilliant light. Just as Rast had done, she blinked several times, making sure the tiny flickering spots were only a temporary phenomenon.

Her vision cleared, and she let out a little sigh. One task down, anyway.

The fingerprints were much easier. Chao took a mold of all her fingertips, then set about making delicate little overlays generated by the 3D printer that were perma-sealed to her fingers.

"Noting will take those suckers off," he told her, as she raised one hand wonderingly in front of her face and peered closely at her new fingerprints. The fusion of the overlay to her fingertips was flawless; if she hadn't known what he'd done, she would never been able to tell.

Rast submitted to the procedure without comment, although she noticed he, too, held his fingers close to his eyes, as if believing he'd be able to note the difference. "Impressive," he finally allowed.

"Best in the business."

"Humble, too," Rast said, his tone so sour that Lira wanted to laugh. For whatever reason, he did not appear to be a fan of Hunter Chao.

A shrug. "What's the point?" He went to a different workstation and picked up a small booklet with a blue cover—an official Gaian off-world travel pass. Archaic, in these days of subspace transmissions and digital information that could be sent from one side of the galaxy to the other in just a few seconds, but there were still worlds that were officially off the grid and required actual paperwork. Next to it was an intricately folded piece of thick vellum that she assumed was the Stacian equivalent.

"Your papers," Chao told them, handing Lira the blue booklet and Rast the piece of vellum. "All electronic files have been processed and disseminated throughout the necessary databanks. As of now, you're no longer Lira Jannholm or Rast sen Drenthan."

Rast made a disapproving noise at that, and Lira supposed she really couldn't blame him. He still had some standing with his people—although she didn't know how much longer that was going to last, with him effectively AWOL at this point. She, however, was glad enough to say goodbye to Captain Lira Jannholm and her record of disgrace. Flipping open the booklet, she saw her new name was Adriana Ayers. That was pretty, and she found herself grateful that at least Hunter Chao hadn't burdened her with something difficult to pronounce or spell.

"Hello," she said, turning to Rast. "Adriana Ayers, new accounts executive for MonAg. And you?"

For a second he stared at her, mystified, and then he bowed slightly. "Janth sen Lhannick, at your service."

"Oh, you kids." Chao was regarding them with an

amused tilt to his head that told Lira he had probably guessed the true nature of their relationship. "Also, here are new handhelds programmed with your fresh identities, and with access to some fairly hefty credit vouchers. Jackson wanted to make sure you could get what you needed when you needed it."

Lira took hers, and, after a brief hesitation, Rast accepted the proffered handheld as well, slipping it into his pocket without looking at it twice.

Chao said, "Well, I think you're set, and Jackson's covering everything, so—"

Up until that moment Lira hadn't even thought of how they would pay for Chao's services, which she knew had to be astronomically expensive. That Jackson was willing to do such a thing for them told her maybe he still cared more than she was willing to admit. Then again, he probably wanted to do whatever he could to ensure their success so he would be entitled to full disclosure once their mission was accomplished.

If it was accomplished.

She began to say something about how indebted they were to Jackson, but in that same moment Chao's handheld beeped, and he reached down to pull it out of his pocket. He held it to his ear, then said, "Sure. She's right here." And he extended the handheld to Lira. "It's for you."

Mystified, she took it from him. "Hello?"

Jackson's voice came through, clear but somehow small. No wonder, since the signal would have to be bounced through a number of subspace repeaters before reaching her here on Miris Prime. "Lira. I have some new information for you."

Her attention sharpened. "Go ahead." From the corner of her eye she could see Rast sending her a quizzical look, and she held up a hand, indicating that she needed him to hold off on any questions.

"So I started doing some digging on those Bath-shevan mercs, as I said I would."

"And?"

"Turns out they were hired by none other than Gared Tomas."

Lira sucked in a breath. Then again, this wasn't completely unexpected. If it really had been Tomas who'd planted the tracker in her makeup case, then it stood to reason that he'd be the one to call in the mercs to go after her on Gaia. "Okay."

"You don't sound surprised."

"I had a sneaking suspicion."

"Hmm." Jackson's tone indicated some disappointment. Clearly he'd wanted to surprise her with this information, and a bland "okay" probably wasn't what he'd been expecting. "Anyway, it gets better."

"Define 'better.'"

He chuckled. "Even more interesting. So, okay, you took off with Tomas's ship, so it's natural enough that he'd be holding a grudge. But what's not exactly natural are the large deposits he's been getting at regular intervals at a certain out-of-sector branch of First Galactic Trust."

"Jackson, Gared Tomas has his fingers in more pies

than I can count. I'd be shocked if he *weren't* getting large deposits in various banks at regular intervals."

"True...but you might be interested to know exactly whose accounts this money was coming from."

She could tell he wanted to amaze her with the information he was about to impart, so she said, "All right...whose?"

"One Admiral sen Trannick."

CHAPTER FOURTEEN

At first she couldn't say anything, just stood there with the handheld pressed against her ear. Then, "You're sure."

"Of course I'm sure. The deposits began approximately three standard weeks ago."

Just when Tomas hired me...

"You there, Lira?"

She cleared her throat. "Yes, I'm here. I got that. Anything else?"

"That isn't enough?"

"It's more than enough, actually."

"Well, I'm going to keep digging. My hacker friend on Gaia apparently took a liking to you. She's sent me some leads on how to dig deeper into sen Trannick's accounts. We'll get this figured out one way or another. Now that I know things point toward Eridani..."

"...You'll know better where to look."

"Exactly." Jackson paused, then asked, "Everything okay over there? Hunter take care of you all right?"

Lira replied immediately, "Perfect. Everything is in order, and he did a top-notch job. I can't begin to thank you—"

Jackson broke in, sounding almost embarrassed, "Hunter's good people. So what's your next step?"

I haven't a clue. But she knew she couldn't let Jackson know how lost she was feeling right then, as if everything beneath her feet had turned to quicksand. She needed to talk to Rast, tell him about these latest developments, and that meant getting back to the *Chinook* where they could talk in private.

"Haven't quite figured that out yet," she said calmly. "But if you come up with anything else, call me on the *Chinook*. We're heading back soon."

"Got it. Can you put Hunter back on the line for me?"

"Sure."

She pulled the handheld away from her ear and extended it to Hunter. He took it from her, then listened in silence to whatever Jackson had to say. Finally he ended the call and shoved the device in his pants pocket.

"Sounds like you two have pressing business else-where, so I'll go ahead and take you back to your ship."

"Thank you," Lira said at once, glad that he didn't seem inclined to stretch things out. Then again, that one-sided convo with Jackson had probably been about payment or something along those lines, so if he felt reassured that he wasn't going to be left holding the bag on this one, he most likely wanted to move them along so he could work with his next client.

Rast was still shooting questions at her with his eyes, but all she could do was lift her shoulders slightly and mouth *later*. After that he subsided and nodded, then went to the hooks by the door so he could retrieve his coat. Lira did the same, while Chao slipped into the alcove he apparently used as his personal living area and got his own outerwear, a bulky coat roughly the color of the perma-crete that composed the apartment building.

Since Lira wasn't inclined to conversation, and Rast seemed to have gotten the signal that any meaningful discourse would have to wait until they got back to the ship, the drive back was a quiet one. Still, she was grateful for the ride, glad that they wouldn't have to suffer another soaking on their return trip to the 'port.

As Chao came to a stop near the entrance to their landing pad, he said, "You shouldn't have any trouble with those credentials I gave you, but if you do, call Jackson, not me. He can get in touch with me if he has to, but at least that way there won't be a direct connection between us. Got it?"

Grimly, Lira replied, "Got it." She didn't bother to add that if someone did discover something dubious about their faked identifications, getting a call out to Jackson might not be the easiest thing to do. But Chao had made it clear that he wanted no further involvement, so there wasn't much else she could do about it. He'd done enough as it was.

She waited as Rast levered himself out of the back

seat. He extended a hand to her, and she took it, glad of the warmth of his fingers against hers, even as the chill rain fell against her exposed skin. Good thing they didn't have far to go to get back inside the *Chinook*; if anything, the storm seemed to have intensified while they were inside Chao's loft.

They hurried through the driving rain to the landing pad, the access stairs lowering at the command she sent through the remote in her pocket as they approached. As soon as they were inside, she palmed the lock with one hand and reached up with the other to start undoing the buttons of her coat, a garment that had gotten slick with rain even during the few steps they'd had to take from the shelter of the overhang at the entrance to the landing pad to the *Chinook*'s access stairs.

"Do you want to tell me what that call was about?" Rast demanded, even as she settled herself in the pilot's chair and began the sequence for takeoff.

"The mercs were paid by Gared Tomas, and Tomas's funding came from your admiral," she replied, fingers tapping out the familiar sequence of commands unerringly.

"*What?*"

"That's about what I thought." Toggling the comm, she said, "Miris Control, this is passenger ship *Chinook* taking off from Sector Three. Request departure permission."

"Granted," came back almost immediately, in the same bored tone Lira thought she recognized from their approach a few hours ago. Made sense, she supposed. Although several things had shifted in her own universe during those short hours, the same personnel who had originally given her permission to land were probably still on duty at Miris Control. "Have a good one."

"Thanks, Control." Since she had no clear idea of where they were going next, she figured the best thing to do would be to head toward the outer edges of the system and hang there in the relatively open space until they decided on their next move.

During all this Rast had maintained a tight-lipped silence, but as soon as they were clear of the atmosphere and flying smoothly out to the dark borders of the Miris system, he said, "So what's your interpretation? You know Tomas. I don't."

Her mind had been picking at the sequence of events, coming up with an explanation she didn't like very much, although it seemed to be the most plausible one she could think of. "I have a feeling your admiral—"

"He is not 'my admiral' any longer," Rast said abruptly. "I am done with that. All of it."

Lira swiveled in her seat so she could look up at him. He stared back at her, jaw set, eyes narrowed slightly. From his expression she guessed this further evidence of sen Trannick's involvement had been the final blow, the thing that shattered his increasingly tenuous connection to the man who had been his superior. Even so, for him to so abruptly renounce everything he had worked so hard for, to make the break with his command—and by extension, his people —shocked her.

Quietly she asked, "Are you sure of that, Rast?"

He reached out to touch her cheek, fingers warm against her skin, and she closed her eyes briefly, recalling those fingers running over her body, stroking her. But now was not the time to be thinking of such things. Her body had had enough—if not to sate it, then at least to keep it more or less content for the time being. She might not be the captain of a ship any longer, but that didn't mean she had to abandon all the self-control that had come along with attaining such a rank.

"More sure of anything than I ever have been," he told her. "But enough of that. I want to hear what you have to say."

A quick nod, a silent acknowledgment of what she knew he had just given up. They could discuss it later... or not. That would be up to him. "The timing is too convenient. I think sen Trannick, for whatever reason, had agents keeping tabs on me. They must have tracked me to Ganymede, and then on to Iradia when I decided I couldn't stay in the Gaian system any longer. Since I was at decidedly loose ends once my one job piloting a freighter was over with, it would have been easy enough for the admiral to decide he could best keep an eye on me by having me take a position with someone right there on Iradia. A big enough payout to Tomas, and there I was, right under both their thumbs and knowing nothing of it. I'd still be there, too, if it weren't for you."

She'd thought Rast's eyes might warm at her words, but he was quiet, expression far away and still graven in dark lines, as if he was thinking of something not very pleasant.

"What I can't figure out," she continued, since it seemed clear he didn't intend to speak, "is why they would even bother in the first place. I had been drummed out of the GDF. I wasn't a threat to anyone."

"Oh, but you were," Rast said then, and scowled. "You see, I made the very great mistake of being concerned for your welfare, once I learned that you had been relieved of your command—relieved of that command because of what I had urged you to do. I felt responsible, and the admiral clearly saw that. He must have seen, too, that I'd already begun to develop feelings for you. So you see, you were a threat. A Stacian, falling in love with a Gaian? It wasn't to be tolerated. You must be kept away. Or so I assume he thought."

Of all this speech, the thing that stood out the most to Lira were the words "falling in love." Had he really meant to say that? It couldn't be true, could it? Oh, she couldn't deny the heat between them, the physical attraction unlike anything she'd ever experienced before. But it was quite a leap to go from such a physical connection to saying you were in love with someone.

Her face must have betrayed her, because he went suddenly on his knees next to her, taking her hands in his, warming her cold fingers with his touch. "Does that distress you, Lira? If I've misinterpreted certain... signs...from you, tell me now."

It had been some time since she'd had anything at all to drink. That must be why her throat suddenly felt so dry and tight, as if choking back the words she wanted to say. She swallowed, knowing he expected her to say something. A declaration of love? Did she love him?

Of course she did. To deny it would be to deny that water was wet, or the vast starry sky beyond the viewscreen anything but deep velvet black.

"No," she said firmly. "You haven't misinterpreted anything. I don't know how it happened, or what it even means, but I've never felt about anyone the way I feel about you, Rast sen Drenthan. I wanted to deny it, but I can't. I do lo—"

And that was as far as she got, because his fingers tightened around hers and he drew her up out of the pilot's seat, pulling her against him, kissing her, his tongue touching hers, the spicy scent of his skin and hair surrounding her, every nerve ending in her body on fire, cramping need striking her low in the belly, her core damp with desire. He pulled away, just for a few seconds, just long enough to murmur, "I love you," before lifting her from her feet and carrying her down the hall to the cabin.

Oh, God, yes, this was what she needed, his hands working at the fastenings of her garments, strong fingers brushing over her breasts, moving down to stroke her between the legs, a little sigh escaping his lips as he felt how wet she was, how ready. She didn't even remember undoing his trousers, but then she had him in her hand, her fingers barely able to wrap around him as she moved them up and down. That seemed to bring him close to the edge, and he pushed her down on the bed, settling himself on top of her, no time for more foreplay, no time for anything except to take him into her, to enfold him in her legs so she could drive him in further, making one flesh of them, one being, even though they had been born on such different worlds.

The climax flared through her and she cried out, fingers digging into the heavy muscles of his back, and he came then, too, a flare of heat somewhere deep within as his seed splashed into her. He relaxed then, but not all the way, probably fearing he would crush her beneath his bulk if he let go completely.

"I love you," she said, since he had cut her short previously, and it seemed vitally important for her to tell him how she felt.

His breath was warm against her ear as he replied, "I love you, Lira. I love you with every cell in my body. You are a wonder, a gift." Very softly, he kissed her temple, and she ached for him all over again, that he could have such passion and fierceness and yet such tenderness, all contained within one marvelous soul.

Then he did roll off her, but carefully, keeping one hand still touching hers, as if he wanted to make sure she knew he was only moving away because that position had become uncomfortable for him. She watched him, taking in the hard muscles under the deep golden skin, the heavy brows, the fine nose and strong chin and the heavy mass of hair that fell down his back, making him somehow more masculine rather than otherwise, even though most Gaian men wore their hair short.

He stared back at her, as if doing the same inventory of her features, her body. She could only hope he found hers as pleasing as she did his. Odd how his alienness only made him more attractive to her, rather than less.

A chime sounded throughout the ship, signaling an incoming transmission. She sighed, wishing she could stay here in bed with Rast, but knowing she should answer it, because it could only be Jackson, and if Jackson was signaling them, then it probably meant he had information he needed to pass along.

Rast seemed to understand, and remained where he was, watching her as she reached down and grabbed her discarded underwear and shirt, pulled them on hastily. As she headed out the door, she saw him reluctantly stirring from the bed and retrieving his own things.

And even though the viewer on the comm unit should only show her from about the middle of the chest up, she was going to make sure she had the visuals shut off. There were some questions she really didn't feel like answering right now.

―――――

Damn intrusive things, comms. Rast had known they couldn't spend forever in bed together—although that was an enticing daydream—but he'd hoped they would have at least five minutes. Still, that minor irritation paled when compared to what had just passed between them.

She loved him.

He had dared to hope, but he hadn't known. On the surface of things, it was rather a lot to expect, that she should have come to love him so quickly, and after his actions—even if completely innocent—had led to her expulsion from the GDF. That flash of fire between them, that chemistry...he hadn't imagined it, but for her it might have been nothing more than much-needed physical release.

But it was more. Much, much more.

Smiling, he drew on his pants and shirt, but left the jacket where it had more or less been flung across the seat of the chair in the corner. They were on board ship, alone, and so he certainly didn't need to be buttoned up and presentable. That suited him just fine.

If only they could be like this always—the two of them, with a fine ship and all the galaxy to choose from. A pleasant fantasy, but not one they could afford to indulge right now. They had set forth on this quest to find the truth, and he knew Lira would not stray from that mission until she was satisfied with the answers she found.

He heard what had to be Jackson Wyler's voice coming over the speaker, and Rast felt his mouth tighten despite what had just passed between him and Lira. No, it was not jealousy, not precisely, but he did wish that the person uniquely suited to help them find the solution to this Eridani-based puzzle was someone other than Lira's former lover.

Not that there was anything remotely lover-like in her tone as she asked crisply, "So the input from our Gaian friend was helpful?"

Rast noticed she was careful not to say Miala's name. As far as he could tell, Jackson had never known the actual identity of his contact on Gaia, and Lira obviously wanted to make sure she didn't let slip anything that would reveal who the hacker genius really was. Yes, Jackson was helping them, and so Lira would give him what she could, but clearly she thought of Miala and her exact whereabouts as off-limits.

As he took a seat in the copilot's chair, he saw Lira flash him a quick smile, then turn her attention once again to the disembodied voice coming from the speakers.

"Extremely helpful. Once I knew how to cut off the heads from that hydra, it became a lot easier to begin to pin things down. I already told you about the connection between sen Trannick and Gared Tomas, but once I started backtracking the deposits in the admiral's accounts, I found they were coming from a shell corporation on Capris 6."

The origins of the money didn't surprise Rast too much; Capris 6 was the Eridanis' original colony, and had become the nexus for much of the Eridani Hegemony's finance and banking. He could tell Lira was thinking the same thing, because she gave a brief nod, as if halfway expecting to hear something along those lines.

"And this shell corporation?" she asked. "Get anything on that?"

"I'm working on it. These things are set up to be quicksand, but I'm making some headway. I did get a name: Daos Senn. Definitely Eridani."

Lira looked pleased by that; something in her face brightened, and she nodded. "And what do you have on him?"

"Not a whole lot so far. Seems like an upstanding citizen by all accounts. A lot of money, but all earned legitimately. Family has been in various forms of mining for generations."

Mining. Rast frowned a little at that piece of information. Could this have all been an end run by an Eridani mining interest to secure better terms for the millenite on Chlorae II? For there was no doubt in his mind that the Eridanis would have had more luck negotiating with the Stacians as primary rights holders for that ore than they would with the Gaians. Oh, the Gaians played at diplomacy and peaceful coexistence and all that—but they also would sell their grandmother if they thought they could make a profit. Not all of them were like that, of course, but unfortunately the ones in power seemed to operate solely on a philosophy of "what's in it for us?"

Whereas his own people still were grateful to the Eridanis, felt indebted to them for the sharing of technology that had allowed them to become something more than half-barbarians on a backwater world no one in their right mind would choose to live on. Well, no one in their right mind who wasn't Stacian...

Rast realized his thoughts had drifted far afield, and he pulled his attention back to the conversation between Lira and Jackson.

"...possible someone could have borrowed his identity to cover what they were really up to?" she was asking.

"Maybe," came Jackson's reply. "Wouldn't be the first time. I'll have to look into it further. In the meantime, would you like information on his whereabouts?"

"Of course," she said at once. "We have to start somewhere. Is he on Eridani itself?"

"He has properties in three different systems, but it does look as if his primary residence is on Eridani. Sending you the information now."

"Great." Somehow, though, she didn't look entirely pleased; that frown was back, the one that made the line appear between her delicately arched brows.

But since Jackson couldn't actually see her, he didn't appear to notice that anything was amiss. "Well, that's all I have for now. It's almost oh four hundred here—I need to pack it in. I'll be in contact tomorrow if I get anything new."

"Thanks, Jackson." She pushed the button to end the transmission and leaned back in her seat, then glanced over at Rast. Her expression softened a little, and she smiled.

It pleased him to know that she felt cheered when she looked at him, but he still knew she was worried about something. "What is it?" he asked quietly. "I would think it would please you to know we're getting close to an answer. And Eridani is one of the few places in the galaxy where a Stacian and a Gaian might be seen together with no one making too much comment."

"You're right, of course." She got up from her seat and, to his surprise, settled herself into his lap. The copilot's chair, already overburdened with his bulk, squeaked in protest, but at least it appeared that it wasn't in danger of imminent collapse. He folded his arms around her, holding her close as she continued, "I just can't help feeling that somehow this is too easy."

"Easy?" That was a word he hadn't been expecting. "I would call this situation many things, but 'easy' is not one of them."

"You're probably right. I'm sure I'm just being paranoid." She was silent for a moment, apparently content to rest there in the warmth of his arms, and he was certainly happy to have her remain there for as long as she desired. Then she said, "It's just that—I know Jackson has ways of getting at data that almost nobody else does, but even so, I can't help thinking that this Daos Senn person should have been harder to find."

Since Rast had no way of knowing exactly which tricks Jackson Wyler had in his personal hacking arsenal, he wasn't sure how to respond. Surely, once Jackson had gotten access to some of the data, the rest would fall into place in an exponential manner. Or at least, that was how Rast hoped these things worked. He smoothed a piece of hair back from Lira's forehead, marveling once more at the silkiness of those wayward strands, and replied, "Perhaps. Perhaps not. Even so, it's a piece of information we need to follow up on."

She sighed, then pushed herself out of his arms. After settling herself back in the pilot's seat and typing a brisk set of commands into the navigation system—coordinates to Eridani, he guessed—she said, "Oh, I know we have to follow this lead. It's the only one we have.

"I just wish I felt better about it."

CHAPTER FIFTEEN

FROM SPACE, ERIDANI DIDN'T REALLY LOOK ALL THAT different from Gaia. Yes, the shapes of the continents under the mottled cloud cover were different, and three moons circled the planet to Gaia's one, but otherwise they were extremely similar. Lira had spent two years here in an accelerated program at the university before moving on to the Academy at Nova Angeles, but she'd had no reason to return to Eridani since then. And anyway, the university she'd attended was located on the opposite side of the planet. This was her first time coming to this particular sector.

The coordinates Jackson had given her for Daos Senn's place of business and his private residence put him in the southern land mass of Zedirani, near the regional capital of Teliir. Lira requested landing permission, giving her false identity and the *Chinook*'s faked registry, and held her breath. After all, she imagined the systems overseeing such things on Eridani would be far more rigorous than those on Miris Prime, which really, if one stopped to consider that dingy backwater world, had very little that was "prime" at all about it.

But the sweet-toned female voice coming over the comm system gave them permission to land in one of Teliir's four spaceports, and to tune to channel 427 if they had any questions about local currency, weather, shopping, or dining.

"Thank you," Lira said, then closed down the channel and turned to Rast. "So which first? Shopping or dining?"

He grinned at her. "What about accommodations? I might like to try out a bed that hasn't been used by Gared Tomas."

She found that a little rich, considering how many times that bed had gotten a workout over the past few standard days. But then she realized he was teasing her, and she smiled back. "It would probably be safer to keep bunking down here."

"You're right," he replied, then looked a little wistful.

"What is it?"

"I suppose I'm looking forward to when this is all over, and we can simply enjoy being together."

No arguments from her on that score. "Well, remember, we've already decided to spend our well-deserved vacation at the Eridani Majesty on Callia."

"Ah, of course." He paused, then lifted an eyebrow. "How is it you know of this place?"

She repressed a grin, wondering if he thought it was

the scene of an early liaison with Jackson. That was a laugh. Back when they were together, neither one of them could have afforded to stay in one of the hotel's bathrooms, let alone an entire room. "Because it's one of the fanciest hotels in the known universe, not because I've ever had the opportunity to stay there. Anyway, we'll order room service and drink champagne and—"

"Champagne?"

"Fizzy wine from Gaia. It's sublime, I assure you." Or at least, she thought she recalled that it was. It had been a very long time since she'd had a reason to drink champagne.

"I like sublime." He rose from his seat and bent down to kiss her, his lips warm and welcome. "I look forward to drinking this fizzy wine with you."

Assuming we live to tell the tale. Something about being here just felt off. She couldn't put her finger on it, though, and so decided to keep her misgivings to herself. After all, Eridani was a highly civilized, safe world. She and Rast wouldn't have to worry about getting shot on the street or shanghaied onto an ore freighter the way they might in some of the more dubious fringes of the galaxy. About the worst they would suffer here was sticker shock from the high prices in the restaurants or shops.

Speaking of which, they really needed to do something about their clothing. Neither she nor Rast had brought more than one change of clothing on this little adventure, and they were both looking a little seedy around the edges. Not exactly the sort of appearance a

MonAg account executive or a Stacian bureaucrat—there was an oxymoron for you—should be presenting to the world.

She said as much to Rast, and although he lifted an eyebrow at first, he then looked down at himself, at his smudged trousers, and at her wrinkled shirt, and reluctantly agreed that they could both use some freshening up.

A quick survey of the districts around the 'port showed that there was a shopping area less than a kilometer away, but luckily not close enough to the area where Daos Senn's offices were located that they needed to worry about anyone from his place of business seeing them before they were good and ready. Once they disembarked and were walking down the street, she realized that Rast had been right about one thing. The Eridanis around them didn't seem to notice anything strange about a Gaian and a Stacian sharing a spot on one of the city's moving sidewalks...or if they did, they were far too well-mannered to show it.

Luckily, the false identities Jackson had provided for them also came with healthy credit lines attached, so it was no problem to go into the first likely clothing store they saw, have their measurements taken, and walk out less than half a standard hour later outfitted in custom-made suits and footwear. A few doors down was a salon, although Rast balked at that.

"No off-worlder is putting a hand to these," he growled, and reached behind him to curl protective fingers around the dreadlocked fall of hair down his back.

"Have it your way," Lira said, knowing this was an argument she'd never win. "I suppose no one's going to think too much of your hair—it's what they expect of a Stacian. But I'm a mess, so give me another half-hour, all right?"

"If you must. But I think you look just fine."

She wished then she could stand on her toes and kiss him on the cheek, but a public display of affection like that between a Gaian and a Stacian *would* raise eyebrows, even here on Eridani. So she just flashed a grin at him and went inside the salon, where she was buffed and polished to perfection, and came out within that standard half-hour feeling like an entirely different woman.

Apparently Rast thought the same, because he stared at her as she approached as if he wasn't completely sure he recognized her.

"Well?" she asked, once it became clear that he didn't intend to say anything. "How do I look?"

He studied her for a few more seconds, then said, "Intimidatingly beautiful."

"Is that a good thing?"

"I think so."

And because they were standing on a busy street, and not alone, she had to content herself with reaching out and giving his nearest hand a quick squeeze. Her fingers did look strange to her, massaged and mani-cured, her fingernails painted a dark sapphire color to match the suit she wore, but she assumed she'd get used to them eventually.

Because she doubted a MonAg exec like Adriana

Ayers would deign to use public transport, she used her handheld to summon them a cab. It slid up to the curb only a minute or so later, driven by a mech. On any other world this would have been extravagant—mechs were far more expensive than biological labor—but the Eridanis excelled at mech building. It was one area where Gaia lagged behind, although the Consortium's scientists and techs were doing what they could to close the gap.

They climbed in, and the cab sped away, the coordinates of their destination already programmed in because of the order she'd submitted to the cab company. Typical Eridani efficiency—everything sleek and seamless, designed to provide as pleasant an experience as possible. Eridanis as a rule did not enjoy conflict and did what they could to avoid it whenever possible.

In fact, Lira had had a friend at the Academy who was half Eridani, and who once commented that her parents had divorced many years earlier. When Lira asked, somewhat diffidently, if it was because they'd argued—she'd thought perhaps their differing backgrounds had become too large an obstacle to overcome—Elith stared at her, laughed, and then replied, "No, it was because my dad would *never* argue. It drove Mom nuts."

Recalling this story, Lira wondered why the Eridanis, who as a rule avoided confrontations, had stuck their fingers into something like the plot involving her and Rast, and by extension Gared Tomas and Admiral sen Trannick. Surely mining rights weren't a big enough incentive for getting their hands so dirty?

Beside her, Rast stirred, then said, "You're very quiet. Contemplating your cover story?"

"I should be, but I'm not," she admitted, and shifted in her seat so she could more or less face him. Even though he'd declined the salon services, she still thought he looked very handsome in his new suit of a dark umber color, his heavy hair pulled back from the fine bones of his face. "I suppose I was thinking of the bigger picture—of why the Eridanis would be involved at all."

Rast made a warning noise deep in his throat then, and his gaze flickered to the mech driving the cab and back to her. She understood his concern; while there was no reason to think the driver was monitoring their conversation, she couldn't be sure of that, either. So she nodded and fell silent, but reached over to him and took his hand in hers, glad of the strength she felt in his fingers. It was atavistic and backward and foolish, she supposed, taking comfort in the presence of the big capable male. Even so, she couldn't help thinking somehow it seemed inconceivable that she should fail when she had him with her.

Even so, a little mental preparation wouldn't hurt. She knew the credentials Hunter Chao had given her were impeccable, so she wasn't too worried about that. Enough ores and their component elements were used in the preparation of agricultural compounds that it would seem plausible enough for her to have an appointment with Daos Senn, and to have with her the undersecretary for agricultural development on Syrinara. And, oh, how strange that the appointment was somehow not in the computer, but perhaps she could reschedule for a later time? At the very least they should be able to learn something of whether he was in Teliir or not, and use that intelligence to decide what their next step should be.

If they were lucky, during that time Jackson—more or less caught up on sleep, she hoped—might have dug up even more information for them, and they could use that with along whatever they learned at Senn's place of business to determine if the trail stopped at him, or whether he was in fact an innocent party in all this. The possibility still existed of his identity having been suborned for a third party's underhanded business, in which case this whole expedition might turn out to be a dead end.

And if it is? she thought. *It's not as if I have pressing business elsewhere...*

Sadly, too true. But at least she was with Rast, and somehow everything else didn't seem quite as bleak when she contemplated a possible future with him, rather than having to face an uncaring galaxy alone. He'd made it more than clear that she was his focus now, the object of his loyalty. She could not—*would* not —underestimate what a mental shift that was for him, what a sea change, in a man who had been raised to believe in his world first, his family second, and everything else a very distant third...if it existed at all.

The cab pulled to a stop in front of an airy confection of a building, all arched steel and many-paned glass, some of it in the blue and lavender and purple hues the Eridanis loved so much. Lira could not imagine a corporate headquarters back on Gaia—or indeed on any Consortium world—looking this fanciful, but the Eridanis had a very different way of doing business from the Gaians. And no need to worry about paying for their transportation here, as the amount due had been deducted directly from the false bank accounts Jackson had set up for her.

They got out of the cab and passed their fingers over the print scanner at the front door of the office building. Lira could feel herself tense as she did so, since this was the first true test of the false fingerprints Hunter Chao had given them, but the scanner only flashed a cool blue light, the doors opening inward.

She lifted her chin and stepped forward, Rast following closely behind. They stood in an immense foyer, probably twenty meters square. Directly opposite them was a pretty Eridani woman in a very chic silver-gray suit who sat behind a desk of inlaid wood. She smiled at them and said, "Welcome to Senn Enterprises. May I help you?"

Lira approached the desk, wearing what she hoped was a confident smile. "Hello. My name is Adriana Ayers, of MonAg, and this is Janth sen Lhannick, agricultural under-secretary from Syrinara. We have an appointment with Mr. Senn at oh three hundred."

Another smile, and the Eridani woman turned her attention to the virtual keyboard built into her desktop, typing in their information before she checked it on the head's-up display to her left. "Ah, very good, Ms. Ayers. Master Senn is expecting you."

What the...? That couldn't possibly be correct. He couldn't be expecting them, because the appointment was entirely fictitious. Lira wished she could turn to look back at Rast, to see if he could give her any indication as to the best way to respond, but she knew that doing so would only reveal her confusion.

"Excellent," she said, in what she hoped was an appropriately breezy manner.

"The lifts are that way," the receptionist said, and pointed to a bank of doors made of some silvery metal and engraved with a swirling design that echoed the fanciful architecture of the building itself. "Floor fifty-two."

"Thank you so much." And Lira headed off in that direction, acutely conscious of the clicking of her heels on the polished stone floor, Rast a pace or two behind her.

She pressed her thumb on the pad between two of the doors, once again establishing her identity, letting the building's security systems know that she had every right to be there. Although she was acutely aware of Rast's presence beside her, she knew she didn't dare say anything until they were both safely inside the elevator. Luckily, she was not forced to wait very long, as it came within the minute.

They both stepped inside, and she pressed the button for the fifty-second floor. It was only after the doors slid shut and the elevator began its ascent that she said, "Rast, what the hell is going on here?"

He shook his head, looking grim. "I have no idea." Then he brightened a little and said, "Perhaps Jackson Wyler hacked into their computers and inserted the appointment."

"That would make sense...except that Jackson doesn't even know we're here. I haven't talked to him since yesterday."

Rast's expression of dismay might have been comical if the situation weren't so serious. He appeared to ponder the problem for a few seconds, then seemed to relax slightly, saying, "I'm sure Hunter Chao sent him all the information about our new identities, though. Is it possible he's been keeping an eye out for our activities, just in case he needed to intervene to help us out?"

That actually did make some sense. Lord knows Jackson could slip into practically any database in the galaxy. Probably he'd gotten an alert the second their thumbprint scans showed up at the Senn Enterprises headquarters. After that it would only be the work of a few seconds to insert the necessary data into the receptionist's feed, to make it look as if that appointment had been there all along.

And if Daos Senn was occupied with another meeting when they arrived, well, then, it was the sort of mix-up that could easily happen. At least it seemed fairly clear that he was here in his office. A stroke of luck there, that was for sure. She'd just have to hope their luck held.

The elevator doors opened, revealing a short hallway that terminated in a set of double doors. Master Senn clearly occupied the penthouse, as above them Eridani's indigo-tinged sun shone through panes of blue and violet and silver-gray duraglass, the pattern repeating itself in paler hues on the floor of polished white stone. Rast reached out and took her fingers, gave them a quick reassuring squeeze before they headed toward Senn's suite.

Those double doors swung open as they approached, and Lira took in a quick breath, willing herself to stay calm. As in the reception area down in the lobby, a desk faced the entryway, and at that desk sat a well-dressed Eridani woman, although this one appeared to be a few years older than the receptionist in the lobby.

The main difference between her and the receptionist, however, was that this woman wasn't smiling... and that she held a stun pistol pointed directly at them. "Good afternoon, Ms. Jannholm, Captain sen Drenthan. We've been expecting you."

The pistol fired, and Lira's world went black.

Even though he knew she wasn't dead, that she'd only been hit with a stun bolt, still Rast lunged toward the woman behind the desk. He hadn't made it two steps before several pairs of very strong hands wrapped themselves around his arms, pulling him back. The curses died on his lips as a new figure stepped in front of him, one he recognized at once, although the penthouse suite of an Eridani office building was probably the last place Rast had ever expected to see him.

Admiral sen Trannick.

"What the hell are you doing here?" Rast snarled, pulling against the hands that restrained him—hands, he belatedly realized, which belonged to a pair of Stacian soldiers. That made sense, as he should have been able to bring a pair of Eridanis to their knees with just one yank of their arms.

"I might ask the same of you," sen Trannick responded. His gaze flickered to Lira's prone form, and his mouth twitched in distaste. "Come, let's go discuss this like civilized beings." He extended a hand, indicating another set of doors behind him.

"I have nothing to discuss with you." Knowing he would have a difficult time freeing himself from the two soldiers who held him—they were even bigger than he was—Rast stood straight and unmoving in their grasp, showing his contempt for them by acting as if they were not even there.

"Oh, I think we have a great deal to discuss."

"Lira—"

"—will be fine." The admiral nodded, a signal to the woman behind the desk apparently, as she leaned over and spoke a few quick murmured words in the comm unit built into her desk. Almost at once a pair of Eridanis in simply cut civilian clothing hurried out from behind another door, then bent to pick Lira up and spirit her away back where they had come from.

The sight of her limp body dangling from their detestable lavender-skinned hands was too much for

Rast, and he lunged forward again, breaking free from the men who held him, an inarticulate growl of rage coming from deep within his throat, deep within his soul. He would save her, no matter what it took.

A flare of violet light, and another, and he found himself falling, body betraying him as he crashed to the stone floor, hitting his head with a crack he heard rather than felt. The last thing he saw before darkness claimed him was the form of the woman he loved disappearing behind a set of polished metal doors.

CHAPTER SIXTEEN

LIRA OPENED HER EYES AND TRIED TO IGNORE THE DULL throbbing in her head. Despite her military background, this was the first time she'd ever been hit by a stun bolt—and she sincerely hoped it would be the last. In addition to the headache, her muscles twinged in places they'd never hurt before, probably because of the way she'd fallen to the floor after being stunned.

As she slowly focused on the world around her, she realized she was sitting upright in a chair, and that her hands and feet were bound. She did note that at least the chair was padded, and that her feet rested on a floor covered with an expensive-looking carpet in shades of deep blue and steel gray.

"Back among the living?" came an unfamiliar voice from somewhere behind her, and Lira turned her head to the right, trying to trace the source of the question.

He circled her then, coming to a stop a few paces away from the chair where she was bound. Since the room was not well lit, it took Lira a second or two to focus on him, to see that she looked at an Eridani male of approximately forty standard, although since Eridanis didn't age precisely the same way humans did, he could have been some years older than that.

She didn't bother to answer his question, instead saying, "Paragraph six, section twelve, of the Eridani Accord states that it is unlawful to hold or confine a sentient being without due cause. Since I have been accused of no crime, I must request that you release me immediately."

Her words only seemed to amuse him, because he let out a bark of a laugh, then shook his head. "I'll have to ask you not to quote my own world's laws back at me, Ms. Jannholm. Not all of us agreed with the Accord at the time it was signed, and so I think I'll ignore it for now."

That did confuse her somewhat, as she'd always been taught that the Eridani people had wholeheartedly supported the Accord, since it set up standards for behavior among the galaxy's sentient beings that were still followed decades later. But she didn't want this stranger to see her uncertainty, or her fear. "Even so, as I've done nothing wrong, or illegal, the best thing for you to do would be to let me go before you face possible repercussions from my government."

"Your government, Ms. Jannholm, doesn't seem to give a damn about you, or it wouldn't have cut you loose quite so quickly."

A retort rose to her lips, but she choked it back, knowing there was some truth in his words. Truly, if the

GDF had valued her at all as an officer, wouldn't it have at least given her the chance to defend herself? She stared down at her hands, held together with a set of professional cuffs—but the humane kind, of untearable fabric that would keep her wrists bound but not chafe or bruise them. How very Eridani of her captor.

"Ah," he said then, as if pleased that he'd managed to land a blow. "No, I think there aren't many people who give a damn as to where you are or what you're doing—not even that thick-headed Stacian in the other room."

Her heart rose into her throat at those words, a flash of dismay, followed by denial. The Eridani could only be referring to Rast. It did sound as if he was at least still alive. As for the insult in the stranger's words, well, she would ignore that. He was obviously only attempting to upset her in any way he knew how, to say whatever he could to increase her feelings of isolation, of abandonment.

If Rast was alive, she had the feeling he'd move heaven and earth to get to her. All she needed to do was keep her cool, and she had no doubt Rast would think of a way to get her out of this place.

Still she said nothing, knowing that it was best to stay silent, to not give this Eridani—Daos Senn?—any more ammunition than she already had. Obviously righteous indignation hadn't worked at all, so she would just hold her tongue and hope that Rast could get to her sooner rather than later.

A flicker of irritation passed over the Eridani's features, and he moved closer to her, bent down so he could gaze directly into her face. She stared back at him without flinching, noting that many would have probably called him handsome, with his straight nose and firm chin, the well-formed brows. But she had never found herself much attracted to Eridanis. Something about the lavender skin and odd little antennae that sprouted from within their gleaming purple hair just didn't speak to her own personal aesthetics of what constituted personal beauty.

Obviously, she had very different feelings when it came to Stacians...or at least one particular Stacian.

"What is it about you," the Eridani said in half-musing tones, "that would make someone such as Rast sen Drenthan, a man who had his entire career ahead of him, throw it all away?" He reached out and took her chin between two fingers, turning her head this way and that, as if inspecting every detail of her visage.

Lira forced herself to stay grimly quiet, to let him handle her as if she were a piece of meat he was inspecting at the market, trying to find a flaw. She wanted to spit at him, bite down on those lavender-skinned fingers, and despite everything she had to hold back a bleak smile. Perhaps some of Rast's temper had rubbed off on her.

"I suppose some would consider you attractive enough, for a Gaian," the Eridani went on. "Still, it can't be only that. Are you particularly talented? Can you suck a ball bearing through a braided-steel hose?"

Breathe, Lira told herself. *He's just trying to goad you. Don't react.*

So she stared straight ahead, not meeting his eyes,

not saying anything, barely even allowing herself to swallow.

He didn't like that, she could tell; his dark purple eyes narrowed, and he let go of her chin. Lira's relief at being released was short-lived, however, because the fingers that had been touching her face then trailed down her neck, drifted over the high collar of her modish new suit, then moved lower down, over the slope of her breast.

It was impossible to stay silent then. A muffled sound of protest came from low in her throat, try as she might to choke it back.

"Does this bother you?" he whispered, bringing his mouth close to her ear. "I must confess to being a little surprised. After all, you obviously had no problem sleeping with a Stacian, as large and rough and uncouth as they are. Here on Eridani we are...more civilized."

"If this is what you call civilized," she retorted, "then it's no wonder I prefer a barbarian."

He laughed. "I'll make sure he knows you called him that. Not that he probably cares overmuch what you think."

"What's that supposed to mean?" Lira snapped, before she realized she shouldn't have replied at all.

The Eridani straightened slowly, then crossed his arms and stared down at her with a satisfied expression on his regular features. "He's played his role well, hasn't he?"

"What role?" She tried to sound indifferent, but despite her admonition to herself not to listen to what this man had to say, to put no stock in his words, trickles of ice began to work their way down her spine.

"The role of ardent lover, of course. He did well to get you to move your ship out of the Chlorae system, but it went much further than that. All this time he's been following our orders. And then when you also led us to a hacker who's been stirring up trouble in various of our other business interests, well, that was just a very pleasant bonus."

Don't listen to him, she told herself. *He's seen that you care for Rast, so obviously he's going to say whatever he thinks will upset you the most. And if that includes dragging Jackson into this...*

But she couldn't let herself think about that, either. Bad enough that she should be caught like this, and Rast as well. Jackson had only been trying to help. If she'd somehow led these people to him, she'd never forgive herself.

So she stared down at the gleaming toes of her pewter-colored boots, and retreated once more into silence.

The Eridani scowled. "Very well. I am not a man to indulge in torture, and you've served your purpose well enough. Some of my...associates...thought you should be disposed of here and now, but that is not the Eridani way. You remember your old compatriot, Gared Tomas?"

Fear flared in her at the mention of the crime lord she'd double-crossed, but she just continued to look down at the tooled leather of her boots, her expression stony. She could only hope that she hadn't betrayed herself with a twitch or a shiver as she realized what the Eridani had planned.

He must have seen something, because the satisfaction was clear in his voice as he went on, "I see that you do. Well, he's expressed some interest in having you returned to him...although I have a feeling he expects you to fulfill a slightly different role than you did previously."

Oh, God. She recalled Tomas's cold green eyes all too well, the way that feral gaze used to travel up and down her body, even after she'd told him she would only be his pilot, and nothing else. And now Daos Senn was going to send her back to Iradia, back to the man whose ship she'd stolen, whose second-in-command she'd murdered. It did not take a great deal of imagination to guess what her fate would be.

Unfortunately, there didn't seem to be a great deal she could do about it.

———

Rast glared at sen Trannick, who stared back at him imperturbably from across a polished glass conference table, and then wordlessly pushed a container of some beverage toward him. "Go on, drink. You need something to clear your mind."

"I will not sit and share a drink with you," Rast said loudly, even though the effort hurt his head. He had awakened in this chair, and realized he had not been bound. Hardly necessary, with those two soldiers flanking him, and four more in the corners of the room—some kind of conference chamber, he realized. Perhaps he'd raised his voice for their benefit as much as that of the older man who faced him.

"Rast, Rast." The admiral got to his feet and came closer, leaning against the edge of the table less than an arm's length away. The proximity was meant to be subtly insulting, indicating he did not see Rast as the sort of threat that required any distance to be maintained between them. "Time to brush the sand from your eyes. You can still salvage your reputation, if you remove your head from where it appears to be lodged firmly up your backside."

Although every cell in his body ached to jump up from his seat, to strike sen Trannick down and take his chances with the other guards in the room, Rast forced himself to remain where he was, to fix an expression of what he hoped was dubious interest on his features. "Explain."

The admiral smiled slightly, as if pleased to see that his subordinate appeared to be softening. "Captain, do you think you're the first man to have his head turned by a female? It seems she got to you more than most, but you need to forget her. You can have your pick of almost any eligible woman on Stacia—and some that aren't quite as eligible, if that's where your tastes lie."

Rast knew exactly where his tastes lay—wherever poor Lira was at this very moment—but he knew better to say that. He raised an eyebrow. "You weren't so successful at that before."

"I suppose you're speaking of Lilarth. Stupid girl. I told her she didn't play that very well, not well at all. Ah, well, the women on that side of the family were never known for their brain power."

Expressing his agreement on that score probably wouldn't be very wise, so Rast only clasped his hands on the table in front of him and asked, "And if I admit my mistake? All is forgiven?"

The admiral's expression brightened at once. "I gave you a month, Captain, and you have not yet over-stepped that deadline. As long as you will agree that your 'family business' has been handled?"

He hated himself for it, but Rast knew he must do and say whatever he had to in order to regain sen Trannick's trust. Only that way could he find out what had happened to Lira. "I believe so, your Excellency."

A clap on the shoulder, and the admiral's scarred lips lifted in what looked like a genuine smile. "Very good. I'll make arrangements to get us off this forsaken planet so we can get you back to Syrinara."

"About that, Admiral—"

At once sen Trannick's gaze sharpened. "What, sen Drenthan?"

Rast knew he would have to tread carefully here. Injecting a certain amount of scorn into his tone, he said, "The Eridanis, your Excellency. Why are we involved with them at all? I thought our goal was to make the Stacian Federation self-sufficient, to show them that we no longer needed their assistance."

"That point of view has merit, Captain, but they have been useful to us. We needed that millenite, so when certain...interests...here approached me about taking it, then I thought it wise to listen. And I'm glad I did, because now the Stacian Federation controls Chlorae II, and the Gaians are left to scrounge where they can."

"'Interests'?" Rast repeated, hoping that the admiral had accepted his change of heart at face value and would give more details.

Sen Trannick gave a feral grin. "You think all the Eridanis are happy to see the Gaians spread like a cancer across the galaxy? No, some have come to realize that a healthy dose of self-interest can only help their cause. And since the Stacian Federation is the only entity with the *gollonth* to stand up to the Gaian Consortium, naturally those more patriotic Eridani were only too interested in working with us."

"Very sensible," Rast agreed, but his mind was churning away furiously. So there was a dissident group here on Eridani that wasn't quite as peace and love and living together in harmony as its leaders would like the rest of the galaxy to think. This conspiracy had been designed to shift the balance of power on a galactic scale, to push Gaia back from its headlong quest to have so many colonies that it would be impossible to contain them.

A month ago, he would have thought that a fine notion, that Gaia needed to be sent running like a *minsk* with its tail between its legs. But a month ago he hadn't known Lira Jannholm, hadn't understood that a Gaian could be as honorable as any Stacian he'd ever met, as fierce, as loyal and brilliant and beautiful. The

Consortium wasn't the monolith that men like Admiral sen Trannick thought it to be, but a place of many individuals, each with their own dreams and hopes and desires. And Rast thought of Miala and Jerem and Eryk Thorn, and the baby, and the little corner of unclaimed wilderness they called their own. None of them were anything close to a cancer...they were just people.

He knew he had to somehow get the conversation back around to Lira, or he might already be too late to save her. "So this Lira Jannholm," he said casually. "Was I just lucky that she was an attractive woman, or would you have made that bet with me regardless?"

The admiral actually laughed at that. "No, her placement was fortuitous. Actually, I was contacted by Master Senn, who said he had a proposition for me that would be mutually beneficial for both of us."

No doubt of that, Rast thought, recalling the enormous sums Jackson Wyler said had been transferred into sen Trannick's various accounts. Well, one mystery solved. Now Rast knew exactly where that money had come from.

"Doubly fortuitous, actually," the admiral went on, "because he knew she had an association with a certain hacker named Jackson Wyler, someone the authorities on several worlds have had their eye on for some time. We couldn't be sure that she would go to him for help, but as she did so eventually, we were able to finally pin down his location."

Damn. Not that Rast had any particular love for Jackson Wyler, but if the hacker had been surveilled for some time, that meant there was very little of their movements that the admiral and his Eridani cohorts didn't know about. Including the Thorns.

As if reading his thoughts, sen Trannick inquired, "That trip to Gaia—what happened there? We lost track of the mercenaries we sent, and they turned up dead some days later. But by then you'd already left the system, and following your movements was the important thing, so we let it alone."

Rast couldn't allow himself to let out a sigh of relief, but he did send an inner "thank you" to the heavens that the admiral's single-mindedness had prevented him from sending additional soldiers to the Thorn homestead. Then again, attempting multiple attacks like that, there in the very heart of the Gaian Consortium, was only asking for trouble. And since his quarry had gone, there was no reason to continue the assault. More than likely, the Thorns were all safe, if perhaps less than happy at having to repair the damage the squad of Bathshevan mercs had caused.

Easily, and with what he hoped was no discernible hesitation, Rast replied, "Oh, we went to visit some relatives of Jannholm's. They gave us shelter for a few days, but they were poor and couldn't manage more than that. Besides, they were less than happy at seeing her with a Stacian in tow."

"I can imagine." Sen Trannick chuckled, and appeared to dismiss the matter, as Rast had hoped he would. To a Stacian it would seem perfectly natural for Lira to go to family members for help, even though things hadn't worked out so well on Ganymede. The admiral's handheld beeped, and he pulled it out and looked down at the message he'd just received. "Excellent. Our transport is ready, and we can leave. Master Senn will dispose of the troublesome Captain Jannholm, and you'll be back on Syrinara in less than twenty-five standard." He pushed himself up to a standing position from where he'd been leaning against the table, and so Rast did the same, even as his gut clenched with dread. Pushing it could cause trouble, but he knew he couldn't let it go. He had to know what the admiral intended for Lira.

He tried to make his tone as deliberately casual as he could as he asked, "So what are you going to do with her? Eliminate her?"

Sen Trannick studied him for a few seconds. Apparently he saw nothing but mild curiosity in Rast's expression, because he said, "That would have been the wisest thing to do, but Eridanis are squeamish. So Master Senn is having her sent back to Iradia in the ship she stole so that both can be returned to the man who owns them. Sensible enough, I suppose. But enough of that. Let us go."

And Rast could do nothing but follow him as they left the conference room, the soldiers who had stood guard all this time falling in behind.

Lira. On the way to Iradia.

To Gared Tomas.

He could not let that happen. *Would* not.

Exactly how, he had no idea. But it would have to happen soon, or Lira would be left in the hands of one of the galaxy's worst crime lords, a man not disposed to look kindly on the theft of his ship or the murders of two of his most trusted lackeys. True, Lira hadn't been the one who pulled the trigger, but somehow Rast doubted the man would concern himself with such niceties, not when given such a golden opportunity for revenge.

Fists knotted at his sides, Rast stayed the proper two paces behind sen Trannick, although he wanted nothing more than to reach out and wrap his hands around the man's neck, choke the black life from him. But that would accomplish nothing, save being shot in the back by the guards accompanying them. No, he would have to come up with a plan to get away from the admiral, get himself to Iradia. How, he had no idea, as he guessed that his superior officer would keep a close eye on him until they were safely bound for Syrinara.

At least Eridani was a travel hub, one where he stood a good chance of finding a ship bound for Iradia. Doubtful that any such a ship would be as fast as the *Mistral/Chinook*, but he'd have to hope that Tomas would want to gloat over Lira for a while, that he wouldn't simply kill her out of hand.

A sleek unmarked transport was waiting for them, and Rast waited for the admiral to get inside, then climbed in himself. A mech piloted this 'car as well, and took them away from the moving sidewalks in front of Daos Senn's headquarters and toward the outskirts of the gleaming city. As Rast had thought, they were going directly to the admiral's personal shuttle. No chance to get away after all; it was clear that sen Trannick was not going to let his formerly mutinous officer out of his sight. Rast also realized that he had nothing with him but the civilian clothing on his back, and frowned, brushing his knees over the pants of the dark brown suit he wore. Everything he had was probably already gone, spirited away with Lira in the *Sirocco*.

Apparently guessing the most minor reason for Rast's disquiet, sen Trannick said, "No worries on that front, Captain. We'll have a proper uniform on your back in no time."

"My thanks, Excellency," Rast murmured. What else could he say?

The admiral seemed satisfied with that, and went on to speak of the increased production of ships' drives once the new supply of millenite began flowing to the shipyards at Ro'herr. Rast listened with only half an ear, tension increasing along every limb as the 'car stopped at the entrance to the landing pad and they both got out, accompanied by the same four guards. The shuttle was already powering up; obviously word had been sent on ahead.

Two guards walked in front of them, and two followed as the admiral and Rast made their way up the walkway and into the sleek little ship, designed expressly for the purpose of ferrying people to and from the larger Stacian cruiser currently in orbit around the planet. Rast wondered a little at sen Trannick making himself so visible, but then realized the Eridanis welcomed everyone, made it clear that all sentient races were free to come and go as they pleased. No doubt the admiral had designed matters so that it would seem as if his ship had stopped here only to give its officers shore leave while on their way elsewhere. Such things were common enough.

The shuttle lifted from the pad and sailed smoothly up through Eridani's blue skies, so similar to Gaia's, and yet subtly different, as if their blue was slightly touched with violet, rather than the faint greenish shade he'd noticed while at the Thorn homestead. As the planet fell away below them, Rast saw the hammerhead shape of the admiral's flagship grow outside the shuttle's windows, until it blotted out the blackness of space, swallowed the much smaller vessel. Then they were inside the hangar bay, surrounded by the complement of fighter craft that all cruisers carried with them.

As he stared at those sleek dart-shaped ships, an idea began to form in his mind. He'd piloted earlier versions of those same vessels as part of his training, but he knew they'd been given much greater flight capabilities during the past few years. Some even had a cruder version of the subspace drive that powered the *Mistral*, though nowhere near as fast.

Still...

He schooled his face to calm as the shuttle came to a stop and the guards once again took their positions around him and the admiral. They moved on into the corridors of the ship, meeting with a younger officer wearing a lieutenant's starbursts on the sleeves of his jacket. He saluted the admiral at once, gave a quizzical glance at Rast, and then saluted anyway, as if deciding that anyone in the admiral's august presence must be worthy of some sort of honor.

"Very good, Lieutenant," said sen Trannick. "See that Captain sen Drenthan is shown to the guest quarters on deck five."

The lieutenant saluted again, and the admiral turned to Rast. "You'll find a new uniform waiting for you there. Get yourself properly outfitted, and then meet me in my ready room in twenty standard."

"Of course, Admiral." He saluted as well, then followed the lieutenant down the corridor to a bank of lifts. The younger man kept shooting furtive looks at Rast's civilian clothing, although every time Rast tried to catch him at it, the lieutenant would shift his gaze forward again, obviously discomfited at being caught.

If the situation hadn't been so desperate, Rast might have laughed at the young man's behavior. As it was, it took all his energy just to keep a carefully neutral expression on his face, one he hoped betrayed nothing of his inner turmoil, of the desperate plan he was formulating even as the lieutenant led him to one of the guest cabins and then left him there after giving him yet another salute.

Although this was the first time Rast had ever stayed in one of these cabins, he knew their appointments well enough, since of course his own ship had possessed its own complement, although fewer and less lavish than on the admiral's flagship. As they were intended for visiting dignitaries, they were outfitted with every comfort possible in such small quarters, with real shower facilities and luxurious fabrics and a galaxy's worth of entertainment available at the tap of a finger.

Of course, he cared nothing for any of these amenities. No, all he cared about was the uniform hanging in the small wardrobe, the one item which might allow him to execute his plan.

If there was one thing he could count on, it was the Stacian appreciation for rank. While he wore that captain's uniform, no one would question him, or ask why he was in a certain section of the ship. If a Stacian attained so lofty a rank as captain, it meant his loyalty was unimpeachable, something as certain as the rising of the sun each morning.

It was that blindness he'd have to count on.

Hastily he stripped off the civilian suit he wore and hung it up, then pulled on the uniform, fingers working the buttons of the jacket with lightning speed. A quick glance at his chronometer told him that he had only fifteen standard minutes before the admiral began to wonder what his subordinate was up to.

It would have to be enough.

Rast fastened the belt and then slipped into the boots that had been provided for him. They pinched a little, but of course he wasn't going to concern himself with a petty detail such as that.

He'd been aboard this ship several times and so knew it well enough that he could easily retrace his steps to the lifts and then down to the hangar bay where the fighters were housed. That took another five minutes, and he told himself to stop looking at the chronometer, or he'd be sure to attract unwanted attention.

A quick scan of the hangar's contents told him that

the ships he was interested in, the newest and therefore most up-to-date models, were off to his left, closest to the enormous doors that allowed the fighters to enter and exit. The stars beyond shimmered, the atmosphere held in by a field of Eridani design, one which allowed ships and their pilots to leave, but kept the air trapped within the hangar bay. Rast didn't pretend to understand how it worked; he just knew it did.

Shoulders squared, he marched toward one of the fighter craft as if he had every right in the world to be there. A few seconds later, a junior officer hurried over to him, trotting along in his wake. Her expression told him she wished it had been anyone but her who'd been on duty at that moment.

Even so, her salute was brisk as she said, "Captain. May I help you with something, sir?"

"This ship," he said, glad it was someone relatively young and inexperienced who faced him. "Is this the new Avari class?"

"Yes, sir," she responded, obviously glad to be asked such a factual question, one that was easy to answer. "We just received the ships two standard months ago. Beautiful, aren't they?"

"Yes." He ran a hand over the sleek underside of the fighter. "I'm supposed to be getting five in the next month, but this is the first time I've seen one in person." A pause, and he flashed her a smile, one he hoped she would find disarming.

Apparently she did, for a dark flush spread along her high cheekbones, and she seemed to have trouble meeting his eyes. "We were very excited to get them, sir."

"I can imagine." He glanced up at the ship, and asked in an off-hand tone, "Mind if I climb in and take a look?"

"Sir?"

"Can't very well send my pilots out in these if I haven't checked one out first, can I?'

"Well, sir, I—" She floundered for a second or two, then said, "I suppose—that is, I see your point, sir."

"Excellent." Rast pulled the handle to extend the little mechanical ladder that would allow him to climb up into the cockpit; it dropped to the ground, powered by gears so smooth he couldn't even hear them working. He didn't dare look over at the ensign as he hurried up those metal rungs, then lowered himself into the pilot's seat. It was cramped, and he didn't want to think what eighteen or twenty standard hours in that position would do to him. Discomfort he could manage. What he could never live with was the fear that he had not done enough to rescue Lira.

"How is it, sir?" the ensign asked, her tone tight with anxiety. It seemed clear she'd begun to realize something didn't smell quite right about the situation, even if she couldn't put her finger on what it was.

"Perfect, Ensign. My thanks for your assistance." And he pushed the button to drop the canopy over the cockpit, even as he reached with his other hand to flip the switches that would bring the engines online. Out of the corner of his eye he saw the ensign take a step back, then shake her head, although he didn't know if that was her way of communicating that he needed to stop, or whether she was actually expressing her disbelief at what apparently was happening.

No time to worry about that, though. He could only hope that she wouldn't get in too much trouble.

Some of the controls were in slightly different positions, but even so it only took him a few seconds to tap in the commands to have the fighter's computer calculating the course for Iradia. He engaged the anti-grav and folded in the ship's landing gear, and then he was moving toward the atmospheric shield, gaining speed, the astonished ensign dropping behind him.

A shimmer of energy, and he was out in space, engines really kicking in now. He goosed them a little more, knowing his only hope was in the element of surprise, of getting away quickly enough and making the subspace hop before any of the other fighters could scramble and come after him. Good thing that they had been orbiting Eridani, a peaceful world, and so the admiral's flagship was not as heavily guarded as it might normally have been.

Even so, two of the dart-shaped ships came up from under the belly of the flagship, heading straight for Rast and his stolen craft. He pushed yet more power to the engines, tearing away from Eridani as quickly as he could go, counting down the precious seconds until he could drop out of realspace and be safe from any pursuit.

The screens in front of him showed the pursuing fighters had attacked, yet they were far enough behind that he knew those shots had been fired more for show than anything else, since he was out of range. If he could just hold that lead for a second or two more...

A bolt flared behind him, dispersing harmlessly as it hit his shields. A red light flashed on the control board in front of him, indicating that he'd lost approximately twenty-five percent of the rear shield from that one hit.

The black of space dissolved into a swirl of colors that were somehow beyond color, rippling hues he couldn't begin to name. Subspace always unnerved him, but he was glad to see it now. He was away. He was safe.

I'm coming, Lira.

CHAPTER SEVENTEEN

THEY'D HIT HER WITH A STUN BOLT AGAIN, SO LIRA didn't know exactly how she'd ended up back in the *Mistral*. Shipped over in the back of one of Daos Senn's 'cars, she guessed. Not that it really mattered how she'd gotten here. What mattered was where she was going.

Iradia. Gared Tomas.

She sat up slowly and put a hand to her head, which ached more than ever after that second stunning. In that moment she realized she wasn't bound, and wondered why they would leave her hands and feet free. Then again, where exactly could she go? The screen over the viewport had been pulled back, showing the pulsing ribbons of light that signaled they were in subspace, bending the very fabric of the universe to arrive at Iradia in hours instead of lifetimes.

The cabin she recognized immediately—it was the smaller chamber she used when Gared Tomas's travels had required a trip of more than a few hours. The mattress on the cot was as lumpy as ever, and she tried not to think of the luxurious bed in the larger cabin, the one that had belonged to Tomas. Now she could only think of it as the place where she and Rast had made love...had come to love one another.

Where he was now, she had no idea. Would he come for her, try to save her? Or would he dismiss the whole episode as temporary insanity, try to salvage something of his life and career, make himself forget her and the trouble she brought with her?

No, she would never believe that. Daos Senn had lied to her, tried to make her believe that Rast had been in on the plot all along, but she knew that couldn't be true. She'd seen how he looked at her, felt his lips on hers, and she knew he loved her as she loved him, insane as that notion might be.

But knowing he loved her was not the same as being certain he could come to rescue her. She had no idea what had even happened to him after she'd been knocked out and then—well, "questioned" was too polite a word, so she'd go with "gloated over" for now—by Daos Senn. For all she knew, Rast had been shipped back to Stacia to await execution for his apparent defection.

So she would have to rely on herself, although she had no idea how in the galaxy she'd ever be able to extricate herself from this situation. She might not be in handcuffs or tied to the cot, but she might as well be. Whoever was piloting this ship, she doubted he was alone...and she doubted any of them would be stupid enough to allow her a single opportunity to escape.

Which meant she was going to have to confront Gared Tomas, no matter what happened.

She'd been trained to subordinate her fear, to never let it control her. An officer controlled by fear could not make good command decisions. But all she'd ever had to worry about was the impersonal death of having her ship destroyed by an enemy, not the far more intimate demise she was sure Tomas had in store for her.

After he'd used her however he wanted, of course. Lira was not naïve enough to believe he would simply kill her outright. He'd wanted her before. Now he could indulge that desire in any way he wished, and she would be powerless to fight back.

Bile rose in her throat then, despite her empty stomach. The thought of anyone touching her after what she'd shared with Rast was bad enough, but a man like Gared Tomas...

She shuddered, and clasped her hands between her knees to keep them from shaking. As much as she tried to tell herself to not give up hope, some part of her realized that hope was quite possibly unfounded. She couldn't rely on a rescue, and she didn't know if she had the resources to come up with any effective way of escaping her captors.

All right, then. If the worst happened, and she was in Tomas's hands, could she endure it? Could she make herself submit to him, if it meant another day of life, another chance to escape, or, failing that, murder him in his sleep?

Once upon a time she'd thought she could never kill another sentient being, unless it was in armed combat. But that was before she knew men like Gared Tomas existed. Now she was fairly certain she could kill him, if given the opportunity. The problem was, she doubted she would ever get that opportunity. He hadn't lasted this long by being sloppy, or foolish.

Probably the best she could hope for was that he would kill her quickly.

She felt a slight bump then, and the skies outside the viewport shifted from the roiling colors of subspace to the velvet black of the real universe, stars twinkling here and there. No chance to try to focus on those constellations, because the *Mistral* shifted course, and ahead she could see the baleful ochre disk of Iradia growing before them, expanding to fill the sky. Then they were falling into its gravity well, the sensation somehow feeling as if she were picking up speed, although Lira knew in reality they were slowing, the shields tuning themselves to protect the ship and its occupants from the enormous heat of re-entry.

Then all she could see was the planet's orange-red sands whipping past, along with a dark beige blur that might have been Aldis Nova, but it was here and gone so quickly that if she'd blinked, she would have missed it. They were following the shadow of Iradia's terminus, moving over to the night side.

That made sense. Whatever was about to happen, she had a feeling it was better suited to the darker watches of the night.

It was black as pitch out there. Lira got up from the cot and went to the viewport, stared out as they coasted lower and lower, through darkness unrelieved by a single light. She knew Iradia was like that—miles and miles of emptiness with only a few population centers clustered around the planet's oases—but she had never made an approach like this before, and it was unnerving. Of course the pilot was flying on all instruments; there were no visuals here to key on.

But they were headed somewhere specific, that was certain. And finally she saw a faint glow of reddish lights marking a landing area, just sufficient to show its outlines but certainly not enough for anyone more than a hundred meters or so away to see. The *Mistral* finished its descent there, landing with barely a thump. Whoever was piloting the ship, they knew what they were doing.

She turned away from the viewport, trying to still the sudden beating of her heart, to will herself to calm. Whatever happened, she would not plead and cry. She would not beg. They might have stripped her rank from her, but she was still a captain of the fleet.

The door opened. Two men she didn't recognize, both Gaian and both outweighing her by about fifty kilos, stood there with pistols trained on her. "Out," one of them said as they both stepped aside to give her room to exit the cabin.

Nothing for it. Perversely, she was glad of the expensive suit she wore, the heels that clicked on the metal floor as she moved past them. She might be a little rumpled, but she certainly didn't look like a whore, even if that was what Tomas intended to make of her. What had Rast called her?

Intimidatingly beautiful. She doubted she could

intimidate Gared Tomas. Still, perhaps her appearance might give him pause, might make him re-evaluate his plans for her.

Well, she could hope so, anyway.

Once she was in the corridor, the man who had spoken said, "Move," and pointed his pistol toward the open hatch and the gangplank beyond it.

Obviously he was a man of few words. She did as he had instructed, walking calmly out of the *Mistral* and into the dry night air, which still seemed to shimmer with the heat of the day. Sweat began to drip down the high collar of her suit jacket, although Lira would have been hard-pressed to say whether the the stifling atmosphere of Iradia was really to blame for that.

They guided her into a low, sprawling building. As soon as they were inside, highly cooled air blasted in from all sides, and she had to keep herself from shivering at the sudden shift in temperature. The floor below was polished red rock, native to Iradia, and the walls on either side were decorated with sconces of intricate dark bronze and stained glass. Very elegant, and not what she would have expected of a structure so clearly out in the middle of nowhere.

Then she realized where she must be, even though this was the one place of Tomas's he had never brought her.

His home.

She swallowed. Gared Tomas kept the location of his actual residence a secret from almost everyone. Of course she'd heard rumors—that it was a near-impregnable fortress located in one of Iradia's most remote deserts, that those of his employees who were trusted with its whereabouts knew that death would be their reward if they breathed even a hint of its location.

If she had been brought to his home now...well, it was a fairly good indication that Tomas intended to keep her here. Permanently.

The two enforcers with her continued to direct her from corridor to corridor, all of which were well-appointed without being garish. Funny that the crime lord appeared to possess some actual taste. Then again, his cabin on the *Mistral*, while luxurious, hadn't bordered on the garish, either.

Well, that's just wonderful, she thought. *Maybe he can chat with you about interior decoration before he rapes and murders you.*

At last they stopped in front of a door that was flanked by more hired muscle, this time a pair of Bathshevan mercs, heads shaved and tattooed according to their custom. Without a word they opened the door and stepped aside.

"He's waiting," said the chatty enforcer, and pushed Lira through the open door before hitting the controls so it closed immediately, barring the pathway to escape —not that she would have been able to get past even one of those men, let alone four.

She stumbled over a thick rug, Menari weave by the look of it, and cursed her heels. Immediately a strong hand was on her elbow, steadying her, and she looked up into Gared Tomas's bottle-green eyes. At once she recoiled, yanking her arm from his grasp, but he only smiled.

"So good to see you, Lira," he said, and pointed to a low table that fronted a divan of soft brown leather. Sitting on the table were a pair of glasses filled with dark red liquid. "Drink?"

Getting hit twice in a twenty-four-hour period with a stun bolt must have done something to her hearing. That was the only explanation she could think of. No way Tomas was smiling at her pleasantly and offering her a drink.

But here he was, bending and lifting one of the glasses from the table, then extending it to her.

"Is this a joke?" she asked finally.

"'Joke'?" he echoed, and seemed to consider her question for a few seconds. "No, I don't believe so. You've had a long journey. I thought you might want something to take the edge off."

Because she didn't know what else to do, she took the glass from him but didn't drink. Instead, she held it under her nose and sniffed, then looked at it sideways to see if she could see anything odd about it, a film along the top, a graininess—any indication to show that it had been tampered with.

"Suspicious, aren't you?" Tomas let out a chuckle and reached for the glass. He brought it to his lips and took a large swallow before handing it back to her. "You see?"

At the moment she really didn't. Up was down, night was day, Gared Tomas wasn't trying to kill her. When she put it that way, a drink sounded eminently sensible. So she allowed herself a sip, and realized it was only wine, something heady and dark and complex…although, considering that she hadn't eaten in hours, even the lightest of white wines probably would have felt heady to her at this point.

"Better," he said. "Now, why don't we discuss the situation like civilized people?"

"All right," she managed. "I truly am sorry about the *Mistral*, but—"

"My people have inspected it and found no damage. It could have been much worse. The important thing is that I have it back."

"A-and your men—"

For the first time a shadow passed over Gared Tomas's face. "Morain was a loss. But you were not the one doing the shooting, were you?"

"No," Lira replied, although she said no more than that. The last thing she wanted to do was attempt to improve her own situation by implicating Rast more than she already had. She took a slightly larger sip of the wine, and wondered if Tomas was going to offer her some food to go along with it. Already she was beginning to feel a little light-headed, the wine clearly going directly into her sustenance-deprived bloodstream.

In fact, she was beginning to feel a lot more than merely light-headed. The room seemed to dip and sway around her, beginning to swirl. Tomas's eyes were like emeralds, boring into hers. He set down his own glass and smiled.

"Wha—" she began, stumbling over the syllable. "But you drank some—"

"I did. I also drank the antidote first."

Antidote…

Her knees buckled, and she slumped to the carpet. Or rather, she began to collapse onto it, only to have Tomas catch her, lower her to the floor, his arms going around her. Those glittering green eyes came closer and closer.

"That's better," he said, his voice a silken threat. "That's how I wanted you."

And the world slipped into a merciful darkness.

Rast glared at the readouts on the console before him and swore under his breath. Still three standard hours to go. This was a good little ship, the best fighter craft he'd ever seen, but it was no *Mistral*.

And being stuck like this, in a single seat for the greater part of eighteen standard hours, was almost more than he could bear. He'd been trained to endure longer than that with no food and no sanitary breaks, so the physical discomfort wasn't the worst of it. No, it was wondering what was happening to Lira while he chased after her, the limitations of the little ship's drive preventing him from crossing the distance between Eridani and Iradia with the same lightning speed the Sirocco-class *Mistral* possessed.

Still, at least he'd gotten away, had managed to give sen Trannick the slip. That was something. As long as Rast was alive and free, there was a chance. He wouldn't let himself believe anything else. He'd fought

THE GAIA GAMBIT   297

too hard for her and given up too much in that fight to abandon hope now.

And so he kept telling himself as those last few hours trickled away, and finally his stolen fighter craft emerged into realspace on the edge of the Iradian system. Anyplace else, and he might have had a difficult time making planetfall in such a vessel, so clearly designed for aggression. But because this was Iradia, he wasn't challenged at all, only told there were docking pads available in Aldis Nova, for the right fee.

Typical. He transferred the specified units to the 'port authority, or what passed for it in that rough frontier town, and didn't even quibble at the amount required. He had more important things to worry about.

As he guided the ship down to one of the pads at the 'port on the settlement's outskirts, Rast wanted to slap himself. True, Iradia's population was far lower than that of many planets, even his own arid and hostile home world. Even so, there were roughly three or four million people living down there, and approximately thirty settlements scattered across Iradia's surface. He'd come to Aldis Nova because that was where he'd found Lira the first time, but there was no guarantee she'd be here. Tomas was rumored to have hideouts and safe houses everywhere, including on Iradia's moon. Lira could be anywhere.

But since he didn't know what else to do, Rast set down the ship anyway and gratefully pried himself out of the cockpit. At the very least he needed to eat and attend to some other pressing bodily functions. He could go days without sleep if necessary, and might have to, but those other matters could wait no longer.

After locking down the ship and double-checking balance on the credit voucher Hunter Chao had given him, Rast headed out into Aldis Nova. Luckily, he had set down in the late afternoon, and so there was still enough light remaining that the true dregs hadn't yet oozed out of their hiding places. Not too far from the 'port he found an eating establishment, ordered a meal, and used its rest facilities—none too clean, unfortunately—while waiting for the food to be prepared.

When his meal did arrive, however, he found himself picking at it, and not only because he was uncertain of the overall hygiene of the establishment. No, he couldn't help berating himself for having no clear plan as to what to do when he arrived here, even though he knew deep down that he'd done the best he could. After all, stealing a fighter craft from the admiral's flagship was no mean feat. But that feat would count for very little if he couldn't discover where on Iradia Lira had been taken.

His handheld buzzed, and Rast scowled. Who could possibly be calling him here? After all, this was the handheld Hunter Chao had provided, and so the only people who had its code were Hunter, Lira, and—possibly—Jackson Wyler.

Rast pulled it out of his pocket at once and looked down into Wyler's grinning face. Surely he never would have said he'd actually be happy to see that smug-faced Gaian, but right now the only visage that would have been more welcome was Lira's. Calmly, though, he said, "Wyler."

"Afternoon, Master sen Lhannick," Wyler replied, using the alias Chao had given him. "At least, I'm assuming from the time/date stamp that it's afternoon where you are."

"More or less. Listen, Wyler, we don't have a lot of time—"

"I know that. But I'm guessing you're probably a little stuck. Typical Stacian, going charging in without any real plan."

Good thing roughly a hundred parsecs separated Rast from Wyler at that moment. But since getting into a war of words wouldn't help Lira, Rast bit back the fifty or so insults that rose to his lips and instead gritted, "Is this your oblique way of offering some help?"

"You could say that. Just understand that this is for Lira, not for you."

"Understood."

Wyler's image on the handheld looked pleased. "First off, she's not in Aldis Nova. She's halfway around the planet from you."

Naturally. Rast swallowed a few more curses and waited for the other man to continue. When no more information seemed to be forthcoming, he growled, "So where is she?"

"At Tomas's main compound, about a hundred clicks west of a crummy outpost called Pathi."

That was all Rast needed. "Thanks, Wyler." He moved to cut off the transmission, but the hacker quickly said,

"Hold up there, cowboy. Even you should think twice about going in there, guns blazing. Just wait—we've got a team on the way."

Rast didn't know what a cowboy was and didn't much care. It was Wyler's other remark that gave him pause, and made him move his finger away from the "end" button on the handheld. "'We've got a team on the way'? Care to clarify."

Wyler's miniature face looked almost abashed. "Well, I might not have been completely truthful with you."

"About?" Rast growled.

"I might not have been working quite as outside the lines as I led Lira to believe."

"Speak plainly, Wyler—I don't need your Gaian double-talk."

A sigh. "I'd forgotten how literal you Stacians can be. All right, then—I've been working with the Gaian authorities for some time in various capacities. Some of sen Trannick's behavior has been under suspicion for some time, but no one could put a finger on what he was up to until he used you to get at Lira so she could be removed from her post in the Chlorae system."

"That was all a setup?" Rast demanded. Good thing that Wyler was so many light-years away, or the Gaian would have run a strong risk of being throttled. "I thought you said Admiral Horner was clean."

"He was—is, I mean. It was one of Lira's crew who reported her, um, activities with you to the admiral's office. He had no choice but to remove her. Turns out that crew member was being paid well by sen Trannick's agents to report anything suspicious about his captain's behavior. He was going to make sure she was removed one way or another...although I'm guessing he came up with that particular scheme because it was the most amusing. But we also knew that Lira wouldn't leave it alone forever, and counted on her getting in contact with me for assistance." Wyler hesitated, and a rueful smile touched his mouth. "What I didn't count on was her detour to Iradia, but that's worked out to our advantage anyway. The Gaian authorities have been trying to nail down Gared Tomas for years, so that's a nice little bonus."

"Wonderful for you. And so you had no idea of the Eridani connection until your hacker friend unearthed it for you?"

"None. As soon as Lira relayed that information to me, I sent it on to the Eridanis. They're working things on their end, but unfortunately weren't fast enough to catch up with Daos Senn before he handed Lira off to Gared Tomas's agents."

Typical. No doubt the Eridani agents involved had to waste precious time to send politely worded communiques back and forth before they decided on a plan of action. While he couldn't deny how much his home world had been helped by the Eridanis, he also knew that having any sort of extended dealings with them made him want to tear his hair out.

He'd heard enough. "Speaking of wasting time, I've already done enough of that. Lira's been here on Iradia in Tomas's hands for almost twelve standard hours. I'm going in to get her."

"But the team—"

"—can mop things up when they get here. I'm out." Rast cut off the transmission and shoved the handheld back in his pocket, then got up from the table and swiped his voucher at the kiosk on his way out of the restaurant before hurrying back to the 'port to retrieve his ship.

Wyler might not have provided exact coordinates, but the information he'd provided should be enough. The stolen fighter craft had fairly powerful scanning equipment and should be able to zero in on Tomas's compound once the ship got within twenty kilometers. After that, well, Rast would just have to see. He hadn't been that impressed by the crime lord's defenses the last time he'd encountered them. True, this time he would be confronting Tomas on his home territory.

On the other hand, he'd also be coming in while flying one of the Stacian navy's most advanced starfighters...

CHAPTER EIGHTEEN

LIRA DREAMED THAT RAST WAS KISSING HER, MOUTH insistent, his tongue touching hers, tasting hers. But something about the shape of his mouth was wrong, and the feel of his lips was wrong, and his very scent was wrong. So her dream self pulled away, and she opened her eyes, and that was when she realized she hadn't been dreaming at all, that it was not Rast pressing his lips against hers, that when she opened her eyes and saw bright green meeting them rather than shining copper, she realized it was Gared Tomas violating her with his mouth.

Gasping, she pulled away—at least as far as she was able. Because then she saw that she lay on a bed in an unfamiliar room, and her wrists were bound to the head posts of shining carved stone. The suit she'd purchased on Eridani was gone, and in its place was a thin-strapped gown of moon-moth silk so sheer she might as well not have been wearing anything at all.

"Bastard!" she spat. "I knew you were low, Tomas, but I didn't realized you'd stoop so low as to take a woman when she's unconscious and can't fight back." Even as she spoke, though, she began to think things hadn't gone quite that far. Her body had none of the usual post-coital tells. Still...

He didn't appear offended, but only grinned and pushed a few strands of her hair away from her neck. The touch of his fingers trailing across her skin made shivers run down her back, and not in a good way. "I didn't 'take you,' Lira, although I was sorely tempted." His hand moved from her neck to the swell of her breasts, its heat penetrating the flimsy silk as if it weren't there.

She forced herself not to react. That was what he wanted, she knew—to see her try to squirm away from his touch. Or maybe his ego was so massive that he thought she would actually enjoy it. Instead, she remained still, glaring up at him. "So why the whole bondage setup? I have to warn you that I'm not really into that sort of thing."

"Oh? Pity." He lifted his hand from her breast and smiled, a smug smirk that made her wish her hands were free so she could wipe it off his face. "I wanted to make sure you wouldn't try to get away."

"And you thought there was a greater likelihood of that if I'd stayed in my own clothes?" As soon as she asked the question, she regretted it, because his gaze flicked downward, toward the obvious outline of her aureolas through the thin silk. She swallowed, trying not to breathe too deeply, to do anything else to draw his attention to places where she really didn't want it.

The grin broadened. "That suit looked very uncomfortable." To her relief, he sat up and moved a few inches away from her.

She would have preferred a few light-years, but any additional distance was welcome at this point.

"No, Lira," he went on, "I made you an offer some weeks ago, and you turned it down. A blow to my ego, but one I got over soon enough."

No real surprise there; only a day after she'd told him she'd be a pilot or a mistress but not both, he'd had her take him and an overly painted local girl to his hideout on Iradia's moon. At the time she'd wondered if he'd done it to let her know that she was certainly replaceable and definitely hadn't broken his heart. If he even had one.

Lira said nothing, though, and only arched an eyebrow at him, trying to show that he might have her bound and all but naked before him, but she wasn't about to let him intimidate her.

"That was some initiative you showed, stealing my ship and running off with that Stacian." Tomas paused, and ran a contemplative hand over his chin. "I have to say that surprised me a little. I hadn't thought your tastes were quite that exotic. That's...promising."

She tilted her head to one side. "Is there a point to all this?"

The amused expression faded somewhat. "The *point*, Lira, is that I thought you were just a down-on-her-luck former GDF captain. I didn't think you had any flair, so to speak. But I still need a pilot, and now that Morain got himself blasted into the next world, I need a second-in-command. And I want someone in my bed I can rely on. I know if you give me your word to execute your...duties...faithfully, then I can trust you."

There could be only one explanation for such a proposition. He had to have gone completely insane. "Gared, I stole your ship. I was accessory to the deaths of two of your men. And now you want me to be your—your—" She broke off, unable to find a reasonable analogue for the concept of pilot/mistress/majordomo.

"I know," he replied calmly. "You've proven that you're not nearly as by-the-book as you first led me to believe. As for the rest?" He bent down toward her, and she forced herself not to flinch, not to give any indication how much she loathed the idea of his mouth touching her again.

Then a distant rumble seemed to echo through the room, and Tomas straightened immediately, eyes narrowing. "What the hell—"

Another rumble, closer, and more obviously an explosion. Across the chamber, a piece of local pottery tipped off a shelf and shattered on the stone floor.

At once the crime lord was on his feet, any thoughts of wooing Lira abandoned for the moment. As he headed for the door, he called over his shoulder, "Don't go anywhere." Then he was gone, and she was left alone.

Her solitude wasn't exactly as welcome as she'd thought it might be, considering that she was still tied to the bed and that the compound was clearly under some kind of attack. A little rush of joy went through her as she thought of Rast. Maybe he really had come to save her, improbable as that might be.

No, that couldn't be possible. Far more likely that one of Gared Tomas's numerous enemies had finally discovered the location of his residence and had come here to settle one of a hundred scores. And if that were the case, the last thing she wanted was for the victor—whoever he might turn out to be—to find her tied up here like a gift just waiting to be unwrapped.

With that thought in mind, she began pulling at the binding on her left wrist, which felt infinitesimally looser than the one on her right. Whatever happened, she wanted to be long gone by the time Tomas came back...or his enemies began to lay claim to everything in his compound.

Including her.

Wyler had been right—the outpost of Pathi was hardly a blink in the darkness of the planet's night side, a small cluster of lights in an enormous well of black. The instruments on board his fighter told him barely a hundred souls called the hamlet home, but at least he knew he was more or less going in the correct direction. A few more minutes, and he'd be pulling up on Tomas's compound.

Once there, he'd have to be careful. Another scan would indicate how much muscle the crime lord kept around the place. The problem was that the scanner couldn't differentiate between species, let alone sex, so he would have no way of knowing where Lira was being held. That meant the buildings themselves would be off-limits. He figured the best thing would be to shoot up the gate—a place like that most likely had a wall, and that indicated the presence of a gate. Anyway, something on the periphery would be the target, to draw attention and hopefully cluster as many henchmen in one place as possible. Such an attack would have to be quite a surprise anyway, if Lira's analysis had been correct and no one save a trusted few even knew of the compound's location.

The scanner beeped, showing lifeforms two kilometers ahead. He slowed the ship, reading the scans. Fifteen altogether, with eight of them clustered near what appeared to be a gate and with the others spaced out at regular intervals along the wall. Perfect. A couple of strategically placed shots at the gate, and he could take out more than half of them all at once. One against seven—*six*, he reminded himself, since of course Lira wouldn't be a combatant—wasn't great odds under normal circumstances, but if these men were anything like the two he'd shot down while stealing the *Mistral*, then six shouldn't be that much trouble, even if one of them was the dreaded Gared Tomas himself.

Rast readied the pulse bombs, flicking the controls over to standby. One touch of his finger, and the bombs would be on their way, bringing a friendly little wake-up call to the crime lord and his lackeys.

With stealth mode engaged, he made one pass of the compound, just to get a visual to supplement what the ship's readouts were already telling him. All around was pitch-black night, and Iradia's moon was on the other side of the planet, but his eyes were far more dark-tuned than any human's, and so he could pick out the outline of a rectangular compound, with a low sprawling structure in the center and several outbuildings off to either side. There was some illumination, faint downturned lights that might provide enough of a guide for foot traffic but weren't strong enough to be seen from very far away.

Time to make the place a whole lot brighter.

He ran a finger over the touch pad, and first one, then a second bomb sped away from the fighter, dropping with deadly speed toward the gate and the cluster of men who stood guard there. Too bad they were looking out to the desert for any incoming enemies, and not to the skies above.

One explosion, and then another painted the night with garish hues of yellow and orange. Even from this height Rast could see the dark shapes of human forms being hurled outward by the force of the blasts. Most lay still, but one appeared to have been far enough outside the radius of the explosion that it hadn't killed him. Ah, well, one more he'd have to pick off at closer range.

Judging it safe enough to land a dozen meters or so outside the periphery of the compound, Rast brought the little fighter down to rest in the desert sand. All such ships were outfitted with several sidearms and spare battery packs, in the unlikely event that a pilot should get shot down and need to defend himself. Even so, Rast wished he had something heavier than a pair of pulse pistols. A self-guided shoulder missile launcher would have been nice.

No time to worry about that, however. A gun in each hand and the spare battery packs shoved into his pants pockets, he climbed out of the fighter and dropped lightly to the sand, then moved quickly to the shelter of the wall, edging along it until he came to the gaping hole that used to be the compound's gate. He heard shouts and a confusion of running feet. Good. As he'd hoped, the attack had taken them by surprise, and it seemed they were still trying to figure out who had hit them, and what to do next.

That worked. Using a swirl of smoke as cover, Rast strode into the gap and shot the man who stood there, shouting for reinforcements into his handheld. He dropped at once, and Rast stepped over him, keying on the sound of another man calling to a compatriot somewhere deeper in the compound, then shooting him in the back of the head. Amateurs. Obviously Gared Tomas cared more about hiring bulk than brains. His loss. It didn't seem as if there was anyone here capable of mounting a coordinated defense.

Five left, one of them the crime lord himself. A pulse bolt flared over Rast's shoulder, and immediately he went into a crouch, eyes narrowing in the darkness as he searched for his attacker's position. Up there, on the roof of one of the outbuildings. Rast raised his pistol and shot the man, whose darker outline against the night sky was visible enough. The silhouette slumped over and then fell to the ground with a thud.

Four to go.

Several bolts hit the wall above Rast's head, indicating that they knew he was somewhere in the vicinity, even if they hadn't quite narrowed it down. Time to move. Halfway bent over—since this was one situation where his height was more a liability than an asset—he scuttled farther into the complex, keeping the wall of the main building at his back. He needed to find an entrance, but the place was built like a fortress. The windows were narrow slits covered with metal shutters, and he'd yet to locate a doorway.

Pausing in a blind spot created by the structure turning at right angles to the wall he'd been following, Rast held his breath and listened. No more shouting, as if the men who'd survived thus far had realized all that did was give away their positions. So they weren't quite as dumb as they looked.

Waiting was excruciating, since he guessed Lira had to be somewhere in the building behind him, but he knew he couldn't be hasty in his actions. He'd done a good job of reducing the number of men he'd have to face, but there were still four left, among them their leader.

A murmur of voices, and the unmistakable hiss of a door opening on hydraulic hinges. A human probably wouldn't have even detected those sounds, but Rast's hearing—Stacian hearing—had been sharpened by millennia of hunting beasts far fiercer than humans, of relying on those senses to keep them alive from day to day. The door was up ahead, approximately fifteen yards away.

Target now selected, he inched along the wall, slowing as he came closer to the doorway and noted the shapes of two men flanking it, obviously providing cover.

Cover for what?

A new sound came to his ears, the unmistakable whine of a ship's engine powering on. It emanated from the opposite side of the compound, near one of the outbuildings, which must serve as a hangar for whatever transport Gared Tomas used to get in and out of this remote location.

Transport. Shit.

Not worrying about stealth any longer, Rast turned and bolted toward the source of the sound.

Her skin was scraped and red, but Lira finally managed to wriggle her hand loose from the cuff that held her to the bed. It was the sort of thing designed for sex play, and not a true binder, or she would never have been able to free herself. Following those two explosions, things had gone oddly quiet, but she guessed that was because the attackers were now trading small arms fire with Tomas's men. The compound was probably large enough that she was too far away to hear anything.

Fine. She really didn't care who or what they were —she just wanted to get away before they found her.

Once the one hand was free, it took less than thirty seconds for her to extricate herself completely from the cuffs and push herself off the bed. She looked down at the flimsy gown she wore in disgust, and wasted a few precious seconds trying to find a more suitable garment in the chamber's large wardrobe, but it was empty except for some spare sheets and blankets, and a rather impressive collection of sexual aids.

Do you really need all that to get it up, Tomas? she thought, but wouldn't waste any more time on the assortment of sex toys than that. Instead, she went to the door and touched the controls to open it, then looked back and forth down the corridor. It seemed empty enough, although she thought now she could hear a few distant shouts and the sharp crack of pulse bolts being fired.

Since they were coming from her left, she decided to head right. Of course she had no clear idea of where she was going, but anywhere had to be better than tied up to that bed, just waiting for someone to find her.

The stone floors were cool underfoot as she hurried along, wishing she had on a proper pair of shoes, some real clothing. Jogging like this only made her breasts bounce under the thin silk gown, and she reached up with one arm to more or less hold them in place as she went.

Then she heard the sound of heavy boot steps, and she pulled up short, looking from side to side for some-place where she could conceal herself. But this stretch of corridor was empty and blank, not even a doorway to provide some shelter or a place to duck into. And as she hesitated, Gared Tomas came around the corner, accompanied by a large, brutish-looking Bathshevan merc.

"Going somewhere?" Tomas asked.

Damn. Damn, damn, damn. Lira stared back at him as levelly as she could and replied, "I might ask the same about you."

"As a matter of fact, I am. And now I don't have to go looking for you, so thank you for that." He reached out and grabbed her by the arm, pulled her toward him. "Barlek, cover us."

The merc nodded and moved ahead, running point as they hurried down the corridor. Toward what, she didn't know, although it seemed clear enough that Tomas had some sort of destination in mind, wasn't simply fleeing whoever had invaded the compound.

They emerged into the warm night air and went toward a small building that seemed to serve as a hangar, since Lira could see the nose of the *Mistral* sticking out of it. Of course it made sense that he would use the fast little ship as his getaway vehicle, but she wished it had been something else, something not quite so hard to catch.

Gared's grip was like a band of iron around her bicep as he dragged her toward the small snub-nosed ship. She didn't even bother to try to wrench her arm away. He was far too strong.

But then a flash of orange-red went sailing over her head, almost grazing Tomas, but hitting the Bathshevan even as he turned at the sound of the pulse pistol being shot. He slumped to the ground, blood pouring out of his seared and blackened eye socket. Gared cursed and spun both of them toward their attacker.

Lira's eyes widened, and she couldn't help letting out a small murmured word of thanks.

Rast had come for her after all.

He'd found her. Too bad at the moment she was being held by that bastard Tomas like a living shield, the crime lord's own pistol held at her temple. Even so, she looked at Rast across the few yards that separated them, and her full mouth curved in a smile.

"Don't do anything stupid, Stacian," Tomas said.

"Don't plan to," Rast replied, staring at the other man in contempt. How like a Gaian to use a woman as a shield, another person's living flesh as a barrier between him and his enemy's weapon. No Stacian would ever do something so cowardly. Then he caught a flicker of movement near the nose of the atmospheric craft behind Tomas, and saw another man, probably the pilot, trying to use the ship as cover as he crept toward the little group, his pistol in hand.

That cover wasn't quite good enough, though. Rast narrowed his eyes and loosed a single shot. The man dropped like a stone, and Tomas cursed.

"Looks like you're out of a pilot, Tomas," Rast said, and couldn't help grinning.

The man's hand tightened on Lira's arm. She didn't precisely wince, but some of her smile faded. For the first time Rast noticed she was wearing a gown of wispy silk that was fluttering in the warm night breeze. It left nothing to the imagination, and despite everything, he could feel his loins tighten at the sight of her.

He had a good idea where that gown had come from, and she looked mightily displeased at wearing it.

"Actually, I've got one right here with me," Tomas replied easily. Rast would say that much for the man; he was no coward. "And she's a much better pilot than the one you just shot, so I'm not all that worried about it."

Stalemate? Rast held the gun steady, not dropping it, but not keeping it pointed at Tomas, either. "You might want to ask how she feels about that."

Surprisingly, the crime lord chuckled, and bent his bald head toward Lira, touching his mouth to her cheek. "What do you think, darling?"

Rast must have learned some control from her, or else he surely would have lunged forward in that moment. She didn't react to Tomas's foul caress, but stared straight at Rast instead, blue eyes intent on him. Some sort of unspoken message seemed to leap from those eyes to his brain, telling him what she planned to do next.

"I think I'm sick of you touching me," she said, and then wrenched her arm from his grasp and dropped to the ground, giving Rast the shot he needed.

The pulse bolt hit the crime lord right between the eyes. They stared forward for a second, blazing green, and then he fell backward, sand spraying everywhere as he landed.

Lira scrambled to her feet and ran to Rast, her arms going around him, body pressing closely to his as if she wanted to make sure they would never be separated again. He held her tightly, marveling at the scent of her hair and the feel of her breasts as they ground into the thick fabric of his uniform. Again his body responded, needing her, wanting her.

Now was not the time, though.

Gently, he took her by the arms and held her far enough away that he could look down into her face. "Are you all right? He didn't—"

"No," she said at once. "He wanted to, was going to —but I think he was dragging it out. To torture me, I suppose."

That sounded about right. Well, he wouldn't argue with the man's perversions, if they'd kept him from laying hands on Lira. Rast ran one finger along her cheek, down to her chin, reassuring himself with that touch that she was safe, that she really was standing here in front of him, untouched and unhurt. Relatively, anyway. Even now he could see a ring a bruises forming around her upper arm where Gared Tomas had held her. Too bad the man was dead, because Rast wanted to kill him all over again.

Shaking away those thoughts, he asked, "So what now?"

She lifted her shoulders, nearly bare except for the

wind-whipped strands of her loose hair, and the whisper-thin straps that held up her gown. "First thing you do is give me your jacket."

"My jacket?"

"If you think I enjoy parading around looking like this, you don't know me very well."

He laughed, loving the fire in her eyes, the challenging lift to her chin as she stared up at him. "Well, I'm enjoying it."

"Rast—"

"Very well." With feigned reluctance he reached up and began to undo the line of buttons down the front of the garment. Once he was finished with that, he pulled it off and handed it to her, smothering a grin as he watched her shrug into it and attempt to push up the sleeves so they wouldn't hang halfway down to her knees. "Oh, yes, that's *much* better."

"I'm not attempting to be stylish, just not naked." She paused then, and squinted up at the night sky, at something behind his head. "Oh, hell—is that some of Tomas's reinforcements?"

Rast turned to look as well, gaze sharpening as he took in the sleek outlines of a Gaian atmospheric hopper, followed by the narrow shape of an Eridani planetary transport. For a second or two, he scowled, puzzled, and then remembered Jackson Wyler's comment about a team coming in to take care of things.

"No," Rast said, and held her close. "I think it's our rescue."

CHAPTER NINETEEN

RAST TRIED TO EXPLAIN THINGS AS BEST HE COULD WHILE they were shuttled up from Iradia's surface to the Consortium ship orbiting the planet, but somehow Lira couldn't quite begin to process it all. Jackson Wyler, a Consortium operative? All this part of a plan to track down the dissidents on Eridani?

It began to make more sense after she was given a chance to change into a set of simple clothes—tunic, narrow pants, low shoes—and have one or three cups of coffee to clear her head. She and Rast were sat down in a cold, spartan conference room and questioned by an equally cold and spartan woman somewhere in her forties or fifties who recorded everything they said and took copious notes on her handheld. At length she thanked them both for their service to Gaia, and got up and went out, leaving them alone.

Rast was scowling. "Nothing I did was in service to *Gaia*," he muttered.

Lira almost wanted to laugh. "Oh, that's just how they talk. Don't let it bother you."

"Hmm." He crossed his arms over his chest and looked around the gray little room with distaste. "How long are they going to hold us here? I suppose if they're thanking us for our 'service,' then they don't intend to charge us with anything. So why can't we go?"

Those were questions she would have liked answered as well, but she didn't know for sure. "Maybe they're just double-checking our story with Jackson. I don't know." She shifted in her seat so she faced him better. He still wore his captain's uniform, the jacket having been returned to him after she'd gotten some proper clothes. Seeing him that way made her think of the first time she'd ever laid eyes on him, when even then he'd impressed her with his barbarian glory, although at the time she hadn't known anything of the wonderful, courageous heart that beat under the carved buttons and the ochre-dyed wool.

He made another sound of disapproval low in his throat, and she reached under the table and laid her hand on his thigh, strong and rock-hard under fingers. Despite their surroundings, she felt a rush of heat between her legs. Rast wasn't the only one who wanted this all over with so they could be properly reunited.

The door opened, and Lira was surprised to see an Eridani man enter. He was older than Daos Senn, with streaks of pale lavender in his dark purple hair, the Eridani form of going gray. His expression was pleasant enough as he sat down across from them and folded his hands on the tabletop.

"This is not a debriefing," he told them. "You've probably had enough of that."

"So what is it?" Rast inquired, tone rough.

The Eridani did not seem put off by Rast's brusqueness. "A thank-you, I suppose. Without your determination to find out why you had been disgraced, Captain Jannholm, it might have taken us much longer to uncover the dissident factions on our own planet, factions that could have caused a great deal of trouble, should the details of their activities ever be discovered by the galaxy at large. I'm happy to say that Master Senn represented a very small percentage of our population, but that made him no less dangerous. Thanks to you, he and his compatriots are no longer a threat."

Lira found herself somewhat discomfited by the Eridani's outright gratitude. The no-nonsense manner of the Consortium operative who had interviewed them somehow seemed easier to handle. "I'm glad we could be of help," she said, after an awkward pause.

"The Eridani government would like to express its thanks in a more...concrete...manner." He looked from Lira to Rast and back again, then continued, "Whatever we can offer is probably not enough, but one must start somewhere, I suppose."

So the Eridanis wanted to give them a reward. That was all well and good, but it wouldn't get her ship back, or her command. And then, as she sat there beside Rast and felt the reassuring bulk of his presence next to her, she realized she didn't want it. Her government obviously had no real need of her, so why would she even entertain the notion of going back to the GDF? All right, if the life of service she'd worked toward for so many years was now off the table, what did she *really* want?

A memory came to her then, of feeling the wonderfully responsive controls of the *Mistral* under her fingers. Making love to Rast in the little ship's luxurious bedroom. Sitting in the cockpit with him and watching the distorted light of subspace stream past the viewscreens.

That was what she wanted. That life with him, for as long as it lasted.

She cleared her throat, and hoped she wasn't being presumptuous in speaking for the both of them. "Well, since the previous owner has no real need of it, we'd really like the *Mistral*."

Beside her Rast stirred. She could almost feel the surprise radiating out from him. Had he thought she'd try to ask for her command back? Not that this Eridani would have been in any position to grant such a request...if she'd even wanted such a thing.

"The crime lord's ship? Interesting." The man folded his lavender-skinned hands on the tabletop and gazed at Lira for a few seconds, as if trying to determine whether there was anything hidden in such a request. Then just the smallest lift of his shoulders. "As you said, he has no need of it. We'll make sure that it has a clear title in both your names. But really, that's a very small request. There's truly nothing else you want?"

Rast leaned forward, meeting the Eridani's serene violet gaze with his own fierce copper-hued one. "Our names cleared. Neither one of us has any desire to go forward with our military service, but I want us to both have honorable discharges, clean records. Nothing that can cause trouble in the future."

She should have thought of that. A slight squeeze of his thigh, just enough to show she recognized the worth of such a request.

The Eridani nodded. "Such things will have to be managed by your respective governments, of course, but I see no reason why they wouldn't consent to your request, especially since it is true that you both handled yourselves honorably in this matter."

So they had a ship, and they had their freedom. It was enough. Almost. Lira began, "Those credit vouchers Jackson Wyler gave us..."

"...will of course remain activated for as long as you have need of them. I'm glad to see that you're thinking of the logistics of your new lives." The man smiled and asked, "Anything else?"

She glanced at Rast, and he gave the smallest shake of his head. "I think we're good here. All we want now is to be able to go. Are we free to do so?"

The Eridani paused, and she saw him touch the band of silver metal at his wrist. At first glance one would have thought it merely a bracelet, an elegantly simple form of personal decoration, but she realized now that it was a communication device, and other ears besides his had been listening in on their conversation.

"Yes, quite free," he said, after a pause. "We'll provide a shuttle back to Aldis Nova, which is where the crime lord's ship is being held. Several teams have gone over it and found no further evidence necessary to closing this case, so there's no reason why you can't take possession immediately."

Lord knows what physical evidence those teams had found of hers and Rast's relationship. Oh, well, she certainly wasn't going to worry about such trivialities at this point. "Thank you," she said simply, but she meant it. She hoped the Eridani could hear the gratitude in her voice.

Rast stood and bowed, one arm across his chest in the formal Stacian gesture of respect. "Many thanks."

The Eridani rose from his seat and inclined his head. "And in return, Captain sen Drenthan." He smiled at them again and went out.

So that was settled...mostly. Lira turned to Rast, opening her mouth to say something about their next step, restocking the *Mistral* once they were back in Aldis Nova or some other trivial practicality, but he stopped her with a kiss, his arms going around her as she tasted him, inhaled the wonderfully spicy scent of his skin, and realized this was going to be her life from here on out. Rast, always and forever.

He wanted to sweep her away immediately, but he hadn't counted on the intricacies of Gaian bureaucracy. They were taken to separate cabins and told that their paperwork was being processed, and since Rast's request for an honorable discharge had to be relayed by the Eridanis because the Gaians of course had no formal diplomatic relations with the Stacian Federation, it could take a little while...which to the Gaian Consortium could mean anything from a few days to a few months. Or worse.

Those fears weren't realized, however, because within one standard day the files had been processed and delivered. Rast suspected the alacrity with which the case was handled had far less to do with his own service and a great deal more with trying to wrap up anything that had to do with Admiral sen Trannick's disgrace. Apparently he'd been removed from command, his entire family reeling from his dishonor. That was the way of things on Stacia—when one man fell, he took the rest of his relations with him. Not entirely fair, perhaps, but it did have the benefit of being a ruthless way to root out a cancer, since a disease often spread far beyond its initial site of infection.

At any rate, after spending a restless night on the cramped bunk in his borrowed cabin and wishing with all his heart that he was on the *Mistral* with Lira, he found himself called to take a shuttle with her to Aldis Nova. Once or twice during the night he'd thought about slipping over to see her, but he'd gotten the impression that, although the Gaian authorities were holding their noses and not mentioning the obvious relationship between their former officer and her Stacian adversary, neither did they want it flaunted in front of them.

So he'd slept alone, and dreamed of Lira, and the next morning got up and took care of his toilette, then folded his captain's uniform away and put on the new clothing that had been provided for him. She met him at the lift that would take them down to the shuttle's hangar bay, her manner almost shy, as if she wasn't quite expecting what his reaction to all these changes would be.

She looked lovely, in a simple tunic and pants in a dark blue-green that complemented her sea-colored eyes, her glorious hair lying loose on her shoulders, just the way he liked it. The shadows were gone from under those eyes, as if she'd gotten a good night's rest. Better than his, he guessed, but then again, she probably fit much better in one of those Gaian-engineered bunks than he did.

There was no formal send-off; the shuttle pilot—a lieutenant, if Rast recalled his Gaian rank symbols correctly—merely nodded at them and said they were ready to go. Both Rast and Lira had only one small duffle bag apiece. They'd been provided with a few changes of clothing along with other necessities, and their new handhelds contained all the data required to prove their identities, as well as their right to the *Mistral*.

Since the shuttle was a small one, with no barrier between the pilot and the tiny passenger compartment, neither one of them seemed much inclined to conversation as the ship left the large Consortium vessel and headed to Aldis Nova. But Lira's hand found its way into his as they sat there, and the feel of her strong but delicate fingers was enough to satisfy him.

For now, anyway.

The sun was setting as they flew into Aldis Nova's largest 'port, the place where the *Mistral* was being kept. Conveniently—although it probably wasn't convenience at all, but maneuvering on the part of the Gaian authorities—the shuttle touched down on the pad right next to the one where the *Mistral* waited. After landing the transport so gently Rast barely felt it meet the ground, the pilot told them, "She's all yours. New locks are keyed to both your prints. Have a good one."

And that was it. In silence he and Lira picked up their duffles and disembarked, then crossed the short distance between the two pads to their ship. She had been cleaned up, it seemed, shining as if she'd been brought here directly from the shipyards. Rast spied the new keypad by the door, and bowed to Lira. "You should go first."

She shot him a hesitant glance, then smiled and stepped forward, pressing her thumb to the lock. It glowed blue, showing it was on standby, waiting for the second authorization to open the door.

There seemed to be something symbolic about that, about the two of them having to combine their prints to make the ship theirs. He placed his thumb in the same spot where hers had been only a few seconds earlier, and the door opened.

A faint chemical smell drifted out—residue from the thorough inspection the Gaians had given the place, no doubt. He'd have to see about getting some pots of *merh* to put around the place. Most likely Lira wouldn't have any objections, since he'd noticed that she appeared to enjoy the scent.

Otherwise, though, the ship didn't seem much altered, although a few pieces in the main cabin felt a little off, as if they'd been shifted from their original positions and not put back exactly in place. He noticed that Lira wore a small smile, pleased that they were here at last.

Even with that, though, she was no-nonsense enough, dropping her duffle bag on the floor of the cabin and then heading forward, as if she couldn't wait to get her hands back on the controls. When she reached the door to the cockpit, though, she hesitated, and looked back at Rast.

"Do you—that is, would you like to take her up?"

He loved her for making the request, even though he knew she was the far better pilot. "No, you do it. I find I prefer the copilot's chair."

Her face lit up, and she went to take her position. He followed, settling himself in the copilot's seat, adjusting the harness as she went through the usual preflight checks. The *Mistral*'s engines thrummed to life, and within a few short minutes they were lifting into the air, Aldis Nova's shabby streets disappearing beneath them, the last of the sunset painting the landscape in shimmering hues of copper and bronze before he could see no landmarks at all, only the disk of the planet as it grew smaller and smaller behind them.

"Where to now?" Lira asked.

He knew she was asking about their next destination, but he had something much closer in mind. "How quiet is it out here on the edge of the system?"

A puzzled expression flitted across her features.

"Quiet enough. Most people going in and out of the Iradian system like to keep a low profile, if you know what I mean."

"Good," he said, and took her hand, lifting her from her seat. "Because where I want to take you, I definitely don't want to be disturbed for the next few hours..."

This was what she had dreamed of—Rast's hands on her, his mouth touching her, tongue savoring her, bringing her to ecstasy over and over again. And the feel of his body, the heavy muscles, the rough texture of his wild hair. All of it was a homecoming she'd only imagined, hadn't really believed would actually come to pass.

Sated at last, body sore in an entirely pleasant way, she lay cradled in his arms, listening to the deep, slow beat of his heart, feeling the warmth of his body envelop her. The *Mistral* hung just outside the Iradian system, before true wild space began, those empty reaches that had at last been defeated with the development of the subspace drive. They were safe here, until they decided what they wanted to do next.

Still, some part of her couldn't understand why he had given up everything to be with her. He still had a position, had a family who must care about him. He wasn't like her, cast out, unwanted.

"Can I ask you something?" she murmured, fingers

playing with one of the golden bands wound in his dreadlocked hair.

"Anything."

Even his voice was a comfort, the low baritone seeming to fill the quiet of the cabin. "Why don't your people terraform Stacia? After the Eridanis helped you with Syrinara—"

"Oh, no," he said at once. "Stacia is our home world, our mother. We would never desecrate her by altering what she is. It's because of her that we are who we are." He paused, and looked down at her. "Do you understand?"

"I'm trying to." Lira was quiet for a moment, considering what he'd just told her. Yes, she'd read that the Stacians had an intense reverence for their planet, one she'd never quite been able to understand, since it seemed that planet had done whatever it could to kill them. Too bad her own people didn't have that same respect. Gaia had been a much more hospitable world, and they'd brought it to the brink of destruction. Slowly they were fighting their way back, but it was a process that would take lifetimes. "Then...I don't understand."

"Understand what, dearest?"

"Us, I suppose."

He shifted his weight so he was able to face her more directly. The copper eyes studied her. "And what is it about us that you don't understand?"

Might as well get it out. Yes, they were here together, and that was a miracle in and of itself, considering everything they'd gone through to get to this point. But she knew she needed these last few nagging concerns confronted once and for all. "You had everything. A career, a family—I know how you Stacians are about family. But you're willing to walk away from all that? For what?"

"For you," he said. His tone was quiet, but very firm. "They were proud of me, proud of what I'd attained, but still it wasn't enough. I had no wife, and no clear desire to have one, although that was expected of me even more than my service in the navy. Women—" He broke off, and let out a short laugh. "I cannot lie to you, Lira, and say there were no women before you. But none of them touched my heart. None of them were *trenalle.*"

The word was beautiful. "What does *trenalle* mean?"

His arms tightened around her. "It's difficult to translate exactly. I suppose the closest I can get in Standard is 'heart's heart.' You are my heart's heart, Lira. You are *trenalle.* Beloved."

Something inside her seemed to break then, hearing him say such a thing to her, telling her that she was what mattered, the connection between them was what mattered, not the expectations of his family or his heritage or his world. She pressed herself against him and said, "You are my heart's heart as well, Rast. Before you—well, I just didn't understand. But somehow you help everything make sense. Even though *we* don't make sense."

He laughed, and bent to kiss her, his lips warm against the side of her head even through her hair. "No,

I suppose most of the galaxy wouldn't be able to make sense of us at all. But I don't care about that. I don't care about anything, except being here with you."

"Neither do I," she replied, and turned in his embrace so she could pull him against her, pull him into her, not wanting the intricate dance of foreplay, not wanting anything except the feel of him inside her, filling her, making their bodies one, moving together as a single entity, as a single expression of need, of desire.

Of love.

———

Eventually they slept, and then some hours after that they got up and squeezed into the shower unit, laughing as they tried for the first time to fit both of them into a space intended for only one normal-sized human. Lira's hands explored him, stroked him, brought him to a climax as the hot water sprayed over them both. Good gods, he was starting to wonder whether she was insatiable, or simply trying to make up for lost time.

Either way, he was the clear beneficiary here.

But at length they made it to the cockpit and stared out the viewscreen together, gazing on the velvet black backdrop with its billions of tiny winking suns.

"Where to?" she asked, an echo of her question from the previous day.

He knew the destination didn't really matter. The

only thing that mattered was that they would go there together.

"You choose," he said.

Lira cocked her head to one side, appearing to consider. Then she smiled and began programming in a long string of coordinates.

"I take it you have someplace in mind."

"I do," she replied. "Do you recall a conversation about Callia, and room service at the Eridani Majesty?"

"All too well. So it's breakfast in bed, courtesy of our new credit vouchers?"

Her eyes twinkled. "Breakfast...and lunch...and dinner."

"Sounds like heaven."

"It will be...if you're there."

Then she put her hand on the controls to engage the subspace drive. He placed his hand on top of hers, and together they activated the engines and watched as the *Mistral* leaped forward into the shimmering light.

All Fall Down

Dragon Rose

Binding Spell

Ashes of Roses

One Thousand Nights

Threads of Gold

The Wolf of Harrow Hall

Moon Dance

THE GAIAN CONSORTIUM SERIES

(Science Fiction Romance)

Blood Will Tell

Breath of Life

The Gaia Gambit

The Mandala Maneuver

The Titan Trap

The Zhore Deception

Refugees (September 2017)

ABOUT THE AUTHOR

Christine Pope has been writing stories ever since she commandeered her family's Smith-Corona typewriter back in the sixth grade. Her work includes paranormal romance, fantasy romance, and science fiction/space opera romance. She fell under the Land of Enchantment's spell while researching her Djinn Wars series and now makes her home in Santa Fe, New Mexico.

Christine Pope on the Web:
www.christinepope.com